Dead, White, and Blue

Berkley Prime Crime titles by Carolyn Hart

WHAT THE CAT SAW

Death on Demand Mysteries

DEATH COMES SILENTLY

DEAD, WHITE, AND BLUE

Dead,
White,
and Blue

CAROLYN HART

BERKLEY PRIME CRIME, NEW YORK

THE BERKLEY PUBLISHING GROUP
Published by the Penguin Group
Penguin Group (USA) Inc.
375 Hudson Street, New York, New York 10014, USA

USA I Canada I UK I Ireland I Australia I New Zealand I India I South Africa I China

Penguin Books Ltd., Registered Offices: 80 Strand, London WC2R 0RL, England
For more information about the Penguin Group, visit penguin.com.

This book is an original publication of The Berkley Publishing Group.

Prime Crime Books are published by The Berkley Publishing Group.
BERKLEY® PRIME CRIME and the PRIME CRIME logo are trademarks of
Penguin Group (USA) Inc.

Library of Congress Cataloging-in-Publication Data

Hart, Carolyn G.
Dead, white, and blue / Carolyn Hart.—First edition.
pages cm.—(Death on demand mysteries)
ISBN 978-0-425-26077-7 (hardback)
1. Darling, Annie Laurance (Fictitious character)—Fiction. 2. Darling, Max (Fictitious character)—
Fiction. 3. Booksellers and bookselling—Fiction. 4. Missing persons—Fiction. 5. Women
detectives—South Carolina—Fiction. 6. South Carolina—Fiction. I. Title.
PS3558.A676D435 2013
813'.54—dc23   2013000482

FIRST EDITION: May 2013

PRINTED IN THE UNITED STATES OF AMERICA

10 9 8 7 6 5 4 3 2 1

Cover design by Jason Gill.
Interior text design by Laura K. Corless.

To Lee Evans Prier,
remembering long-ago happy days
in Southern California.

Dead, White, and Blue

1

Anger sharpened Vera Hurst's features, emphasized the determined line of her jaw. She had never quite been beautiful, her jaw was too strong, her deep-set eyes too commanding. There was something primal in Vera that Wesley found irresistible. Flaming with rage, she had never been more desirable. Once she had been his wife, but he had squandered her trust. He'd lost what mattered to him and now he was trapped in an empty marriage.

"Shell said she'll bring suit for adultery." Wesley Hurst stood with his back to the hotel room door. He felt caught in a nightmare, his life spinning out of control.

Vera folded her arms. "I see. The slutty home wrecker is the little woman betrayed. That's almost funny. But not quite." Vera's cool voice was controlled, acerbic.

"She won't agree to a divorce." Wesley still grappled with disbelief at Shell's response. He shifted uncomfortably from one foot to the other. Damn, women were a lot of trouble. He felt bewildered and obscurely resentful as he faced the woman who had been his wife, who was not now his wife. He'd never intended to have more than a fling with Shell. In a moment of unrelenting honesty, he faced up to shabby motives that made him feel small and inadequate. He'd wanted to score off Bucky and maybe he'd wanted to shake Vera out of her complacency. And, he felt even smaller, maybe he was attracted to Shell because she was openly, flamboyantly powerful where Vera's force was concealed beneath a veneer of Southern charm. Shell, voluptuous, sexy, and inviting, pulled him further than he'd intended to go. Vera gave him hell and he got his back up and now everything was all screwed up.

When he dug down deep enough, he knew he couldn't live without Vera. She'd never been more passionate than in their clandestine meetings. Again, uncertainty pricked his pride. Was her passion created by the lure of the surreptitious, by a vindictive pleasure in besting Shell, or because she needed him as well? He poked the question layers deep, but on sleepless nights, he knew he'd wonder.

Vera's gaze was cold, demanding. "What did you tell her?"

"I'll countersue. I know damn well she'd been screwing around with Dave."

"Did you tell her that?"

"Yes."

Vera's cold green eyes studied him. "You never could lie worth a damn. What else did she say?"

He walked closer to Vera, put a hand on her shoulder, found it rigid. His hand dropped away. "She'll tell everyone you and I are having an affair." He wouldn't repeat Shell's exact words, which had been short, pungent, and explicit. What curdled him inside was Shell's amusement. She wasn't angry or regretful or, God knew, jealous. She laughed. Damn her. If she carried out her threat . . .

"Look at me, Wesley."

Each word was like the flick of a whip. Slowly, reluctantly, he lifted his gaze.

"What else did she say?"

He didn't want to answer. But he did. "She said she might borrow the mic from the bandleader, tell everyone at the dance. She said maybe you should wear a special dress tonight, embroidered with a scarlet *A*."

Jed Hurst stalked up the stairs. He heard Hayley's music, a hot salsa, "Mi Cascabel" with trumpets and drums and the urgent, enticing lyrics. Was he the only person in the whole family who saw what was happening? Ever since Dad moved out and married Shell, Mom didn't want to hear a word about Shell, but he couldn't explain what was going on with Hayley without talking about Shell. Besides, Mom and Hayley were always crossways, especially after Hayley got buddy-buddy with Shell.

He had a flash of adult understanding. Maybe Hayley tried to act like Shell because she thought that's what Dad admired. Maybe Hayley was trying to get back at Mom because she divorced Dad. As for Dad, he'd gone from a guy with the hots for Shell to disappearing. Not for real. Dad was actually next door in an even bigger, splashier house, but it was like he pulled on an invisible suit when Shell was in the room. Yesterday Jed followed him out to his car, tried to tell him, but the minute Jed started talking about Shell, Dad's face got that closed look and he peeled out of the driveway. Dad seemed to spend more time than ever on the *Vagabond*, nosing out into the Sound by himself.

Somebody had to do something before it was too late. Jed reached Hayley's door. He knocked hard three times, turned the knob. The door was locked. "Hayley, let me in." He pounded, didn't stop.

He didn't hear a click, but finally the panel opened maybe an inch. "Get lost, Jed."

"Hayley, you got to let me in. Kevin's mom and dad saw you."

Abruptly, the door was flung wide.

Jed stared at his sister as the drums boomed and trumpets blared. He didn't know what bothered him most, the makeup that made her look thirty instead of fifteen, the too-tight red sateen blouse, or the silver lamé leggings. "You look like a slut."

She tossed her head, rolled her eyes, heaved a dramatic sigh. It was an echo of Shell the day Mom ordered her out of their guesthouse. Uncle Bucky had brought her with him on a visit. Uncle Bucky claimed to be a Hollywood producer, but he'd heard his dad say that Uncle Bucky was just a guy on the fringe who'd managed to meet some people because he had money. Dad and Uncle Bucky always clashed. Jed didn't see where either of them had ever amounted to much. They both lived off their trust funds, and what was the difference between hanging around Hollywood and spending all your time on your boat? He wasn't going to be like that. Maybe he'd go to Clemson, and if everything broke right, he'd be a golf pro. He was going to be somebody, do something with his life. He wasn't going to be a fake like Uncle Bucky. Dad wasn't a fake, but he didn't have to work so he'd never tried to do anything. He was a good sailor, but so were a lot of rich guys. As for Uncle Bucky, every time he visited, there was trouble. He thought the island was backward and stupid. Jed wanted to ask him why he bothered to come. But he knew the answer. Uncle Bucky wasn't a big deal in Hollywood, but on the island he bragged about his Hollywood connections and how he had lunch with some big star or other. The last time he'd brought Shell Vitale, his new discovery, and nothing had been worth a damn ever since. Of course, he hadn't come back, not since Mom and Dad divorced and Dad married Shell. Only a year ago, but everything had been lousy ever since.

Especially Hayley.

"Take that stuff off. Where'd you get clothes like that?"

Hayley gave another long-suffering, world-weary sigh. "So plebeian. Utterly bourgeois. Mired in mediocrity. Juvenile." Her dark eyes gleamed with malice. "Pimply."

Jed hated the splotches on his face. He'd popped a yellow zit near his right eye this morning, and the blemish was all he saw when he looked in the mirror. Usually, Hayley's taunt would have been enough to send him off in a rage, but he kept on, dogged, determined, scared. "The Buccaneer Bar's a dive. You're underage. You danced with guys you'd never met. Kevin's mom and dad were on a scavenger hunt for a beer coaster last night and they couldn't believe it when they saw you."

Hayley struck a pose, overdrawn lips pouty, shoulders lifted, arms akimbo, one hip higher. "They should mind their own business. What right did they have to say something to the manager? Now I can't go back. The manager told me to take a hike."

"How'd you even know about a place like that?"

Hayley stretched her fingers, admired bloodred nail polish. "Shell and I had lunch and she told me about it. She said it was hot and the music was swell and nobody'd ever guess I was underage because I know how to flaunt it."

"I'll call the cops. That's contributing to the delinquency of a minor." Jed knew he was blustering. The cops would probably ignore him. How could he prove anything? Hayley would lie.

Hayley's eyes flared. "Don't you dare. Shell's wonderful. Shell says I can handle myself. Shell says rules are for the boring masses. Shell says you have to dance to the beat you hear in your heart. Shell says—"

Jed felt hollow inside as he turned away. *Shell says* . . . He had to do something.

Maggie Peterson smiled brightly as she crinkled the red crepe paper streamer. Inside she fought wave after wave of panic and desolation. She tossed one end to Claire Crawford. Claire's nonstop chatter flowed around Maggie like the sounds of city traffic or the surf, always there, negligible, requiring no comment or attention. How could this be happening to her?

She bent to the task of thumbtacking the streamer to the edge of the bandstand. She felt numb, empty. Like her life. The shock when she'd found out was like the moment when they'd told her the tumor was malignant. Dave had been a rock then, seeing her through the surgery, taking her to chemo, helping her pick out a wig, deep black just like her hair. Her hair grew back a dull brown and she felt diminished. Her black hair had emphasized the rich brown of her eyes. The color rinse she now used didn't match the glory of the original. When she'd been declared cured, he'd bought a magnum of Cristal to celebrate. They'd danced, the two of them, on the terrace of the house, Dave big and blond, loud and powerful, she too thin and conscious that she wouldn't seem whole again until she had the implants. Champagne always went to her head and she'd giggled through the evening and Dave had raised toast after toast, "To us. Now. Always."

She could hear his voice, deep, robust.

That was last fall. It was the New Year's Eve dance when Wesley first brought Shell. She remembered that night, Wesley ruddy from a jaunt he and Shell had taken to Australia, Shell spectacularly lovely in a gold lamé gown that every woman there knew cost thousands. There was perfection in the styling of the lacy bodice and high ruched waistband above a swirling layered skirt. Shell's reddish brown hair and classic features were Hollywood perfect, but her magic wasn't that she was beautiful. Several women in the room were beautiful. None of them possessed Shell's breathtaking aura of untamed wildness and careless confidence. No one who looked at her, woman or man, ever doubted that Shell would do what she wanted when she wanted and never count the cost. To herself or to others.

From the instant Dave saw Shell, nothing was ever the same.

The crepe paper streamer was yanked.

Claire's high voice was insistent. "Maggie, I swear I've asked you three times. Do you want white or blue for the next row?"

Maggie stared blankly at Claire's long face with its untidy mop of brown curls and a nose that quivered.

"White or blue?" The nose twitched.

Maggie stifled a hysterical laugh. Claire's world had shrunk to the all-important decision, a white streamer or a blue one. What would she do if Maggie told her red was for blood, white was for hearses, and blue for the gun in Dave's desk?

D ave Peterson was good at figuring angles and stresses. He'd built bridges all over South Carolina and Georgia and nobody had to worry about a fracture. He'd planned everything, secretly cashing out stock, selling property. Half and half. He'd take half, leave half for Maggie. Fair was fair.

He pushed away a quick memory of Maggie, her black tresses gleaming in the sun, her dark eyes gazing at him with open passion. Another picture slid in its place, Maggie thin and wan, weak and sick from chemo, wig askew. But pulsing in his veins was the memory of Shell in his arms, tangled chestnut hair, sloe eyes, an enigmatic smile.

He frowned. He didn't know what to take from her farewell at their last meeting. He'd told Shell the plan, instructed her to bring her passport, he'd take care of everything else. She'd given her light rippling laugh, paused in the doorway only long enough to murmur, "Spoken like an engineer. Black or white. Up or down. In or out. Life's never that simple, *cherie*," and then she was gone, the door closing behind her.

He remembered the championship game his senior year. Hot, sweaty, aching, the shouts of the crowd as the final seconds ticked, coming off the field, a wild melee, the icy shock when his teammates upended the ice-filled cooler over him. For an instant, it was like his heart stopped. He'd felt that same instant of shock at Shell's parting words.

He sat stone still, eyes narrowed, face hard. Nobody screwed him over.

The early-morning sun slanted through the live oak tree, turning tangles of Spanish moss from dull grayness to silky gray green. Eileen Marsh Irwin avoided direct sunlight in July, but she enjoyed starting the day on the terrace in a cushioned teak chair with her own Cornish tea. On a small table beside her sat a china teapot, a plate of scones, clotted cream, and raspberry jam. Eileen lowered her newspaper enough to watch her husband. Middling height, middling appearance, his hair now graying and thinning, glasses, a rounded face that might have inspired confidence as a family doctor or genial salesmen if you didn't look too closely, see the gleam of avarice in faded brown eyes, the hint of weakness in his mouth.

Edward stood on the putting green. Their rambling home overlooked the country club golf course. He held a putter in his hand, but he was immobile, slump shouldered, as if braced against a gale wind. Poor Edward. So transparent. He'd forgotten that he was on the green. Instead, his mind was racing, trying to figure out what to do. She knew the signs. Edward was in big trouble.

They never had much to say to each other. Pleasantries. A careful skirting of any topic likely to cause distress. A former Latin teacher, she enjoyed reading Catullus, Horace, and Lucan. She often thought in Latin. *In omnia paratus.* With Edward she had learned to be ready for all things.

Eileen's gaze was cool and thoughtful. She had no illusions about her husband. Edward thought he was clever. He wasn't. The last time Edward was in trouble—a matter of buying on the margin and an unexpected call—she'd warned him. She would not invade her trust fund again. She wondered what he'd done this time. He always thought the next risky investment would make him rich. There had been the car dealership that cratered, the string of second-class movie theaters, the smelter in China.

Her fine brows drew down. He'd been worried since last winter. Spring came and he had appeared more relaxed, actually looked smug, almost cocky. But this morning he'd come out to the terrace pale and distraught, poured a mug of coffee, muttered something unintelligible, left the coffee to grow cold on the table, and bolted to the green where he now stood, obviously a man with demons nipping at his heels.

Eileen finished her tea, folded the newspaper, rose. She crossed the terrace, strode to the library, her face furrowed. She and Edward didn't share a room. When she glimpsed him coming down the stairs this morning, his rounded face appeared untroubled. As she had stepped onto the terrace, the phone rang. She permitted nothing to interfere with her morning tea. The ring ended in midpeal and she knew Edward had answered.

Eileen stepped into the library. She cherished the warmth of the cypress walls, the slight ripple in the old heart pine floor, the gilt oval frame over the fireplace that held a faded painting of her grandfather. The mahogany desk had been in the family for generations. Her great-grandfather had sat there to keep the books of his lumber company. She'd resisted a modern telephone with caller ID and an answering system until she realized the small window afforded her the pleasure of choosing whether to answer the telephone. Caller ID provided a record. She stood at the desk, looked down.

Shell Hurst had called at eight seventeen A.M.

Shell Hurst automatically counted the strokes as she brushed her hair . . . Forty-five . . . forty-six . . . As always, her reflection in the mirror pleased her, glistening chestnut hair, smooth gardenia-petal complexion, large green eyes, straight nose, full lips, firm chin. She scarcely needed makeup, her eyebrows naturally dark, her long eyelashes the envy of other women. She favored a light coral lip gloss.

Today was going to be very satisfying. She looked forward to seeing proud, arrogant, dismissive people squirm. Most delicious of all was the fact that she had nothing to lose. Her prenup was solid. No wiggle room for Wesley there. She'd been careful about that. But he was just a stop along her way. The days of cramped living in a trailer in Bakersfield were a distant memory. She'd been smart enough when she got to Hollywood to know that beauty wasn't enough and she didn't have enough skill as an actress. But she was skilled enough to play the role of aspiring ingenue with Bucky Hurst, who was as bogus a producer as she was an actress. She'd figured from the first that bald-headed, burly Bucky was all blow and no show, but he had money. He'd been too wary to ever agree to marriage, but her investment paid off handsomely when he brought her to the island. Henpecked Wesley had been ripe for the picking. Last night Wesley had about collapsed when she told him she knew all about his secret little meetings with Vera. She had him in a sweat. And some others, too. She'd warned each of them that she intended to make some public announcements at the dance. Their reactions had been highly entertaining. Tonight she would hold all the strings in her hands. The puppets would move at her direction, Wesley and his oh-so-perfect ex-wife, Dave who'd been easy to seduce and never realized he was simply a means of provoking Maggie, who'd treated her like pond scum because of Vera, pompous little Edward who had made a fatal error in judgment. Would she jerk the strings or let them dangle?

A nnie Darling felt haunted by the old adage: Be careful what you wish for. Yes, she wanted to have the best, most successful mystery bookstore north of Delray Beach. Yes, she wanted to hear *ka-ching ka-ching* as vacationers bought beach books. This summer had some sizzlers: *The Big Cat Nap* by Rita Mae Brown, *What Doesn't Kill You* by Iris Johansen, *50% Off Murder* by Josie Belle, *Miss Julia to the Rescue* by Ann B. Ross, and *The Cat, the Wife, and the Weapon* by Leann Sweeney. Yes, she wanted to celebrate holidays. Yes, she wanted to dance the night away with the handsomest man in the room. Tonight he would wear a white dinner jacket. Her knees turned to water when she saw Max in a white dinner jacket, Joe Hardy all grown up and sexy as hell.

But maybe, just maybe—she drew a deep calming breath—her plate was too full. Nose-peeling tourists who'd neglected to reapply sunscreen packed Death on Demand, and all of them were suckers for the Fourth of July display in the front window featuring *Murder on Parade* by Jessica Fletcher and Donald Bain, *Exit Wounds* by J. A. Jance, *Star Spangled Murder* by Leslie Meier, *Iron Ties* by Ann Parker, and *Can't Never Tell* by Cathy Pickens.

"Annie, I can't find that special order for Emma." Ingrid Webb, narrow face imploring, spoke in a tone of doom above the hubbub wafting from the coffee bar, including a Marlene Dietrich–husky voice crooning "Come on-a My House." Speaking of things wished for . . . Annie added to her tally. Yes, she wanted her lively, sparkling, always unpredictable mother-in-law to be happy. Laurel, a blond beauty who attracted men from nine to ninety, rarely passed a day without originating something totally surprising to those around her. But Laurel's decision to strum her guitar (who knew Laurel played the guitar?) and sing haunting melodies (only Laurel could make a Rosemary Clooney hit seductive as a lace teddy) several evenings a week in the Death on Demand coffee bar—for free, of course—was way too much of a good thing.

Max was no help. When Annie tried tactfully to suggest that perhaps dear Laurel was too generous with her time and shouldn't feel compelled to come in so often, he'd gazed at her with dark blue eyes reminiscent of his mother's. "Not to worry. She's having the time of her life and look at the crowds!"

Annie had resisted the impulse to point out that the crowds were all male and they took up all the tables in the coffee bar and they weren't interested in books. They were interested . . . But some things were better left unsaid to a man about his mother.

"The order for Emma." Ingrid's voice was anguished, stricken by the possibility of riling Emma Clyde, the island's famous mystery writer and staunch patron of Death on Demand. Emma was an irascible force of nature when her expectations were not met, blue eyes icy and strong jaw jutting.

Annie was counting. ". . . and five makes twenty." She waggled a hand at Ingrid to indicate she'd address the missing order in a moment. Annie flashed a welcoming smile at the next in line. The smile changed from automatic to warm when she recognized Police Officer Hyla Harrison. "Hey, Hyla."

Hyla was as no-nonsense in her leisure clothes, a white short-sleeve cotton blouse, khaki shorts, and white sandals, as when attired in a crisp French blue Broward's Rock police uniform. As always her carroty hair was drawn back in a neat ponytail, her freckled face composed and reserved, but her quick smile was sweet. "Hey, Annie."

"Ready for the holiday?" As she spoke, Annie was also listening to Ingrid's plea, "Emma's on her way and I can't find the book!" Annie entered Hyla's selections: *I'm a Fool to Kill You* by Robert Randisi, *Blindside* by Ed Gorman, *Dead Low Tide* by Bret Lott, *The Retribution* by Val McDermid, and *One Blood* by Graeme Kent.

"I don't go on duty until ten tonight. The chief's beefing up the night patrols. Lots of booze on the Fourth. We're ready."

Annie made change and slid Hyla's books into her cotton book bag. "Those are great titles."

Hyla tapped the Death on Demand logo on the black cotton bag, a silver knife with a dot of red blood at the tip. "Crime in books"— sharp emphasis—"is okay. They always catch the perp. I'm glad the store is keeping you busy."

As Hyla turned away, Annie nodded at Ingrid. "I'll look for Emma's order if you'll take over for me."

Annie wormed her way down the center aisle toward the back of the store. She felt a tickle of amusement. Clearly, Hyla was inferring that Annie on the loose posed a danger to the public safety of Broward's Rock. It wasn't Annie's fault that sometimes she became entangled in people's problems. After all, good citizens assisted the police if it was within their power to do so. Annie felt sure that Hyla could rest easy and enjoy her stack of excellent books when she got off duty tonight. Annie was much too busy to get involved in anybody else's trouble. Between the summer tourist crush at the store and her mother-in-law's presence, which lured nonbuyers (of books, any one of them would be eager to purchase dinner, drinks, and very likely sweet mementos for Laurel), she scarcely had time for anything else.

Which reminded her of the table centerpieces for tonight's July fourth dance at the club. She and Max were in charge of decorating the tables. It was already a quarter past six and she needed to dash home, dress, carry pots of red, white, and blue carnations from the coolness of the house to her trunk, and arrive at the club in time to place pots, each with a decorative American flag, on the tables that rimmed three walls of the dance floor.

Flowers . . . car . . . book . . . dance club . . . She dashed into the storeroom, scanning the metal shelving with special orders. Nothing on the A-B-C shelf. Uh-oh. Emma Clyde would not be pleased if her special order wasn't found. She, too, would be at the country club tonight, though not attending the Fourth of July dance of the Lady Luck Dance Club. She was hosting a small dinner party to celebrate the birthday of Henny Brawley, who was both a close friend and Emma's sharpest competition in the monthly contest at the bookstore to identify the books pictured in watercolors above the mantel in the coffee bar. Henny was a mystery expert as well as a gifted amateur actress and active in island charities and clubs.

Annie practiced deep breathing and began a slow, careful, not panicked, certainly not, survey of the storeroom. Her patience was rewarded when she spotted an oblong package wrapped in layers of tissue on the P-Q-R shelf. She carefully unwrapped the book and, ta-da, here it was, a first edition of *The Circular Staircase* by Mary Roberts Rinehart. A summer employee had deposited the book by author's name rather than purchaser. Annie couldn't resist carefully turning the pages for a glimpse of the color frontispiece by Lester Ralph with a filmy, still-perfect tissue guard. Gorgeous, gorgeous, gorgeous.

She felt a swirl of delight, one of those lovely moments in life when everything is right. Henny and (thankfully) Emma would be happy tonight as well as Ingrid, who would be ecstatic with relief when Annie handed over the collectible. Sales were going to top last year at midsummer. Now Annie could race home, change into a cocktail dress, and soon dance the night away in the arms of the handsomest man in the room.

2

Color spots illuminated the dance floor. Max Darling took pleasure in the ease with which he and Annie moved together in a
sinuous tango. As they walk-stepped through a silver spot, he enjoyed
the glimpse of her filmy chiffon dress that emphasized the deep true
gray of her eyes and the sun streaks in her sandy hair. But he also
glimpsed a poignant awareness that their happiness wasn't shared
by all.

In a dusky vale between spots, he murmured, "The night is young
and so are we. Let it go." They turned and stepped, turned and stepped.

"Honestly, why did he even come?" Annie was looking toward
the bar, one area of brightness.

Wesley Hurst hunched at one end of the temporary bar. He held
a half-full glass in his hand. He looked toward the main doorway, his
usually affable face drawn and weary. His bow tie was uneven and

his red cummerbund looked bunched. Of course, it always helped a guy to have a lovely lady on hand to straighten and admire.

"Where is she?" Annie's cool tone left no doubt about her feelings toward Shell Hurst, Wesley's current wife.

If Wesley's face foretold the future, Max doubted the marriage would last much longer. "Timing her entrance, of course."

Annie's nose wrinkled. They half turned together as the band played the haunting and subtly erotic "El Choclo."

"Since when do couples arrive separately? We've been here an hour and not a trace of her."

Max grinned. "The better to heighten suspense."

"Why did he dump Vera for her?"

Max's answer was light. "Stupidity." He spun Annie to his right and her dress swirled and then they were lost in the beat and the rhythm.

Annie sat alone, watching the dancers. The other couples at their table were on the dance floor. Max eased around the next table and arrived triumphantly with their drinks. Tonight she'd opted for a Tom Collins. Max always preferred beer and he carried a glass foaming with a Full Sail Amber from a Savannah brewery. Annie smiled her thanks and took a refreshing sip. She was ready to enjoy a quiet moment and savor the evening. She wasn't sure she liked the colored ceiling spots that left most of the room in semidarkness, including the tables where her lovely centerpieces looked like shadowy clumps.

Usually three chandeliers shed creamy light. She liked seeing people's faces and noticing other women's dresses. Most of the women chose cocktail dresses or evening slacks with dressy tops, though occasionally a woman appeared in a gown. Annie hummed as the band played "In the Misty Moonlight." As couples moved near the perimeter of the floor, they passed for a moment beneath a red spot. Elaine Jamison was slender and lovely in a raspberry stretch crepe sheath. She smiled up at Burl Field. They planned a September wedding. Island newcomers Don Thornwall, the retired navy captain, and his wife, Joyce, seemed equally happy as they whirled by. Maggie and Dave Peterson were next.

Annie's delight in watching the dancers ebbed. It would take time before she forgot Maggie's strained expression, eyes staring, cheekbones prominent, body rigid in her husband's embrace. Dave's heavy face was somber. He seemed oblivious to his wife. His gaze was searching. They danced away into darkness. She had the same thought as when she'd noted Wesley Hurst's glum face. Why come? What brought unhappy people to a party?

Max settled next to her, looked at her quizzically. "I left to go to the bar and you were having fun. I come back and you look forlorn."

"Did you see the Petersons?"

"More candidates for marriage counseling?" Max took a deep swallow of his beer, glanced toward the floor.

"They looked grim."

Max shrugged. "That's their problem. Here's to us." He lifted his glass.

The band always took a short break at nine. Tonight the break was earlier, about a quarter to nine. The dances usually ended at ten. Tonight the last dance was scheduled for nine forty-five because the fireworks would start at ten. The dance before the break ended, before the musicians rose, before any sound or movement distracted, a French door swung open and Shell Hurst stepped inside from the terrace just as the chandelier lights illuminated the room.

Max looked sardonic. "Like I said, waiting to make an entrance."

Shining chestnut hair fell in an enticing swoop down one side of her face, was drawn back on the other, emphasizing the swaying grace of the large silver loop earring in her visible ear. Only Shell could have worn the spectacular dress and not been overmatched. Instead, she and the dress molded together, the brushstroke-print silk caftan exquisite and dramatic. The caftan covered her shoulders and arms, swept to the ground, and that reticence emphasized the plunging V of a neckline that touched the black band at her waist. Black banding marked the flowing sleeves and the caftan side seams and the hem.

There was an instant of silence like the hitch in an old-fashioned reel film.

Before the soundless moment could end, Shell's silvery laugh rang out. "Sorry to be late, everybody. I took a walk on the beach. To think things through. Lots of decisions to make. Oh, there you are, Wesley, right by the bar. You can bring me a drink. Then I'll say hello to all my special friends."

Wesley was still near the bar, face hard. He gazed at her as if she were a stranger. His tie was even farther askew as if he'd yanked at the collar. Now his glass was empty.

In the sudden brightness of the overhead lights, some dancers streamed toward the tables, some toward the terrace for a moment in the moonlight. The usual rumble of men's voices and light high chatter of women began.

Joyce Thornwall, flushed from dancing, slipped into a chair across from Annie. "I suppose he's embarrassed. Aren't the Hursts tonight's host couple?"

One couple served as hosts at each Lady Luck dance. Their primary duty was to welcome couples brought as guests. A second couple—this time Annie and Max—were responsible for the center-pieces. The club provided tablecloths and napkins. A buffet was provided for dinner at seven fifteen. Dancing began at eight.

Annie put two and two together. Wesley Hurst was probably angry at Shell's late arrival and that accounted for his dour presence at the bar. But, as Max had pointed out, the night was young and so were they, and it was time to think about fun. Joyce Thornwall, always adroit and charming, leaned across the table. "I wanted to tell you how much I'm enjoying that clever series about the young royal."

Annie smiled happily, "Rhys Bowen's a wonderful writer. She writes another terrific series set in turn-of-the-century New York City." Annie felt happy, talking about books she loved. She veered to other favorite authors of historical mysteries: Sharan Newman, Kathy Lynn Emerson, Sheldon N. Russell, Jacqueline Winspear, Charles Todd. She had scarcely tasted her drink when the band returned and once again she was on the floor with Max.

Near the bar, Annie looked over Max's shoulder at Eileen and Edward Irwin as they took the floor when the band returned. Eileen was statuesque in a long-sleeve black blouse with gold sequins and dressy black slacks. Her silk shawl swayed as they danced. Annie gave a slight head shake. The black shawl with its fiery dragon motif was a mistake. A bit too much glitz for a woman as pale as Eileen. A white or silver blouse and shawl would have been better. Annie found Eileen austere and daunting. Ice blond hair drawn back from her face emphasized the severity of her features, high forehead, straight nose, prim mouth. She danced with her husband but she might as well have moved alone. Shorter than Eileen, Edward looked as if he was endur-ing the dance, his rounded face solemn.

Shell Hurst came from out of the darkness into the patch of light by the bar. Her expressive face was amused. "Edward, I haven't had a moment alone with you and my heart is breaking." She placed a possessive hand on his arm. "Eileen, you will let me borrow him for a dance, won't you? Wesley isn't in a dancing mood tonight and my toes are tapping."

Eileen and Edward stopped. Other couples flowed around them and Shell.

Edward looked stricken. Suddenly he seemed to shrink, rounded shoulders drooping.

Eileen managed an icy smile. "Of course." She slipped free of Edward and turned toward the tables, her shawl fluttering.

Edward stared after her, his eyes huge behind the lens of his glasses. His mouth sagged open.

Shell stepped near, placed one hand on his shoulder. The other lifted his arm. "Let's not waste our moment." And her carefree laughter could be heard after they moved into the dimness between spots.

Annie stared. Occasionally couples switched partners. It was more customary to dance with your husband or wife. The tempo of the music increased as the band segued into a cha-cha version of "As Time Goes By." No one else appeared to have noticed the quick exchange of partners, which was not surprising as dancers focused on the rhythmic triple step.

Max twirled Annie to a stop near the open windows to the terrace. "There's something about a cha-cha," he murmured, opening a French door to the terrace.

Annie smiled and moved with him. They walked hand in hand to a honeysuckle-draped trellis at the end of the terrace and entered the fragrant bower. She stepped into his arms, lifted her face to his. His fingers trailed across her bare shoulder, down one arm. "Time to go home."

"Aren't we staying for the fireworks?"

"Our fireworks are better than theirs."

Max Darling loved golf, but he didn't love the game enough to make a seven A.M. tee time, which was the only faintly civilized way to play a round on a sea island in July. Sweating like a pig had never been high on his list of priorities, and by eight A.M., any physical exertion guaranteed buckets of sweat. He bent his knees, leaned slightly forward, waggled his new Callaway putter. Nice weight. *Thock.* The ball curved over a simulated hump in the indoor green, ran true to the hole. But what else was new? When a man takes refuge in his office from sweltering heat and has nothing to do but putt, he gets pretty good on the indoor green. Not that it ever translated to the course.

Max retrieved the ball, returned the putter to his red leather golf bag propped next to the door, wandered disconsolately to his desk, tossing the ball in his hand. To say things were slow at Confidential Commissions was an understatement that bordered on the absurd. To be painfully honest, he hadn't had a project since he'd helped an islander trace some gold stocks found in a trunk in the attic. Instead of a gateway to a fortune, Max told him the ornate gold-leafed stock certificates were suitable for framing as mementos, but in terms of cold hard cash, they were maybe worth five bucks apiece at a flea market.

Max plopped into his red leather desk chair. Another hour to go before he met Annie for lunch at Parotti's. Actually, she'd offered him a salad at the bookstore coffee bar, but he well knew that he'd scarcely have a minute with her. He wanted companionship, encouragement. He wanted out of an office that had all the excitement of watching a slow drip from a faucet. His ebullient secretary Barb was gone on a three-week holiday to the coolness of Minnesota, which made him the sole lonely occupant of the office. It was a deep dark secret from Annie, who believed life was real and earnest and work meant *work*, but he and Barb played a mean game of chess on slow days. He picked up a yellow legal pad. Maybe he needed to create a new ad for Confidential Commissions. The one currently running in the *Gazette* obviously wasn't producing clients. Something jazzy. He began to write: *Need to Know? Confidential Commissions handles the most delicate questions with complete confidentiali*—He scratched through, started again. *Got a Problem? Confidential Commissions Specializes in Discreet Inquiries . . .* He X-ed out the line. Sounded too much like a PI agency and he was not a private detective. The state of South Carolina had specific requirements to be a licensed PI, and he didn't qualify because he had no experience in law enforcement. Max considered himself a problem solver, which was a nice, ambiguous term. Max squinted, wrote fast, then nodded in satisfaction as he drew a box around the copy:

Anxious?
Need to know?
Come to Confidential Commissions

Perfect. He ripped off the sheet and turned to his computer to e-mail the new ad to the *Gazette.*

A bell sang as the front door opened. A quick clip of high heels.

Max came to his feet. He believed in karma. Was a bewildered, threatened young woman—preferably beautiful and wearing too much makeup—hurrying to him with an appeal? If she wore a red pillbox hat preferably with a black mini veil, a popular style in Erle Stanley Gardner tales, his day would be complete.

His visitor rushed through his office doorway.

Max's eyes widened. Young, that was for sure. Very young. A girl, actually, despite the absurdly high heels and tight cream jersey blouse above a cerise miniskirt so short he quickly raised his eyes to her face. Max grew up with three sisters and was familiar with brushes, pencils, and palettes of beige, brown, and black. Annie was slapdash with makeup, a quick brush with an eyebrow pencil, a whiff of powder, lips lightly touched with gloss. The girl in the doorway had likely spent a good deal of time at her bedroom dressing table. Her eyes were rimmed with black. Purple crescents beneath the lower lids melded into a thick tannish orange covering. Crimson lip gloss was drawn overlarge. Bright blond hair in tight curls reached to her shoulders.

Max looked beyond the garish makeup and saw a roundish face that still held an imprint of childhood. The violet eyes looked desperately uncertain, the overdrawn lips defenseless. "Hello." His voice was gentle. "I don't think we've met. I'm Max Darling. Can I help you?"

She clasped her hands together. "You find out things, don't you?"

He looked at her gravely. "Sometimes. What do you want to know?" And who are your parents and why are you here? But surely this information would come. He gestured toward the comfortable rattan chair that faced his desk. "Come and sit down and introduce yourself."

She edged past him, settled in the chair, gripped the arms. "I'm Hayley Hurst."

Max made the connection. He had been vaguely aware that Wesley Hurst and his ex-wife Vera had teenage children.

The girl looked at him, her eyes huge. "I know Rachel at school. I've heard about you and Annie."

Max smiled inside. Annie adored her young stepsister and was always eager to know the latest at Broward's Rock High School. The admiration was mutual, and Max didn't doubt that Rachel had over-sold both him and his abilities.

Hayley stared at him with disconcerting intensity. "Rachel says you figure things out. Rachel says you're smarter than any private detective. I need somebody to find out something for me. How much do you cost?"

Max felt uneasy. What possible reason could a kid have to ask for the kind of inquiry he could make? He watched her closely, but kept his tone light. "That depends upon what I'm asked to find. A Honus Wagner baseball card? Who Justin Bieber's dating? Time of high tide tomorrow morning?"

She ignored his effort at humor. "I want you to find out where somebody's gone. I've got five hundred dollars."

He wasn't going to take a child's money, probably her savings from birthday and Christmas presents. In fact, he very likely shouldn't encourage her to tell him whatever worry had brought her here. She had a family. He leaned forward. "Look, Hayley, whatever the problem is, you better talk to your folks. I doubt that I can help you."

"I can't." Her face drew down in misery. "Mom won't ever let me talk about Shell, and when I try to talk to Dad, he gets mad. And ever since the Fourth, Jed gets this funny sick look when I mention her and he tells me to shut up. He hates her for helping me be who I am. He's awful about her. That last day he was threatening to—Well, he was mean. Anyway I can't talk to anyone about her and I only want to know where she went." Her lips wobbled. "And why she hasn't called me."

"Shell's gone somewhere?" It wasn't smart to get mixed up in family squabbles, but if all the kid wanted was a phone call, maybe he could help. Frankly, nothing Shell Hurst would do would surprise him, and certainly she and Wesley weren't on good terms at the dance.

Hayley nodded energetically, scooted to the edge of the chair. "She's been gone since the Fourth." She reached into an oversized rainbow-hued plastic beach bag. "I brought some pictures of her. I thought maybe you might need them if you look for her." She held out three photographs. "I took them out of one of her scrapbooks. She's a movie star. Maybe she's gone back to LA."

Max had heard the island gossip about Bucky coming to the island with a "starlet," but he doubted that Shell qualified as a movie star. He picked up the photographs. All were excellent: Shell holding a tennis racket with a breeze stirring her magnificent mane of reddish brown hair, the tennis blouse and skirt flattering to her leggy figure; Shell in a bikini looking seductively over one shoulder; Shell astride a horse in a costume reminiscent of a John Wayne Western. She might not be a movie star, but she had looks and sex appeal.

Max took the photos, placed them neatly in the center of the desk. He couldn't envision wandering around the island, showing these pictures. Wesley Hurst had always seemed like an amiable man, but Max had no trouble picturing Wesley charging him like an enraged bull.

"You haven't talked to her since July fourth?" Max didn't need to look at a calendar to know today was Monday, July 9. "That's not very long ago. When did you last see her?"

"That night. She went out a little before eight and she never came back. Dad doesn't care. He said she doesn't need to ever come back. He said he's damned sure she will when she stops raising hell wherever she is."

Max wondered if Hayley realized how much she'd revealed about her father's second marriage. Wesley Hurst was clearly at odds with his wife and not just at the dance. The fact that he wasn't upset suggested Shell might have left following an argument.

"She didn't give any hint about where she was going?"

"I didn't know she was going anywhere." Hayley blinked back tears. "I was at Dad's house and I saw her go out that night on her way to the club and she was gorgeous. She was wearing the prettiest silk dress with big, wide sleeves and the skirt almost to the floor and lots of colors. I went over to the club for the fireworks but I didn't try to look in at the dance. I was with some girls. Anyway, the next day I waited until noon to go over to Dad's house. She wasn't anywhere so I went up to her room and she wasn't there. Her bed hadn't been slept in and I didn't find the dress in her closet."

Max didn't change expression. He doubted that Wesley Hurst would want anyone to know he didn't share a bedroom with his second, much younger wife. "Did your dad look for her?"

"He was already gone. I didn't know what to think when I didn't find Shell. I asked Wilma. She's the housekeeper and she said she didn't know from nothing and maybe I shouldn't say anything to anybody. Wilma said Dad had left early to go out in his boat, the *Vagabond*. I can see Dad's new house—I mean, it's not new, but Dad bought it after he married Shell—from my room in our old house. It made Mom pretty mad to have him next door, but he liked being on the beach. Anyway, I was in our old house, that's where Mom and Jed and I live. I watched out my window all the rest of the day. When Dad came home, I ran over there and asked him about Shell. That's when he said he didn't know where she was, but as far as he was concerned, wherever it was, she could stay there with whoever she was hanging out with. Then he slammed his car door and told me to go home."

"So"—Max kept his tone matter-of-fact—"you last saw her the evening of July fourth. You've called her but have had no response."

"I've called her cell a bunch of times. She never answers. Of course"—her voice wobbled—"maybe she sees it's me and she doesn't want to talk to me, but I just want to know she's all right."

"She may have left the island for a week or so. Maybe she'll come back soon." Max thought his comment was singularly unhelpful.

"I guess so." Hayley twined a wiry curl around one finger. "Dad thinks she's run away with somebody. But see, if she did, they went in her car." Hayley leaned forward. "She drives a new green Porsche Carrera. Why wouldn't she leave in the guy's car? I think Dad has it wrong." Hayley's eyes skittered away. "But sometimes she talked to some guy on the phone. She called him *cherie*, but it was kind of like she was having fun with him. I didn't see her take a suitcase when she left that night."

Max didn't change expression. If Shell planned a getaway, she could easily have packed earlier and put a suitcase in the trunk of her car. "I expect she'll be back in a few days."

"Won't you help me?"

Max cleared his throat. "Hayley, sometimes grown-ups need a little space. It sounds like Shell and your dad may be out of sorts with each—"

She jumped to her feet. Tears spilled down her cheeks. "Rachel said you were wonderful. I guess not." She teetered across the room in the high heels, and in an instant, the front door slammed.

Parotti's Bar and Grill was packed. Wide-eyed vacationers stepped gingerly in the sawdust on the bait side of the restaurant, wrinkling their noses at the aroma released when a fisherman lifted a cooler lid, seeking black bass, grouper, squid, snapper, or chicken necks. Opposite the row of coolers was a wooden bar that would have looked at home in a dusty B Western.

Max looked across the table at Annie. "Hayley brought pictures of Shell. Hayley says Shell's car hasn't been back at the house. Shell drives a new green Porsche."

Owner Ben Parotti, dapper in a Tommy Bahama Hawaiian shirt and navy slacks, hurried up to refill their iced tea glasses. "Everything up to snuff?"

Annie doubted that his better half, Miss Jolene of the tea shop background, would have approved of the inelegant query, but Ben's transformation after a late marriage from a bibbed-overall gnome to a snazzy restaurateur was miracle enough. Ben had agreed to expand the menu to quiches and add tablecloths, but he had drawn a line in the sawdust over the bait shop. Bait he had always sold and bait he would always sell, and the smell be damned.

Annie made a happy circle with a thumb and forefinger. "Tell Miss Jolene the new seafood stew is the best ever."

Ben beamed. "She's the best ever." And he was gone.

Max waited until he was out of earshot to finish his summation. "I feel like a rat. She ran out crying. But this has to be a matter for the family."

"What are you going to do?" Annie added butter to a slice of jalapeño corn bread.

Max laughed. "Maybe I'll check InTrade to see what the odds are Shell flounces back looking like the cat that ate the canary."

Annie understood his lack of concern. Shell and Wesley were obviously at odds. Shell was the kind of woman who wouldn't care what anyone thought, and if she wanted to get away for a while and let Wesley stew, she would be gone in an instant.

But if all the kid wanted was a phone call . . . "Max."

His smile slipped away, replaced by a quizzical, wary expression, the kind a man gets when a woman says, "Honey, there are a few things I want you to do this weekend."

Annie tried a winning smile. "Of course you won't get involved in a family dispute, but that doesn't mean we can't try and find Shell and ask her to give Hayley a call."

Max folded his arms. "Shell Hurst got the kid's calls. If she wanted to answer, she would." Max shook his head. "Annie, if there's one thing we all know, it's butt out of people's marriages."

Reluctantly, she knew he was right.

Annie raced ahead of Max on the oyster-shell path to the gazebo, moving fast to elude the kamikaze attacks of mosquitoes and no-see-ums. Mosquitoes honed in on her like honeybees to nectar. Max strolled without hurry, not a man to run in the heat. After dinner on summer nights, especially in muggy August, they sometimes went to the beach for a nighttime plunge, but often they ended the day in their screened-in gazebo, looking out at the moonlit-dappled garden, aromatic with sweet-scented pittosporum and honeysuckle.

Just for an instant, she remembered another August when Max had disappeared and police dogs sought his scent at a cabin where a beautiful young woman lay battered to death. She turned, waited for him to catch up, and reached out to grip his hand. For a time, she'd thought he was dead. For a longer time, she'd feared that he would be tried for a murder he hadn't committed. Now she knew that safety and permanency were always an illusion, that happiness could vanish without warning.

His arm slipped around her shoulders. "I'm here."

Her words came slowly. "I was thinking about that August."

"Don't." His tone was gentle. "Think about now."

Now, this minute, she was safe and happy with Max's arm around her shoulders. In a while, no hurry, they'd return—okay, maybe she'd dash ahead of him to avoid the after-sunset swarms of mosquitoes—to their antebellum house, a welcoming house with comfortable furniture and heart pine floors and books everywhere. All was well for them, but Hayley Hurst's visit to Max evoked a past filled with hurt and fear. She took a deep breath and looked at Max. "When you disappeared"—the words were hard to say—"I looked for you. Everywhere. I would never have stopped looking. Max, nobody's looking for Shell."

"Annie"—he was impatient—"if ever a woman can take care of herself, it's Shell Hurst."

3

Annie leaned against the railing and looked out over the marina, admiring boats small and big. Someone had told her the gleaming white tri-deck motor yacht that had arrived from Singapore was valued at more than ten million dollars. Crewmen were washing the decks, and water from several hoses glistened in the sunlight like arcs of diamonds. She scanned small boats and found her favorite, *Just Plain Vanilla*, a twelve-foot yellow-hulled sailboat. A family with three teenagers was readying to cast off. The scene changed every day, but there was a sameness, too, water slapping against the pier, the satisfying scent of the sea, porpoises frolicking in the Sound. This morning she couldn't take her usual pleasure in the familiar, cherished view.

She frowned and hurried to the boardwalk that ran in front of the crescent of shops. At breakfast, Max had refused to even consider quiet inquiries seeking Shell. Annie felt an urgency to do something. Maybe she felt guilty that she didn't like Shell. Maybe she empathized too much with a teenager's plaintive request. Maybe she was having a Pam North intuitive moment. Men dismissed women's intuition. The facts, ma'am. Pam North in the Frances and Richard Lockridge mysteries was ditzy, but she made unexpected mental connections because of what she had seen and heard.

Annie stood very still. When she looked back at the evening when they'd last seen Shell, she had a sense of darkness, of wrongness. An evening designed for fun against a romantic backdrop had held dark moments, and that was the evening when a woman known to stir passions was last seen. The more she thought about the Fourth of July dance, the uneasier she felt.

"Cool it," she said aloud as she unlocked the front door to Death on Demand. Her subconscious thumbed its nose, muttering, People don't just disappear into thin air. Annie ignored the mutter and concentrated on the tasks that lay ahead. She had a half hour before the store opened at ten to check e-mails, orders, arrivals, and possibly open and shelve several boxes of books, including new titles by Rita Mae Brown and Cleo Coyle. Next month there would be a signing for Emma Clyde. The island mystery author was nothing if not prolific. She was still writing two books a year. Annie felt a qualm. It was getting harder to round up people to attend a signing for Emma. In January, Annie had combined the signing with a luncheon. Emma had been grudgingly pleased with the turnout. In late summer many people they knew were on holiday. She would make a note to remind herself to call regular customers. She could offer a discount on books bought that evening . . . It would be helpful to know when Shell last used her cell phone.

Annie stepped inside, wrinkling her nose at the familiar and delightful scent of new books and old. She turned on the lights and the overhead circular fans. She loved the light swish as they revolved.

At the dance, Shell timed her entrance for maximum effect. Annie took a moment to glance at a new display by the cash desk. The top three slots in the cardboard display stand featured Emma's newest, *The Case of the Charismatic Cat*. The lower slots featured *The Last Minute* by Jeff Abbott, *Some Like It Hawk* by Donna Andrews, *As the Pig Turns* by M. C. Beaton, and *Wicked Autumn* by G. M. Malliet. Maybe a ten percent discount on these titles for everyone attending Emma's signing next month—

A sharp nip at her ankle was a reminder that Agatha, the world's most gorgeous, imperious, and regal bookstore cat, didn't hold with lollygagging around when it was feeding time.

Annie looked down at her glossy black feline, but she started moving at the same time. No one could say she wasn't cat trained. "Sorry, Agatha. Just for a teeny minute I wasn't thinking about you."

Agatha was right behind her. Any instant sharp incisors might clip her bare heel. Annie refused to admit that she was running, but her sandals slapped against the floor. She reached the coffee bar, skidded around the end, and retrieved Agatha's bowl. Why did Shell and Wesley arrive separately?

Agatha landed lightly atop the counter. Her green eyes gleamed, her tail switched.

Annie measured out kitty salmon, placed the bowl in front of Agatha. She'd swab the counter with Clorox wipes later. Removing an irritated Agatha to the floor wasn't an option. By the time Annie had made a cappuccino, Agatha was content.

Annie came around the counter, settled at one of the tables. She should be doing many things, but she'd relax and enjoy a peaceful moment. Wesley Hurst had too much to drink that night. Determinedly, Annie looked up at five watercolors hanging above the fireplace. One of the store's most popular promotions was the monthly contest to identify the title and author featured in each painting. It would, she thought regretfully, be even more popular if someone other than Emma Clyde and Henny Brawley would occasionally win. That wouldn't be the case this month due to Annie's clever ploy of inviting Henny to suggest titles to the artist, thus removing Henny from the competition.

Henny had enthusiastically complied. However, she had succumbed to the temptation of choosing books with, Annie feared, the sole goal of exposing Emma Clyde as deficient in her knowledge of the mystery genre. In fact, Henny had slid a triumphant look at Emma when she'd said oh-so-casually, "You may want to sit this one out, Emma, since it requires a knowledge of earlier best-selling authors," the clear implication being that Henny truly knew the mystery field and Emma did not. The result, of course, was a flash of bloodlust in Emma's eyes as she gruffly replied, "No one knows more about mysteries than I do." The gauntlet was flung. Emma was determined to provide the answers.

In fact, Emma had taken to arriving every morning, ordering a double shot of espresso, and pacing back and forth beneath the watercolors, muttering to herself.

Henny had added insult to injury in midmonth by adding publication dates beneath each title, saying again oh-so-casually, "This may help readers who are mystery challenged."

Annie herself didn't know the titles and authors. She was pretty sure she'd figured out the answers for paintings one, three, and four. Two and five had her stumped. She looked up at the watercolors.

In the first painting, fog swirled around the London cab stopped on cobbled stones. The headlights scarcely penetrated the mist. The cab's dim interior light revealed a smallish round gentleman in evening dress slumped against the cushions, a dark bruise on his temple.

Standing at the open rear door, his intelligent, sensitive face mirroring recognition, a handsome man stared in shock at the dead passenger. 1938.

In the second painting, a hand holding an automatic poked through parted velvet curtains into a small, cozy living room that contained deep armchairs and a table with a plate of ham and cheese and tankards of beer. A brown-haired, slim, midthirties man in a double-breasted blue suit stared in shock as blood streaked the head of a taller man standing near the mantel above a gas fire, and a third man slowly collapsed to the floor. 1946.

In the third painting, a large, imposing woman, conservatively and tastefully dressed, stood among the tables in a seedy nightclub, midway between the back bar and front staircase. She held open a fur coat, offering cover for a beautiful young blonde wearing a red cloak that reached only to her thighs, and little else. 1949.

In the fourth painting, the figure inching up the side of a château wall, high above ground, was a dark shadow, gray sweater, gray flannel trousers, and form-fitting gray leather slippers almost indistinguishable from gray stone. The man moved fluidly, one hand reaching higher to search, patiently and carefully, for a crevice, enough for a fingerhold to ease higher toward the overhanging eave. 1953.

In the fifth painting, a dark-haired young woman, tears of joy streaming down her face, rushed across the courtroom to the counsel table to hug the ruggedly handsome, broad-shouldered man just picking up his briefcase. A border beneath the scene featured small inset drawings of a shoe box with the lid askew and greenbacks visible, heavy dark glasses, a folding wheelchair, and a swarm of teenage boys cleaning a sedan. 1961.

Annie finished her cappuccino. Why wasn't Wesley Hurst trying to find his wife? As she washed the mug, she gave a decided nod, quickly swiped the mug dry. She hurried to the storeroom for her cell. In an instant, she'd touched the number for Hyla Harrison.

Hyla answered, her tone formal. "Officer Harrison."

Annie knew Hyla was on duty. "Hyla, it's Annie." Of course, Hyla had caller ID and was well aware of her caller's identity. "Do you have a minute to talk?"

"A couple of minutes." Hyla was businesslike.

"You covered traffic the night of July fourth. Where were you working?"

"Bay Street. Bumper to bumper to the ferry."

Annie thought quickly. She'd last seen Shell at shortly before ten P.M. "Did you see a new green Porsche Carrera between ten o'clock and midnight?" The last ferry left at midnight. If Shell took the ferry, they could try to trace her on the mainland.

There was a pause. "You know how many cars we had on Bay Street? But maybe I can help you out. I keep an eye peeled for any cars reported stolen so I give the cars going on the ferry a good look. I only remember one Porsche in the ferry line. It was black. Got to go."

Annie sounded as if she had looked into a mist and seen something frightful. "People can't just disappear into thin air."

In one part of his mind, Max took pleasure in Annie's presence, her shining sandy hair and steady gray eyes and kissable lips—very kissable. But this wasn't a moment to suggest they slip home for morning delight. He considered his options. A soothing tone? Grave interest? Instead, he chose an uncomfortable truth. "People disappear all the time."

"Maybe that's because no one really looks for them."

Max tried for sweet reason. "There's nothing to indicate she didn't leave the island willingly. Certainly there's no evidence of a crime. That's the choice, isn't it? Either she left the island in her car or something happened to her after the dance. If she's the victim of foul play"—his tone made clear that he discounted that possibility—"why hasn't anyone found a body or found the car?"

Annie was undeterred. "Hyla says her car didn't board the ferry."

Max jerked his thumb toward the marina. "There's more than one way off an island. Maybe she went on board one of those snazzy yachts. Maybe she's on her way with some Brazilian millionaire." Knowing Annie's tendency to be literal, he added, "Metaphorically speaking."

Annie didn't even glance toward the marina. "Where's the Porsche?"

"There are places on the island where a car could be hidden for years and nobody would find it. Miles of forest."

Annie persisted. "Okay, let's say she's skipping the country with a Brazilian millionaire. Why not leave her car at the marina?"

Max felt that he was, metaphorically speaking, being backed into a corner. "To throw people off the track."

"The track," she said drily, "that nobody's even noticed except a teenage kid."

Max turned his hands palms up. "Whoever knows what's in the mind of a woman?"

Annie's eyes narrowed. "Sexism—the last resort of a man who can't answer a question."

Max grinned.

Annie didn't grin. Instead, she perched on the edge of his desk, her short skirt pulling up to reveal an enticing length of thigh.

Max reined himself in. There was a time and a place. Hopefully, soon. Right now, he assumed a suitably serious expression. "You have a point about the car." What it was, he didn't know, but he knew when to make nice. "What do you suggest we do?"

Annie looked relieved and pleased. "We need to plan a campaign."

Max raised an eyebrow.

She hurried on. "It's up to us to see if we can find out where she is."

Max kept his tone mild. "Why us?"

"We were at the dance. We were among the last people on the island to see Shell. There's lots we can do." She took a breath, blurted, "Besides, she may be a mess, but somebody should care enough to figure out if she's okay."

Max got it. Annie, as usual, was charging to the succor of the downtrodden. He had difficulty picturing Shell Hurst as downtrodden, but Annie had it right that no one apparently gave a damn about Shell and her whereabouts except a screwed-up teenager. That was enough to galvanize Annie into action.

She leaned forward, said eagerly, "Somebody always knows something. We'll start with the day she was last seen."

Max had no doubt that Shell Hurst was off island, very likely with a lover. But Annie was clearly determined to find the woman. "Look"—he tried to be tactful—"you can't go around saying Shell's disappeared. People will get the wrong idea."

Annie looked stubborn. "Maybe the idea there's something wrong will shake loose the information we need. Sure, she's probably in Rio right now, but there's a chance she's not. If we don't look, no one will ever know. We can't just leave it that, oh well, she's left the island and who cares. Hayley cares." Her brows drew down in a frown.

Max knew that Shell was volatile and selfish, and maybe leaving without a word to anyone amused her. But it was possible that Shell was a victim. Yeah, people sometimes disappeared into thin air and were never seen again. Judge Crater. Jimmy Hoffa. And too many others, often young and female. Maybe they went on to better things. Maybe not.

Annie plunged ahead. "We need to find out more about Shell and about that last day. If she left deliberately, there has to be a reason. Or, put it another way, if we can find out why she would leave, we'll know if she left."

Max started to reply, stopped. Annie had already accused him of sexism. It wouldn't be smart to suggest that her logic was both circular and exceedingly feminine. He simply nodded.

"You can find out more about Shell."

Max was relieved. That sounded innocuous enough and perhaps he would make contact with someone who had seen or spoken to Shell after the Fourth. "Okay."

"Then you can talk to Wesley."

"Excuse me?"

Annie was impatient. "Obviously, Wesley thinks she had a reason to leave or he would have started looking for her. Wouldn't he?"

Max looked down at the legal pad, realized he'd been doodling as Annie talked. He'd sketched a shadowy dance floor and scarcely realized moving figures, a low-slung sports car, and, below the penciled images, the dark circles of a vortex. Anything, everything could disappear in the maw of a whirlpool. That's how he would feel, flung to destruction, if Annie walked out of his life.

When Hayley asked for help and told him her father had made no effort to find Shell, Max was convinced Shell had simply chosen to walk away. Any man who cared for a woman would surely move heaven and earth to find her. Wesley had certainly cared a lot at some point. Even if now he was glad she'd left—Max remembered his hard, angry face at the dance—he might have a very good idea where she'd gone. And why.

In between waiting on customers and unpacking boxes of books— the most recent by Lee Goldberg, Dorothy Howell, and Victoria Thompson—Annie arranged for backup at the store, calling on Pamela Potts, an old friend and utterly reliable. Pamela's blue eyes regarded the world without a trace of humor, but she knew mysteries and would shepherd customers to the kinds of books they liked.

Pamela arrived, delighted to be of help. Her blond pageboy was, as always, perfect. She joined Ingrid at the front counter and Annie was free. She walked down the center aisle, automatically straightening books as she went. The Joan Hess titles were out of order in the caper/comedy section. She smiled as she noted the new editions of wonderful M. M. Kaye titles in romantic suspense. She swerved toward the coffee bar and took a moment to survey glass shelves with mugs that carried the name and title of famous mysteries in bright red lettering. Annie chose *Lady, Where Are You?* by Hugh Desmond. She carried a mug of Colombian coffee to the storeroom, firmly shut the door behind her.

She settled at the worktable, pulled a legal pad close, wrote fast:

Need to Know

1. Who is *cherie*?
2. So far as is known, Shell Hurst was last seen at the July 4 Lady Luck dance.

3. Did anything significant occur at the dance?
4. Who was the last person to see her?
5. When did she leave the club?
6. Where is her car?

Annie sipped the hot, strong brew. Did she know anyone who could give her some insight on Shell Hurst? Regretfully, Annie shook her head. She and Max had been members of the dance club for four years, but that was their only real social contact with Wesley Hurst, his first wife Vera, and his second wife Shell. The Hursts were part of an affluent island milieu that lived off inherited wealth, jetted around the world on a whim, enjoyed yacht journeys to the Caribbean. Annie, true to her Protestant ethic upbringing, believed work, if not the road to salvation, was surely the highway to happiness, which, of course, accounted for Max's devotion—possibly too strong a word—to Confidential Commissions. Max also enjoyed inherited wealth. Though not averse to work, he didn't equate effort with worth, but he applauded Annie's ideals and took pleasure in their mostly middle-class friends.

In short, Annie wasn't on speed dial with island socialites.

However, there were other avenues to obtain tidbits about the rich. She retrieved her cell phone, called.

"Your appointment's not 'til next week, Annie."

Annie's short hair was good to go after a quick shower so she went to the beauty shop once a month for a trim. "I'll be there. Daisy, you have a second?"

"Annie," her deep voice boomed, "for you, I got a whole minute." Big and buxom, Daisy Casey talked fast and always said what was on her mind in a honey-sweet Southern accent.

"You know everything there is to know on the island."

Daisy's laugh was husky. "You got questions, ask the beautician, the banker, or the mortician. We cover it all. What's on your mind?"

"I wondered if Shell Hurst—"

"That woman's cruisin' for a bruisin'. Stand me up like I'm white trash! She has her regular appointment, two hours' worth, every Monday morning, and not a peep out of her yesterday. She better not show her face around here again, and she'll have to go all the way to Savannah for someone who can handle the kind of rinse she needs. Why, bless her heart, she'll look like the hind end of a bee-draggled pound dog."

Shell was definitely on Daisy's blacklist. Annie grinned. "So you won't mind giving me the lowdown on Shell."

"Sweetie, I'll rain on her parade like a Lowcountry downpour. Talks pretty as you please but she kind of has a sneer in her eyes."

"How about a lover?"

The silence on the line was stark.

Annie's hand tightened on the cell.

Daisy spoke slowly. "I don't like to cause nice people any grief."

Annie was sure that Daisy didn't mean Shell. Annie picked her words carefully. "I'm not planning on causing grief to anyone nice. But I have a real reason for asking. I'm trying to figure out if Shell's off on a vacation with somebody from the island. She left July fourth and someone's trying to get in touch with her."

"Is it important?"

Annie thought about a teary teenager waiting for a call. "I think so." And in the back of her mind, there was the green Porsche that hadn't left the island.

"Men can be the biggest butts. And after he was such a rock when Maggie was so sick—"

Annie felt a twist inside. Maggie Peterson and her fight with cancer and the distance between Maggie and Dave on the dance floor.

"—I swear if I was Maggie I'd castrate him like a wild hog. That poor honey just keeps holding on. But, mind now, don't you let on to Maggie what I said." Another pause. "Some of the ladies was talking and you know how Loretta Bailey chatters. I swear words come tumbling out of her that would make Leon queasier than eight-foot swells. She said Leon was right puzzled how Dave had sold out a bunch of stuff and put about half his money in cash accounts. Sounds like a man up to no good. Everybody knows cash don't earn any money these days. Oh, here's my next appointment. Gotta go."

Max used his one–eight hundred number for the call to Bucky Hurst. ". . . representing a producer who wants to get in touch with Shell Vitale."

"The lady doesn't live here anymore." Bucky sounded bored. "You can call her on Broward's Rock—"

Max interrupted. "Apparently she's left the island. The matter is fairly urgent. Can you suggest friend or family who can help me out?"

"Left?" There was a rumble of laughter. "I told Wesley boy she wasn't the kind you marry. He was too dumb to listen. As usual. Yeah. She's got a sister in Bakersfield, Edna Vitale."

Annie took a deep breath and tapped numbers on her cell.
"Peterson Construction. How may I help you?"

A muted thump sounded at the storeroom's closed door. Annie came to her feet, carrying the cell. She opened the door, and Agatha marched in, tail high.

"This is Annie Darling. May I speak to Mr. Peterson, please." Annie closed the door, returned to the worktable.

Agatha followed and sailed to the tabletop, landing lightly.

"He's on a conference call at the moment. May I have him call you back?" The receptionist was pleasant and professional.

Annie left the number, slipped back into her seat.

Agatha stepped onto the legal pad, turned around twice, sat. She rubbed the side of her face against Annie's arm, staking claim and effectively preventing Annie from making notes.

"Not enough cat attention? Right. First things first." Annie stroked soft, fine black fur.

A faint purr indicated approval.

"I thought I'd cornered a fat juicy mouse, Agatha. Guess again. Dave Peterson may be *cherie*, but he obviously isn't off island with Shell. Unless Shell has been a very busy lady and quite discreet, there isn't a Brazilian millionaire with a yacht. Agatha, if she didn't leave the island with a lover, where is she?"

Five Vitales later, Max listened to Edna.

". . . sure miss Willie Kay. Oh, I know she likes Shell better, even went to court to get her name changed. But she'll always be Willie Kay to me. Cutest little girl you can imagine. See, I'm twenty years older and our mom died when Willie Kay was a little girl so I raised her. And she can dance and sing like an angel. But I was so glad when she got married and decided not to stay in show business. I don't believe in how a woman has to show off her body to get places. But I don't hold with marrying a man who's been married before. I'm awful afraid Willie Kay's run into trouble there. She didn't tell me much, just said she'd be leaving the island after she took care of some matters. She said she was coming back to California but first she was going to make sure nobody there forgot her. I told her I didn't like the sound of that, the good Lord always says to turn the other cheek, and she laughed and said she was just going to pop holes in some fancy balloons and then she'd be on her way."

"When did you last talk to her?"

"I think it was Sunday before last. In the afternoon."

"She may be on her way now. If she gets in touch, will you ask her to call me?"

"Sure. I'll be glad to. But let me give you her cell number. You can call her yourself."

Max wrote down Shell's cell number, left his number.

He made quick notes: *Shell told sister of plan to leave. Departure didn't sound imminent but that was a couple of days before the Fourth. Did she change her mind? Was she on her way to California?*

As he wrote, he felt encouraged. Here was confirmation that Shell intended to leave the island. Maybe he could find Shell and ask her please to give Hayley a ring. He tapped Shell's number. Five rings later voice mail interceded.

"Double, double, double dare." A towheaded teenager bellowed through cupped hands at a skinny girl wavering uncertainly at the end of the country club's high dive. She edged forward, squealed, jumped.

Annie stood on a flagstone terrace between the pool and the French doors of the dining room. The wing that included the two rooms combined for the Lady Luck dance extended to the left. The wing also afforded access to the terrace through French doors. Shell had entered the dance from the terrace. Annie and Max had walked out onto the terrace through a French door for their close encounter of a personal kind before leaving Wednesday night.

That night she and Max had parked in the overflow lot. Parking in the main lot and the swimming pool lot had been full because of the Fourth. The overflow lot was accessible from a blacktop that bounded a portion of the golf course. Underbrush had been cleared but cars had to squeeze between pines to park. The golf course lot was on the other side of a stand of pines at the end of the terrace. That lot would also have been the choice of latecomers.

Shell made her entrance when the band stopped playing at a quarter to nine. Very likely she'd either found space in the overflow lot or the golf course lot since she entered from a terrace door.

Annie crossed the terrace and opened a door into the hallway that ran between the dining room and the wing. She stepped into coolness and quiet. She closed the door and raucous shouts from the swimming pool weren't audible. The slap of her sandals against the cypress flooring was the only sound. The dining room was to her right. A closed double door to her left offered access to the site of the dance. She reached the end of the hallway. Straight ahead was the central two-story atrium. To her left, another hall led to private meeting rooms on one side, and, on the other, larger party rooms. For the dance, a partition was opened to combine two rooms.

Annie looked down the shadowy hall. That night the only means of access to the dance were the door in the cross hallway and the French doors to the terrace. The door opposite the dining room had been used by waitstaff and the band members.

She hurried across the atrium, passed the cloakroom. She stopped at the third frosted-glass door, the office of the service manager, Gerald O'Reilly. His door was open. He sat at his desk, his usually pleasant face creased in apologetic defensiveness. Jerry, as he urged club members to call him, was redheaded, ebullient, smooth, efficient, and always respectful. He wasn't obsequious, but he deferred to the members, a subtle reinforcement of their affluent status. "Nothing like this has ever happened at the club. Absolutely I understand your outrage. I intend to find the responsible party." Another defensive pause. "Certainly the club will pay for all damage—" He winced and held the phone away from his ear.

The bellow over the phone reached Annie in the doorway, the deep male voice apoplectic. ". . . don't you understand? She was in perfect condition, never even been repainted, not a scratch on her. Worth a fortune. Now she'll have to go to a body shop. She won't be the original."

Jerry tried again. "Colonel, I understand your distress. Sir, we want to—" Jerry's shoulders sagged. He clicked off the phone.

Annie hesitated in the doorway. Not a cheerful conversation and obviously the other speaker had hung up on Jerry. It was a reminder that everyone had challenges and maybe this wasn't a good time to talk to Jerry.

He looked up and his face reformed into a semblance of welcome though his cheeks were still flushed. "Mrs. Darling." He came to his feet, moved around the desk. There was the air of a maître d' ready to offer the best table. "What can I do for you this morning?"

Annie smiled. "Jerry, I want to have a word with some of the waitstaff who served the dance club Wednesday night, especially those on duty between eight fifteen and nine thirty."

His genial expression eroded. "Believe me," he spoke emphatically, "I've already asked everyone who was in the dance rooms and no one saw that shawl." He shoved a stubby hand through his thinning red hair and looked both exasperated and beleaguered.

"Shawl?"

He took a deep, steadying breath. "Aren't you here for Mrs. Irwin? She's called five times already."

Annie didn't know whether to offer smelling salts or suggest a mantra. Instead, she gave him a reassuring smile. "I am not seeking a shawl and I haven't talked to Eileen Irwin."

Pink again tinged his cheeks. "I'm sorry. Every time anybody brings up that night, it's trouble. Colonel Hudson's livid. You might know"—his tone was aggrieved—"some kid on a joyride would use the colonel's car to trench two holes." He shook his head. "What a mess. The greenskeeper's in shock. Ruts six inches deep on eight and nine. Even worse, the damn car apparently skidded on that hump-backed bridge over the lagoon by nine and knocked down a post. I mean, it's only a scratch on one fender. Well, I guess a headlight was cracked. But the colonel's lucky the whole car didn't go into the lagoon. Now the colonel wants all the valet parking kids fired. That's not fair. Anybody could have taken the keys from the board. Anybody could spot his Air Force Thunderbird key fob if they hankered to drive an MG."

"Someone took the car from valet parking?" Annie felt sorry for Jerry. Crusty, seventyish Harry Hudson had three passions in life: his military career, his classic yellow MG with running boards, and golf.

Jerry swiped again at his mussed hair, looking even more like a bird with a red crest. "There were cars everywhere Wednesday night. The MG wasn't really gone that long." Again he was defensive. "But it was an hour of hell when the colonel asked for his car and we couldn't come up with it. I thought he was going to have a stroke on the spot. We were just lucky somebody walked home across the course and found it. And the next day Mrs. Irwin was here and you'd think she'd lost the crown jewels. She swears she wore a silk shawl to the dance and she left it on her chair when they went out for the fireworks, and when they got ready to go home after the fireworks, she couldn't find it. I thought she'd complained to you." He wrinkled his snub nose.

"You want to talk to the waitstaff. Was there something else wrong that night?"

"Everything was lovely. The dance was a great success. The staff couldn't have done a better job." He looked visibly happier with each reassurance. Annie scrambled to think of a tactful reason to speak with club staff. "This is another matter entirely. I'm trying to find out when Shell Hurst left that night and I hoped some of the staff might have noticed. She was wearing a distinctive dress. A friend is trying to get in touch with her."

Jerry stared at her and she could see the questions running through his mind . . . *What difference does it make when Mrs. Hurst left the club Wednesday night? Why not call and ask her? Something screwy here. Mrs. Darling's always nice to deal with* . . . And his quick decision . . . *Nothing to do with the club. What harm can it do? The Darlings are active members. I can get rid of her and talk to the club president, ask him to deal with the colonel* . . .

"Sure." Jerry's tone was hearty and now his face didn't reflect anything but eagerness to be of service to a member. "Let me get our personnel list and I can suggest staff members to contact."

4

Max raised an eyebrow. "Am I supposed to charm the ladies while you vamp the men?" He lounged comfortably in his red office chair.

Annie's laugh over the speakerphone was lighthearted. "I find you irresistible so I figure other women will be happy to talk to you. You check out the girls. I'll talk to the guys. I'll be a sweet lil' ol' Southern girl counting on a big, fine man to solve my problem for me."

Max pulled a notepad close, sketched a knight flinging down a cloak. "Two small details."

"Yes?"

"In South Carolina, I don't think a girl from Texas counts as Southern."

Annie drawled, "Honey, a girl from Texas is Southern with a dash of picante."

Max grinned, but continued. "Bigger detail. I don't think we have

53

a problem." Quickly he recounted his conversation with Shell's sister. ". . . so Shell intended to leave the island."

Annie's silence was not so much resistant as thoughtful. "Why leave secretly? And you can't say this wasn't pretty secretive. We haven't found a soul who's seen her after the dance."

Max sketched a pair of big staring eyes. "Hold on, Annie. We haven't exactly canvassed everyone she knew."

"That's my point."

Max shook his head in puzzlement and scrawled on his pad: *Channeling Pam North again.* He decided to move on. "Your solution?"

"We need to check the waitstaff, find out who Shell talked to and whether anyone saw her leave and, if so, whether she was alone."

Annie took a deep gulp of air-conditioned air smelling strongly of fried onions as she stepped into the Meet 'n' Greet Diner, a few blocks from Parotti's Bar and Grill. Its specialty was onion burgers, which Ben Parotti dismissed as grease on a bun. She slid onto the red leatherette seat at the counter, facing a hooded grill and shelving with glasses and dishes. The club staff phone directory was a gold mine of information, indicating which employees were part-time and held other jobs during the day. Steve Castle had bartended at the dance. Daytimes he cooked at the diner. His dark face was thin, intense, and reserved. He was pleasant but quiet. He handed Annie a menu.

"Hello." She smiled. "I'm Annie Darling. You worked at the Lady Luck dance on the Fourth."

He gave her a quick, curious gaze. Annie thought she saw recognition, but he only said, "Yes, ma'am. What would you like to drink?"

She ordered iced tea. It was still early enough that only a few of the booths were taken and she was one of three customers at the counter. He brought the tea and held the order pad. "Onion burger with everything, coleslaw." Before he turned away, she said quickly, "Steve—"

His eyes narrowed.

"Jerry O'Reilly suggested I check with you. I need some information about that night."

He regarded her steadily. "Like?"

"Did you see the woman who came in just as the band took a break? Young, beautiful, she called out to her husband who was standing at the bar. He'd been there most of the evening. Looks a little like Brad Pitt. Sunburned. He spends a lot of time on his boat."

There was a flash of something in Steve's dark eyes. Maybe disdain. Maybe envy. "Right."

"Did you see her with other people between that time and the end of the dance?"

His brows drew down in a frown. "You were there. Why ask me?"

"My husband and I left early."

A bell pinged. He jerked his head at the grill. "Got to go."

She watched him as he flipped burgers, moved them to buns, added lettuce, tomato, relish, placed them in paper-lined plastic baskets with mounds of French fries. When he'd delivered that order, he came back behind the counter.

"I was too busy at the bar to watch the dance floor. She came up once, talked to the guy you said was her husband. I happened to hear a little bit. She kind of flounced that dress, said, 'Maybe tonight.' I think she was gigging him about something. Then she said, 'Maybe not.' He looked like he'd like to belt her a quick one. She laughed, then turned and walked away. He stayed at the bar. Next time I looked around, he was gone."

"Did you see either of them again?"

Steve shook his head. "Ma'am, it was pretty dark in there. And"—his tone was sardonic—"I didn't care where they went."

Max walked down the boardwalk. Beyond the sea oats on the dune, green water stretched to the horizon. Pelicans in a V skimmed above the water, seeking a school of menhaden. The air was heavy with heat and the scent of the sea. Sleek gray porpoises glistened as they rose in graceful arcs only to disappear again. He felt conspicuous in a polo and slacks and loafers. He wished he had on trunks and could race to the water and splash out to the first wave.

Maybe Annie would be satisfied that they'd done all they could do when they finished talking to club staff about that night and he'd entice her to the shore. He loved thinking of Annie and the beach and how he'd surprised her when he first came to the island. He'd found her sunning on a towel, eyes closed. He'd given a frankly erotic whistle. Anybody who doubted he could make a whistle erotic didn't understand the allure of Annie in an oh-so-brief swimsuit. He jerked his thoughts back to the present, passed the fried shrimp booth, a saltwater taffy booth, and stopped at the cotton candy booth. A dark-haired girl in her late teens used a cone to collect the fluffy candy, this batch in a truly appalling shade of chartreuse.

"Be right with you." She had a soft, sweet voice. When the confection was in a plastic cover, she said rapidly, "Dollar seventy-five each, on sale today, dollar and a half, four bags for three dollars. Pick your favorite shade: blue, purple, pink, green, or black."

Max was diverted. "Black?"

Her smile was infectious. "The manager has a thing for *The Addams Family*." She hummed a bar from the musical.

Max almost asked the manager's age, but focused on his objective. "I'm looking for Lindsay Hamilton."

Her brown eyes widened. She seemed to take in his non-beach attire. "Are you here about that shawl? Mr. O'Reilly said that woman might go to the police. I think she's horrible. A dumb old shawl. I don't care if it's worth a hundred and fifty dollars. It isn't fair to look at me and Rhonda like we're thieves just because we're new. Well, Rhonda's not exactly new but she only works there occasionally. We didn't even work in the room until after the dinner was served and cleared. We weren't even in there very long. All we had to do was pick up dirty glasses."

The girl looked ready to cry. "I thought it was great to have a chance for a job at the country club and now this happens. I wouldn't take something that belongs to someone else and I think it's mean that she's blaming one of us."

"For starters, I'm not a policeman. My name's Max Darling, my wife and I were at the dance, and I'd like to visit with you about something else entirely. Jerry O'Reilly said you were working that evening. You look smart and bright and I hope you can help me. I'm looking for information about one of the guests."

Lindsay's tense posture slowly relaxed. "One of the guests? I'll help if I can, but I don't know anything about those people."

He described Shell Hurst's arrival. "Did you see her?"

"Everybody did. That was a gorgeous dress." Her eyes shone. "She's somebody you don't forget."

"Did you see her after that?"

"A couple of times. She went to the bar first. She talked to some guy, medium height, sandy hair. He wasn't pleased to see her. When she walked away, well"—Lindsay gave a little shiver—"I don't know what was wrong but I wouldn't want a guy to look after me like that."

"Like what?"

"Mad. Bad. Mean. He was kind of good-looking if his face had been nice. Then I was busy picking up glasses. I was in and out. I saw her again in a corner across from the band. She was standing under one of those silver spots. The neckline of the dress"—her eyes widened—"went in a V to the waist. I've never seen anything quite like that. She was laughing." Lindsay frowned. "The man standing near her was in the shadow, but something about him, I don't think he was the first guy."

So far, Max thought, Shell's evening didn't appear to offer much indication of where she might have gone.

"Just after the dance broke up for the fireworks, I saw her out in the hall. She had her back to me. I knew who it was because of the dress. That's the only reason I noticed. I was coming out of the dance room and turning right to go to the kitchen and I just happened to look down the hall. That was the last time I saw her. She was about twenty feet away. I only caught a glimpse of the person she was talking to. Another woman. She wasn't in evening dress."

"Can you describe the other woman?"

Lindsay shook her head. "The lady in the fancy dress—" She looked at him inquiringly.

"Shell Hurst."

"—blocked my view. She was taller than the other woman. I just got a quick look. I know it was a woman. I could see a portion of her arm." She looked uneasy. "Maybe they were disagreeing about something. The woman's hand was all curled up in a tight ball. Like this." She dropped her right hand to her side, made a taut fist. "She had on a heavy link gold bracelet."

◆ ◆ ◆

Annie always enjoyed the luncheon buffet at the country club. She'd already eaten at the diner, but dessert and coffee would be fine. She smiled hellos to several friends and settled at a table near the door to the kitchen. This particular table was partially screened by a potted palm.

She took small bites of key lime pie, watched the swinging door. She spotted her quarry. Richard Ely was thirtyish, sharp featured, dark haired, always polite, an excellent waiter. He was attentive, courteous, but reserved. Some of the waitstaff she'd come to know as individuals: portly Sam Maguire who raised bloodhounds, cheerful Dana Jenkins who was proud as punch of her bright, smart daughter who was on a Fulbright to China, Jason Hoover who wrote poetry. She didn't know diddly about Richard Ely.

He came near the table, carrying a tray with soiled dishes.

"Richard?" Her call was pleasant.

He swerved to the table. "Mrs. Darling." His gaze took in the half-eaten pie, the carafe of coffee. "Would you like fresh coffee?"

Annie shook her head. "If you have a moment, I have a question. Jerry O'Reilly told me you and a couple of new employees took care of us at the Lady Luck dance after the intermission."

"Was there a problem?" His dark hair was cut close to his skull. His face was angular, deep-set eyes, jutting cheekbones, thin lips.

Annie shook her head. "Not at all. I wanted to know if you saw Shell Hurst?"

"I might have." His face was impassive, but his eyes held a definite memory.

Annie had no doubt he'd noticed the plunging neckline of Shell's dress. "When did you last see her?"

"I was out on the terrace during the fireworks. I took a little break. I saw her then." His gaze was suddenly probing. "I've heard some talk. Some people are saying she didn't go home that night. I heard no one's seen her since the dance."

"Who said that?"

He was bland. "Some of the women in the health club overheard some ladies talking. I didn't pay any attention to who told me." His gaze was faintly defiant. He shifted the tray to one hip. "During the fireworks Mrs. Hurst was near the French doors for a while. Later she crossed the terrace to the path to the overflow lot. I saw her in the light from the torchieres." There was a flicker in his eyes. Shell's dress may have been almost sheer in a brief shaft of light.

Golden-hued lanterns marked the walks around the club and the paths to parking lots, offered dim illumination among the clumps of towering pines and live oaks.

"Was anyone with her?"

There was curiosity and quick calculation in his dark eyes. "Not with her. She was the only person on the path then. People were all over the terrace, watching the fireworks."

"But you saw some people?" Was he being deliberately vague?

"You can't recognize anyone unless they stepped right next to one of the lights." He shifted his stance and there was a clatter on the tray he held. "Does it matter who was around the path?"

Annie felt uncomfortable, but if island gossip was already bubbling over Shell's whereabouts, probably her answer didn't matter. "Possibly someone who spoke with her that night may know where she's gone. It would be helpful to know when she left the overflow lot."

"Maybe somebody knew where she was going, is that the idea?" Again that flash of calculation. It was as if he picked up cards from the table, studied his hand.

"Right."

He cleared his throat. "I'll ask around, Mrs. Darling, see if I can find out anything useful to you." He spoke in the same tone as if he'd promised to arrange the serving tables for a book club luncheon. He walked to the swinging door, pushed it with an elbow.

Annie almost called after him. There had been a flicker in the hooded dark eyes beneath the heavy frontal bone just before he turned away. Was it excitement? Interest? Knowledge?

She made a mental note. She'd check back with Richard tomorrow, see if he had any more information to share.

Max caught up with a small woman pushing a laundry cart on the third floor of the Sea Side Inn. "Mrs. Chase, if you have a moment, I'd like to visit with you about the Lady Luck dance at the country club. I understand—"

"I didn't take that woman's shawl." Rhonda Chase was thin, wiry, middle-aged, and bristling. She stood quite rigid in her neat gray uniform. "I've worked at the inn for fourteen years and nobody's ever missed a thing on my rounds and I don't appreciate being chased down about that shawl. I been working some nights at the club for years, too. I can tell you me and that nice girl Lindsay didn't do anything but clear up. What would either of us do with a fancy shawl like that? I don't think you'll find either one of us at a rich folks' dance. If you people cause me any trouble here at the inn, I'll get me a lawyer. And how did you know I was up here on the third floor doing my work like I'm supposed to? Did you ask the manager to see me? What's she going to think?"

Max wished Eileen Irwin hadn't treated the shawl's disappearance as grand theft. Obviously, she'd insisted that Jerry O'Reilly put

61

pressure on staff who had been in the rooms. Max understood Eileen's assumption that the thief must be a club employee. The likelihood of a member taking the shawl, unless in error or malice, had to be minuscule and that left employees. Jerry would certainly look with more suspicion on new or occasional employees.

"I told her I'm looking for a missing woman and that my questions have nothing to do with you personally, simply that you were at an event where the woman was last seen and I'm checking with everyone who was there."

Her indignation ebbed. "Missing? Who's gone missing?"

"At the dance, a young woman in a dress with a noticeable cleavage—"

"Mrs. Hurst. She came in at the intermission. Everybody saw that dress. And lots more." Her tone indicated disdain. Her dark eyes held no warmth, but she was curious. "Is she missing?"

"As far as we know, she hasn't been seen since that night. How do you know her?"

"I've worked plenty of parties. I know all those folks." Her brown face reflected disdain. "Funny thing, they never recognize me, but I know them when I see them, know more than they'd ever guess." She closed her mouth and pressed her lips together in disapproval.

"What do you know?"

She lifted her shoulders, let them fall. "Maybe they all deserve each other. That's all I got to say."

Max recognized a boundary. Rhonda Chase was a smart woman who had no intention of risking trouble from people who had money and power. "That's fine. I'm really trying to find out more about Mrs. Hurst at the dance. She hasn't been in touch with anyone since the dance. In fact, she doesn't appear to be on the island. A friend is trying to find her. I'm hoping to talk to people who chatted with her and perhaps someone will know where she is. If you saw her in conversation with anyone, please tell me."

The maid's eyes narrowed. "There's no law against people talking to people."

Max smiled. "Right. Perfectly respectable and if you can give me some help there, no one could complain about that."

She studied his face, slowly nodded. "I don't suppose anyone could. I kind of eyed her close. She looked like a cat with whiskers in the cream, pleased with herself. I figured that meant trouble for somebody. She came up to her husband at the bar. Didn't stay long. Next time I looked she was dancing with Mr. Irwin. He looked scared to pieces." There was a little note of surprise in her voice. She gave a puzzled head shake. "I saw him a few minutes later. His face was kind of gray. Mrs. Irwin came up and took him by the arm and they walked away. Later Mrs. Hurst and Mr. Peterson were dancing. About halfway through a dance, he stopped. Another couple bumped into them. That retired navy man and his wife. He started to apologize but Mr. Peterson turned away and headed toward the terrace. He looked like he was fixing to smack somebody. Mrs. Hurst was left standing there on the floor. She was casual as could be, just smiling and gazing around. She must have seen somebody she wanted to talk to because she started across the floor in the other direction. That's the last time I saw her."

The July-hot air sagged with humidity. Dark clouds bunched on the southern horizon where earlier the sky had been a cloudless blue. The weather forecast called for late-afternoon and early-evening thunderstorms with likelihood of intermittent showers for the next two days, but what else was new in July. Annie started to perspire though she stood in the shade of an awning. Oyster-shell paths led in several directions. Annie knew the club grounds well. If she turned to her left, she would reach the pool. The path to her right led to the golf course clubhouse. Instead, she went straight, passing between the apron of the pool and a picnic area where a grandstand had been set up to view the fireworks. The path curved through live oaks and tall loblolly pines. In the windless air, Spanish moss hung still and straight from branches of the live oaks. Annie loved the silvery moss, which, to her, added an exotic touch so different from the windswept plains of Amarillo. Beyond the live oaks, underbrush had been cleared from among sixty-foot-tall pines to provide parking spaces. The sandy ground showed the impress of tire tracks. It was catch as catch can for those who used the overflow lot, but perhaps thirty or forty cars could squeeze between trunks.

At night the pines loomed as dark sentinels with occasional lights affording enough illumination to park and walk to the path. Now the empty lot was gloomy in the shade of the trees. On the night of the Fourth, the lot was likely full. The center drive curved to the north to the exit and the blacktop that bounded the back of the club. Anyone walking in the darkness would be dimly seen. Even if she found someone who had been in the lot when Shell came for her car, it was unlikely she would have been recognized. Moreover, Annie doubted many left in the middle of the fireworks.

What prompted Shell to leave then?

Annie shook her head. Who knew? Shell was bored. Shell was going somewhere. Shell planned a private moment with someone.

Private . . . It seemed very private here, very quiet. On the night of the Fourth, exploding fireworks would have been audible, though muted. If everyone was watching fireworks, the lot might have been empty. Except for Shell.

Annie heard a distant rumble of thunder.

It didn't take a girl from Amarillo long to get away from tall trees when a thunderstorm was coming.

Annie clapped her hands together. "Poof! She's there and then she's gone."

Lightning flashed. The lights in the house wavered. Thunder boomed. Rain sheeted down, obscuring the garden. From the safety of the back verandah, Annie enjoyed the heavy wet smell, the gurgle in the drainpipes, the drumrolls in the heavens. Light spilled cheerfully—when the electricity didn't falter—onto the porch. Max was a comfortable presence beside her in their cushioned porch swing, his arm resting across her shoulders. The July heat was tempered by the rain. Usually they were accompanied on the swing by Dorothy L, a plump, affable white cat. Not tonight. Annie was sure Dorothy L was upstairs, burrowed beneath their spread. Dorothy L loathed thunder, dogs, and turtles.

"It only seems that way." Max's voice was untroubled. "Obviously Shell went somewhere. She drove the Porsche to the club. The Porsche is not at the club. When we discover where she went, there will be nothing sinister about the overflow lot."

Annie realized he'd picked up on her feeling of unease about the lot. Even now she didn't like to remember the stillness and the quiet. "I don't see how we can find out where she went."

Max said abruptly, "Maybe we're being stupid."

Annie twisted to look at him.

"We've gone here and there, asking about Shell, hoping someone has some idea where she's gone. According to Hayley, Wesley said he expected she'd come back when she was good and ready. Maybe she's been in touch with him since Hayley came to see me. I'll go in and get Wesley's phone number." He returned in a moment to the porch swing and made the call. "Hey, Wesley. How are you? . . . May I speak to Shell?"

In the light from the kitchen window, Max's face was . . . interesting.

". . . actually someone wants to get in touch with her and I—" Max frowned. "If you hear from her, I'd appreciate it if you'd ask her to give me a ring . . . That's confidential infor—" He returned the cell to his pocket. "He doesn't know where she is. He doesn't give a damn where she is. Who's trying to find her? When I declined to tell him, he clicked off. He sounded okay until I asked for Shell. From then on, he was combative, surly, and maybe a little worried."

"Worried about Shell?"

"I don't think so."

Another flash, another boom.

Annie reached up, gripped Max's hand. "I know she went somewhere but why can't we find her?"

"Hey, Annie." His tone was warm, reassuring. "Let's build on what we've got. The overflow lot spooked you this afternoon. That's because a storm was building. Atmospheric pressure and all that. But we know for sure that the Porsche left the lot." He banked on that fact. Yes, Shell was gone but so was her car. "Anyway, we learned a lot today. We connected Shell to Wesley, Edward Irwin, Dave Peterson, an unidentified man, and a woman who wasn't in evening dress. We know after Dave deserted Shell on the floor, she looked at someone across the room and set out in that direction. Tomorrow we'll find out more. If we don't find anything, maybe we can ask Billy Cameron to make a few inquiries."

Maybe it was time to call on the island chief of police. Billy was a good friend and he could make some quiet inquiries.

As for the Porsche, Annie wanted to know where the car was. Yes, the Porsche had been driven out of the overflow lot, but Broward's Rock had large swaths of heavy forest where a car could be left undiscovered for years. Perhaps forever. Shell could have left in someone else's car, but in that event where was her car? They'd keep looking.

D eep in the night an explosive peal of thunder startled Annie into wakefulness. She opened her eyes. A moment later wavering brilliance bathed the bedroom in an unearthly glow, followed immediately by another huge clap of thunder. An odd remembrance slid through her sleep-drenched mind, swift as an eel. She sank back into slumber.

5

Annie paused in the doorway to the kitchen. Rain pattered steadily against the windowpanes, but the kitchen was welcoming, the walls a warm yellow, the calico curtains fresh and bright, the overhead light turned on full force. There was a delectable scent of baking. She sniffed.

Max turned from the stove, spatula in hand. "Bacon, scrambled eggs, and oat scones with raisins and dried cranberries." He gestured at a basket with a red-and-white-checked napkin on the breakfast table. "You're just in time to get out the whipped cream flavored with vanilla." His eyes told her he very much liked her shorty pajamas. Or perhaps it wasn't the pajamas . . .

Annie sent an admiring gaze his way as well. Blond hair rumpled, unshaven and barefoot, Max in a tee and boxer shorts made it hard for her to remember what she'd hurried downstairs to tell him.

She placed the chilled bowl of whipped cream on the table, added a container of unsalted butter, poured herself a mug of coffee. "Max, last night the thunder woke me up—"

He slid bacon onto two plates, added a heap of eggs, carried the plates to the table. "Breakfast is served, madam."

She slipped into her place, picked up a chilled glass of orange juice in a toast. "To the chef." Not only was Max Joe Hardy handsome and sexy, he loved to cook. She wondered idly if Joe Hardy had grown up to cook breakfast for his wife. If his adventures were being spun today, he might rival the kitchen skills of Robert B. Parker's Spenser.

Max bowed and joined her.

Annie drank freshly squeezed juice from Florida oranges, felt a jolt of pleasure. "Last night I woke up and I knew there was something funny about what Mrs. Chase told you."

Max took a bite of a scone topped with whipped cream. He raised a blond brow. "I would say the redoubtable Mrs. Chase was singularly lacking in humor."

Annie picked up a slice of bacon. "Not funny that way. Odd. Strange. Tell me again what she said about Edward Irwin."

Max was casual. "She said he looked scared to death when he was dancing with Shell and then she looked surprised."

Annie put down her fork. "Why?"

Max took another bite of bacon, mumbled, "Why what?"

"Why did Mrs. Chase look surprised?"

Max grinned. "Most men don't find their dance partners scary. Shell may be many things, but I don't think she *scares* men."

Annie accurately read his expression. "Push your libido back into the primal swamp and concentrate on Mrs. Chase. There's a difference between scared and uncomfortable. Maybe she would have noticed if Edward looked stiff and even embarrassed. But scared? She did say scared, didn't she? Is that what she meant?"

Max paused as he added a dash of unsalted butter to a scone. "Mrs. Chase," he spoke thoughtfully, "is precise. I think if she said scared, she meant scared. She said Edward looked 'scared to pieces' and obviously his response surprised her. That is odd, isn't it?"

"Very odd. What does she know about Shell and Edward that she was surprised that he seemed scared. You can talk to her again and I'll go over to Eileen and Edward's house."

Max grinned. "I hate to mention unpalatable truths, but I can't see this encounter proceeding smoothly. Let's see, are you going to open with, 'Edward, why are you scared of Shell?' or perhaps, 'Eileen, your husband's a wuss and what's his panic over Shell?'"

Annie looked at him with dignity. "I have the perfect excuse. Eileen's obsessed with finding her shawl. I'll explain I'm updating information about Lady Luck members for a new directory and if she'd like I can ask everyone about the shawl. You go back over to the inn and see Mrs. Chase."

Annie popped her umbrella as she hurried up the bricked sidewalk to the rambling ranch-style house. Last night's storm had morphed into a steady rain. The dim day muted the color of the impatiens in the front flower beds. Midway up the walk, Lady Banks' rosebushes formed a backdrop to a small pool with a stone nymph. The sodden breeze carried the sweet scent of pittosporum that screened the garages from view. Annie was grateful to reach the covered porch. Big-petaled pink tea roses flourished in a blue terracotta urn. Annie pressed the doorbell.

The door opened. Light white bamboo flooring stretched down the hallway, a cheerful contrast to the outdoor gloom. A small chandelier bathed Eileen in soft white brightness, emphasizing her fairness. Annie didn't miss the flash of surprise in Eileen's cool gaze. Eileen, much taller than Annie, looked trim and youthful in a navy turtleneck and white slacks.

Annie hurried to explain. "I was out this way and thought I'd take a chance on catching you. I could have called but it's so much easier to talk to someone in person."

Eileen might be surprised, but she had good manners. "Won't you come in?"

"Thank you." Annie furled the umbrella, propped it to one side of the door.

The central hallway gleamed beneath the lights of the small chandelier. A dining room opened to the left. Eileen led the way down the hall to turn through an archway into a formal living room with several sofas, an easy chair, a Windsor rocker. A large mirror in a Danish modern frame hung over the bricked mantel. A low glass coffee table was bare of magazines, emphasizing the austerity of the furnishings. At their house, Dorothy L would be ensconced atop a tennis racket Annie had dropped on the coffee table over the weekend. Their table also held a stack of books she was eager to read, including new titles by Robert Crais, Katherine Hall Page, Jeffery Deaver, Meg Gardiner, and Carolyn Haines.

Annie skirted the oh-so-bare glass coffee table and decided her untidy, we're-busy-and-having-fun living room was much more cheerful. She dropped onto a green-and-yellow plaid sofa that faced the fireplace. Eileen settled opposite Annie in an easy chair with blue linen upholstery.

The chair and pale blue walls and straight cream drapes were a perfect background for Eileen. Today her white blond hair was in coronet braids, accentuating the sharp planes of her face. One blond brow was slightly raised in inquiry.

Annie hurried to explain. "I promised to put together a new directory for the dance club, so I'll be contacting everyone. I understand you lost your shawl and I'd be glad to ask everyone if they saw it."

"The shawl was not lost. I would not lose a hundred-and-fifty-dollar beaded silk shawl." Eileen's tone was icy. "The shawl was stolen. I have spoken to Jerry O'Reilly several times and I am not satisfied with his response."

"I saw you dancing and noticed the shawl, but I didn't get a good look." Annie leaned forward, tried for a just-us-girls-chatting bonhomie. "I'm afraid I was too taken up with Shell lassoing Edward. That was a surprise. I didn't know she and Edward were friends. Does he usually dance with her? Maybe I hadn't noticed."

There was no answering smile on Eileen's thin face. "I wouldn't presume to know what was in Shell's mind. I suppose poor Edward was the nearest man at hand. I think she was trying to irritate Wesley, make it public that they weren't dancing. Later I saw her dancing with Dave."

"I wonder if she said anything to Edward about her plans that evening." Annie lowered her voice. "This is just between us, but it seems that Shell's run away and no one knows where she's gone."

"Very few"—Eileen's tone was cold—"likely care. I'd think her departure would be a huge relief to Wesley, considering the way things are."

Annie saw a prurient gleam in her hostess's eyes. "How are things?"

Eileen raised an eyebrow. "Certainly I don't want to spread gossip—"

Annie glanced past Eileen at the mirror over the mantel, which reflected the back of Eileen's chair, the glass coffee table, Annie on the plaid sofa, the herringbone-patterned carpet that stretched all the way to the archway, and the light white bamboo flooring. It took her only an instant to decipher the dark splotches on the floor that were reflected in the mirror. Someone stood out of sight beyond the archway, casting a misshapen shadow. The back of the sofa where Annie sat was high enough to block Eileen's view of the hall floor. The shadows were visible to Annie because of the higher vantage point of the mirror.

"—but everyone knows what's going on." There was an edge of disdain in Eileen's cultivated voice. "You'd think Vera would know better. Once burned, twice shy. Instead . . ." An expressive shrug. "I suppose Wesley doesn't think it's adultery this time since he and Vera used to be married."

Annie tried to concentrate on two separate thoughts: Wesley was cheating on his current wife Shell with his former wife Vera, and a hidden figure listened to their conversation. "I suppose that might explain Shell leaving." Annie gave another swift glance at the mirror. The elongated shadow in the hall shifted.

"I would think it might." Eileen looked curious. "When did she leave?"

"The night of the dance. A friend asked Max and me to find her. Did you see her when you and Edward left that evening?"

Eileen made a dismissive gesture with one long, elegant hand. "We weren't together but I'm sure he doesn't know anything about Shell's activities. I'm afraid the music gave him a headache and the fireworks made them worse. He went on home. We'd walked over on the golf path. Our house backs up to the seventeenth hole. I stayed for a few minutes more, then went back to the dance floor to look for my shawl. I couldn't believe it when it was gone. I asked several of the waitstaff." Her lips thinned. "I must say no one was very helpful."

"Do you suppose"—Annie made the question light, almost as if inconsequential—"I could talk to Edward? Perhaps"—Annie managed to speak the rest of her sentence without changing her tone though she was abruptly aware of incredible tension—"Shell said something that might give a hint of her plans."

Eileen looked amused. "I doubt Shell confided in Edward. That dance was one of the few times he'd ever spoken with her. She was simply making a show to aggravate Wesley. In any event, he's not home now. I'll check with him and let you know if he can be helpful. And"—clearly she was ready for her guest to leave—"I'll appreciate your asking everyone about my shawl. It's pure silk, twenty by sixty inches, a golden dragon spouting flame, hand beaded in gold and red beads."

Annie rose. "I'll be glad to ask everyone. If you hear anything about Shell, give me a ring."

The shadow disappeared from the mirror.

Eileen walked with her to the door. "I certainly hope someone finds my shawl."

Annie looked past Eileen down the hall, but it lay empty. As the front door closed behind her, she carried with her a memory of the tension she'd sensed after she saw the shadow in the mirror and Eileen's revelation about Wesley and Vera.

Jerry O'Reilly looked uncomfortable but determined, his rounded face uncommonly serious. "I don't want to be uncooperative, but I'd like to know what's going on. The club has a right to protect itself."

Max tried for a reassuring tone. "I'm not going to make trouble for the club."

Jerry's reddish face folded in a tight frown. "I told those women at the spa that we don't talk about our members. The last time anyone saw Mrs. Hurst, she was fine, just fine."

Max raised an eyebrow. "I gather word's out that Shell Hurst hasn't been seen since the night of the dance."

"That's what I mean." Jerry was explosive. "That's like an accusation. Then people get to whispering and they say, 'I wonder what happened to her at the club.' That's bad."

"The best thing to do is to find her, right?" Max made his smile easy and friendly. "We can squash those rumors if we trace her movements that night. We know she was here. We know she was driving a Porsche. She arrived late so she probably parked in the overflow lot. The Porsche isn't in the lot. So we can reasonably conclude that Shell drove the Porsche out of the lot and that puts the club in the clear." Max leaned forward. "Just to be thorough, I'd like to have some names of the boys doing valet parking that night. If she used valet parking, that would prove when she left the club. In any case, my point in talking to club employees isn't to cause anyone a problem. There's no reason to think any club employee had any kind of personal contact with Shell Hurst. I just want them to tell me what they saw. Hopefully, I'll find out who talked to Shell. Perhaps she gave someone an idea where she was going. That's all I'm looking for, Jerry." Max turned his hands palms up. "So here's what I need, the names and addresses of the valet parkers plus the home address of Rhonda Chase. I spoke to her yesterday at the inn. I dropped by a while ago because I have a couple more questions but this is her day off. And Annie told me Richard Ely might have some information today. While I'm here at the club, I'd like to talk to Richard."

Jerry abruptly looked irritated. "So would I. He hasn't shown up this morning and he didn't call in. You can tell him he'd better get on the horn to me ASAP." He opened his desk drawer, lifted out a directory. "About the others . . ."

Annie eased through a clot of damp people near the front cash desk. Death on Demand was jammed. Many would soon stream outside since the rain had ended. But the crush from the morning rain was a definite boost to sales. There was a lovely smell of books, coffee, and sodden vacationers. Pamela Potts was stacking a pile of books, enunciating in a clear voice, ". . . and *Affairs of Steak* by Julie Hyzy. That makes a total of . . ." Ingrid Webb flashed a thumbs-up from the other cash register. As Ingrid often noted in a wry tone, "They come in the rainy season and then they're morose because it rains. But the more it rains, the more we sell."

Annie's objective was the storeroom. With the door closed, she intended to make a list of couples who had attended the dance. She reached a snag in the center aisle near the romantic suspense section. A woman with flushed cheeks clutched Deanna Raybourn's *The Dark Enquiry*. "I saw it first." A middle-aged woman with a baleful stare stood with arms akimbo. "It was on top of the bookcase. I put it there while I was looking for more books. It's mine."

Annie edged between them. "Ladies, let me help. I have more copies in the storeroom. And we have other wonderful romantic suspense writers, Mary Stewart, Nora Roberts, Maya Banks."

They were right behind her all the way to the storeroom. It took Annie only a moment to find a new shipment. She sent both of them off with two Raybourn titles each. They headed up the aisle toward the cash desk, ostentatiously ignoring each other.

Annie turned to go back into the storeroom and stopped. Emma Clyde stood in front of the fireplace, glowering at the watercolors. The island author's spiky hair was an unusual shade of mauve today. Her caftan was a dark, dull purple.

"Damn unfair." Emma never took her eyes off the first painting, but Annie knew the comment was aimed at her.

Annie was almost certain Emma had been in the store every day this month standing in front of the watercolors. Was Emma thinner? Was there a haunted glaze in her primrose blue eyes? Enough was enough. Annie joined her. "Emma, let me get you a mug of Colombian."

Emma didn't budge. "Why didn't you let me pick the titles for the month?"

Annie felt like a goldfish gulping for air. It wouldn't do to point out that Henny had won last month so it seemed that the honors should be hers. "You can choose the titles next month. As for these"—she waved at the watercolors—"I know you'll figure them out."

Emma gazed morosely at the first watercolor. "I have every one but that one." She spoke in a tone of deep loathing. "Nineteen thirty-seven. Likely a Brit. Not Tey certainly. It doesn't look like Christie. Michael Innes sometimes had that kind of man, with an almost military bearing but cultivated—"

Annie interrupted. "Emma, you are dear to spend so much time on the contest, but you mustn't neglect your work. How's the new book coming?"

Emma turned a glum face toward her. "Between books." She gave a huge sigh.

At once Annie understood. Emma was obsessing about the contest because she didn't have an idea for a new book. "It will come."

Emma sighed again, heavily. "Marigold's turned her back on me."

Annie knew authors had a peculiar faculty for treating their imaginative creatures as real. Honestly, didn't writers know the difference between actuality and make-believe? She looked at Emma's droopy appearance, spiky hair scarcely brushed, craggy face wan and pensive, somber caftan. The answer came swiftly. In a word, no.

Annie loathed Emma's detective. Red-haired Marigold Rembrandt was didactic, controlling, and supercilious. It pained Annie to speak of Marigold as if she were in the next room, but poor Emma needed a boost. "Marigold's probably turning a corner right now and bumping into something really mysterious."

Emma shook her head slowly, with finality. "She's gone." The whisper was almost a croak. "Sometimes she returns on *Marigold's Pleasure*. We sail tomorrow but I have little hope."

Marigold's Pleasure was Emma's palatial yacht. "Sea air will help."

A doleful head shake.

"You've done the Rubik's cube?" Emma often bragged about sparking creativity by focusing her thoughts on anything other than a plot.

"Four hundred and sixty-nine times."

"*New York Times* crosswords?"

A weary wave of Emma's hand was her only answer.

"Anagrams?"

Emma stared dully at the floor.

"Emma, you are brilliant." Praise was life's blood to Emma. She soaked up encomiums like a parched desert welcomes downpours. The more, the better. "Insightful, clever—"

Blue eyes slowly lifted to gaze at Annie.

"—able to discern what matters—" Annie broke off. Annie didn't know what mattered in the search for Shell. Was it her estrangement from Wesley, Wesley's liaison with his former wife, Edward's panic at the dance, Dave leaving Shell in the middle of a dance, the woman Shell spoke to in the hallway? Annie gripped Emma's elbow, tugged. "Come to the storeroom with me. I need your help."

There was a spark of outrage in now chilly and very sharp blue eyes. "I do not unpack books."

Annie resisted pointing out that if somebody didn't unpack Emma's books, they wouldn't be sold. "Not books, Emma. A real mystery."

Yeah. I'm Ross Martin. I was working the night of the Fourth." The chubby dark-haired teenager stared at Max out of anxious brown eyes. He had the air of a kid who tried to please and who was always afraid he wouldn't get it quite right. "We were swamped, me and Mike and Luis. See, we hang the keys on the board." He pointed at a rectangular wooden board, three feet by four, studded with hooks. "There's no reason we'd have noticed the colonel's keys were gone. If we looked, we'd just think he'd grabbed the keys while we were out getting cars. The idea that one of us took his MG and trenched the course and smashed the bridge is crazy. And besides, I was thinking about it." He pulled a crumpled sheet of paper from a back pocket of his Bermudas.

Max had no interest in either the colonel or his car but decided to let the boy vent. Maybe recalling the drama of the evening would sharpen his memory.

They stood beneath the porte cochere at the front of the country club. The rain had ended for the moment. Soon the air would be steaming. There was still a freshness from the moisture. Big drops clung to the flaring petals of huge red blooms on six-foot-tall hibiscus shrubs on each side of the walkway.

Ross gestured toward the U-shaped drive in front of the porte cochere. "We park the valet cars over there in those first rows."

Max looked obediently at perhaps a dozen cars in the big lot. A row of palmettos partially screened the cars.

"The lots on either side of the driveway hold about a hundred cars each. There's more parking by the pool and by the golf course, and then there's the overflow lot past the trees behind the swimming pool." He looked to see if Max understood. "Okay. The MG rutted up the greens on eight and nine and the fairway between eight and nine, then crashed on the bridge over the lagoon right by the ninth green. Here's the deal. Somebody took the car out of valet parking. For sure, they wouldn't drive it right by the front of the club and over to the golf course. Too many people know that car. But there's a back way to the golf cart path that leads to the eighth hole. You go"—he pivoted and pointed—"out the rear of the main lot onto a blacktop road that kind of circles the club. It passes the parking for the swimming pool, curves around by the overflow lot, and ends up on the far side of the golf course. There's a stretch where the road goes through deep woods. At that point, the golf path isn't close to any houses. All the guy had to do was drive off the road and onto the golf path right by the tee for the eighth hole. Whoever did it was counting on the fact that those two holes are really far away from the main club and nobody would be out there." He looked stricken. "I can't believe somebody deliberately slammed the MG into the bridge. Man, that was a beautiful car."

"Do you like sports cars, Ross?"

"Oh yeah. Did you know Mrs. Carlisle has an Aston Martin V12 Zagato?" His voice was awed.

"Are you familiar with Mrs. Hurst's Porsche Carrera?"

He nodded. "Cool. But that Zagato's the prettiest thing I've ever seen."

"Did you park the Porsche the night of the Fourth?"

He shook his head. "She drove by right around eight. She must have been on her way to the overflow lot. By then everything else was full, even the lot by the pro shop."

"Did you see her car leaving the club midway through the fireworks?"

Ross looked surprised. "No. Not many people went in or out until the fireworks ended. Then cars were everywhere." He frowned. "Did something happen to that car, too?"

"No. We're trying to figure out for sure which lot Mrs. Hurst used that night."

Ross didn't ponder why anyone would want to know. Instead, valet parking not under fire, he tried to be helpful. "Since she went that way, I'm pretty sure she must have ended up in the overflow lot because the swimming pool lot filled up early. You might ask Jed. Poor guy."

"Poor guy?"

Ross abruptly looked uncomfortable. "I shouldn't have said anything. He was kind of watching out for his dad, that's all. I guess I thought maybe he knew where his stepmother was. He was looking for her earlier. I mean, he asked me if I'd seen her Porsche. I told him she probably parked in the overflow lot. But what people do isn't my business." His lips closed.

Max knew Ross wouldn't say more. As for Jed . . . Max remembered Hayley Hurst's plea for help in finding Shell and how Jed didn't want to talk about her being gone. He heard her thin young voice, *Jed gets this funny sick look whenever I talk about her and he tells me to shut up.* Jed had threatened . . . What had he threatened?

Max kept his tone casual. "Any idea where I might find Jed?"

Ross looked out at puddles and a faint haze of sun behind thinning clouds. "He plays every day but they won't open the course now 'cause it's too wet. He's probably on the driving range. He's on the golf team. He usually spends the day here."

Emma's startlingly blue eyes were alive with interest. "Not seen since that night?"

"Not a trace."

"She's not a thoughtful person."

Annie agreed. "Keeping quiet out of spite?"

Emma nodded. "A possibility. After all, the car is gone." Emma tapped the stubby fingers of her right hand on the tabletop, a staccato accompaniment to rapid thoughts. "As Marigold always instructs Inspector Houlihan, the first task is to determine the parameters."

Annie maintained a pleasant expression, though she quailed inside, knowing she'd brought this moment on herself. Emma taking charge was bad enough. Emma citing Marigold affected Annie like fingernails on a blackboard. Marigold was rude, obnoxious, and overbearing with the inspector, whom she treated as a cross between a lackey and a dunce.

Emma gave Annie a commanding look. "Take notes."

Annie almost rebelled, but she had sought assistance. She picked up a pen, pulled a notepad close.

Emma sat across the table, arms folded, face creased in thought. "Shell Hurst was last seen at the Lady Luck dance at the country club. At various times during the evening, she was observed talking to her husband, to Edward Irwin, and to Dave Peterson. After Dave walked away, Shell apparently moved across the room as if with a specific purpose so we can reasonably conclude she saw someone with whom she intended to speak. Just before the end of the dance, she was in the hallway talking to an unidentified woman not in evening dress. Mark an asterisk there."

Annie held the pen over the pad. "Asterisk?"

Emma gave a long-suffering sigh. "Marigold always finds it necessary to dot every *i* and cross every *t* with the inspector. To wit: It may be necessary to query those not connected to the dance club to discover the identity of the unknown woman in the hall. Tell me again what Max learned from the young waitress."

Annie obediently described the waitress walking toward the kitchen. "She saw Shell talking to another woman. She must have been smaller because Shell blocked her from view. She wasn't in evening dress and the waitress thought she might have been angry because one hand was clenched into a fist. She wore a heavy link gold bracelet."

"Heavy link . . ." Emma murmured. Abruptly, her eyes glinted with mischief. She pulled her cell from a caftan pocket. "Henny, this is Emma. I thought you might be interested in our very own little mystery, i.e., Where, oh, where is the lovely Shell Hurst? I'm sure you've heard she's nowhere to be found. Let me bring you up to date . . ." Emma succinctly summarized everything Annie had told her. "You can help by finding out who Shell talked to in the hall. We're looking for a woman shorter than Shell who was not attending the dance. She wore a heavy link gold bracelet on her—" Emma paused.

Annie knew she was picturing the hallway and Shell standing with her back to the waitress.

"—left wrist . . . Oh, certainly."

Emma thrust the phone at Annie.

"Henny, how are you?"

Henny's tone was cool. "You enlisted Emma to search for Shell Hurst?" Implicit was the question of why Annie had chosen Emma and ignored Henny.

Across the table, Emma's expression was angelic. Who could possibly accuse her of one-upping Henny?

Annie longed for the good old days when phones didn't record missed calls, making it impossible to claim that contact had been sought earlier. "Emma happened to be in the store, trying"—said with emphasis—"to identify the watercolors." That should please Henny. "I thought it might distr—interest her to know that Max and I are looking for Shell. If you could lend a hand, too, it would be wonderful."

"So she can't figure out the paintings." Henny almost managed not to sound smug. "She was probably moping about and you took pity on her."

Annie felt a swell of relief. Henny was not only a brilliant mystery reader, she was insightful. "Exactly." Annie's tone was fervent.

A soft murmur of laughter. "Would you really like help?"

"Absolutely." Annie knew there was one more base to cover. "Please ask Laurel to pitch in. Between the two of you, I'll bet we know the owner of that bracelet within an hour."

"Ah, a challenge. Will do." The connection ended.

Annie handed back the phone and gave Emma a chiding look.

Emma smiled blandly. "Probably the woman in the hall is totally peripheral but it will be a nice exercise for Henny and Laurel while we attend to serious business. Now"—she hitched her chair closer to the table—"for the important work. As Marigold always insists, 'Determine the first task.' In this situation, our first task is to discover whether Shell spoke to anyone else. Our second task is to ask Richard

Ely to elaborate on his observation of Shell as she walked toward the overflow lot."

"Max is out at the club. He said he'd talk to him. And he's going to ask Rhonda Chase to explain why it surprised her when she thought Edward Irwin was afraid of Shell."

"Very good. We'll concentrate on Shell. Plus, that leaves us a third task. Stir the pot." Emma looked at Annie expectantly. "That's what I did in *Death Knocks Twice*. You'll remember the story—"

Annie felt a quiver of panic. Emma expected Annie to be au courant on each and every book, all eighty-seven of them. "Twice," Annie murmured hopefully.

"—it was very clever." She looked at Annie expectantly.

"Very clever." Annie spoke as if overwhelmed at the magnitude of the achievement.

"One of my best plots."

"Wonderful plot. The twist was simply fabulous." For readers who didn't mind coincidences.

Emma looked like Agatha basking in the sunlight. "I was truly inspired."

Annie remained reverentially silent. She knew better than to push her luck.

"Ah, yes." Emma reveled in glory for a moment longer, then said briskly, "As Marigold told the inspector, get their attention. Enough of subtlety. That's what we'll do. We'll shock them into cooperating. We'll confront people face-to-face. You learn a lot from expressions. As Marigold always observes—"

Annie tried very hard to keep her face pleasant and admiring.

"—'The smoother the liar, the sweeter the tone.'" A pause.

Annie gave a moment for Emma's self-adulation. "Right. So?"

Emma's eyes narrowed, but she continued. "We announce at the outset that we're hunting for Shell. Shell disappeared after the dance. Did you see her? With whom? When? Where? What did you observe?"

Annie hesitated. If she and Emma announced Shell was missing, the news would wash over the island like a storm surge. "Max and I've been keeping it low-key."

"Why?" Emma demanded. "If she's fine, no harm done. If she's not fine, somebody may get nervous."

Last night Max had suggested they might talk to Billy Cameron today. Certainly that contact would make it publicly known that Shell hadn't been seen since the night of the Fourth. Annie and Emma might as well see what they could discover. Possibly they would get a lead to Shell's whereabouts. "I'm in."

Emma nodded approvingly. "Now"—she was businesslike—"who attended the dance?"

Since many members were out of town in July, the summer dance always had the lowest attendance. Annie wrote down names as she spoke. "There were twelve couples that night. When we subtract Max and me and the Hursts and the Irwins, that leaves nine couples. Teresa and Harold Baker, Joyce and Don Thornwall, Maggie and Dave Peterson, Camille and Caesar Hernandez, Wendy and Alan Carlson, Lou and Buddy Porter, Rose and Jake Wheeler, Claire and Roscoe Crawford. Elaine Jamison and Burl Field were guests of the Bakers."

Emma was didactic. "Wesley Hurst is the last person to contact. We'll wait on the Irwins until Max talks to Rhonda Chase." Emma whipped granny glasses from her capacious pocket and perched them on her nose. She peered over the rims at Annie. "We'll also wait on the Petersons. We know Dave appeared angry with Shell. Anger suggests a strong personal connection. Our queries may provide some information there." She pursed her lips. "Let's look at our pool of possible informants."

Annie was grudgingly admiring. Emma did make everything clear.

Emma pointed a stubby finger at Annie's list. "Scratch the Bakers and Elaine and Burl. They left Monday for the Amazon." Her blue eyes gleamed. "But we have Joyce and Don Thornwall—"

Annie interrupted. "Let me talk to them." Annie admired the newcomers to the island, Don a retired naval captain, Joyce the epitome of the finest of military wives. Both were smart, charming, intelligent, and, most important now, observant.

Emma was reluctant. "Hardly sporting to take the best possible witnesses for yourself. Let's split them up. I'll talk to Don. Now, Camille and Caesar Hernandez." She shook her head. "I doubt we get much from either of them. We'll put them in reserve."

Annie agreed. Camille was a fund-raiser for an island charity and circumspect in her opinions. Caesar was hearty, raised bird dogs, and was oblivious to social nuances.

Annie's cell phone played the "Army Air Corps." "Hey, Henny." Henny had been a WASP during WWII, one of the glorious women who ferried bombers about the country and tested new fighters.

Henny's voice held a smile. "Vera Hurst."

Annie blinked. "Excuse me?"

"The woman wearing the heavy link gold bracelet was Vera Hurst. She was having dinner on the terrace with several friends. They were vague about the time, but she drifted away a little while before the fireworks began. Laurel said to tell you that Vera was wearing a short-sleeve navy ruffled blouse and belted floral skirt, peonies on white, and navy sling back pumps. Anything else you need to know?"

Annie glanced at the legal pad. "Emma and I are going to fan out, talk to people who were at the dance. We're going to be up front, tell them we're hunting for Shell, and ask: Did you see her? With whom? When? Where? You and Laurel can help. I'll call in a few minutes, give you the names. Okay?"

"Reporting for duty. Awaiting orders." The connection ended.

"That was Henny. She and Laurel found the woman seen talking to Shell. It was Vera Hurst."

Emma was thoughtful. "According to Eileen Irwin, Vera and Wesley are having an affair. I wonder if Vera approached Shell or Shell approached Vera. Either way, it must have made for an interesting encounter."

Annie said slowly, "Vera's hand was clenched into a fist."

Emma tapped the tabletop. "That end of the hall has a doorway out onto the terrace. If Shell and Vera went out that way together, Vera may have seen Shell walking toward the overflow lot. We can compare what Vera saw to what Richard Ely tells Max."

"We'll talk to Vera after we hear from Max."

Emma nodded agreement. "All right. Let's see who we have left. Wendy and Alan Carlson. Not promising."

Wendy Carlson taught first grade and was gentle, sweet, and never gossiped. Alan was a lawyer and very likely quite careful to parse his words. "I'd say let's skip the Wheelers, too." Rose Wheeler was a poet and spent most of her time wandering the beach near their home in a straw sun hat and flowing white dress, barefoot and immersed in her own world. She had an ethereal smile and rarely evinced interest in anything but poetry. Jake was tall, taciturn, gruff, and humorless.

Emma frowned. "As for Claire and Roscoe Crawford, she's silly and he's sly."

Annie wasn't ready to dismiss them. "Silly people rarely think before they speak. And sly people watch everyone and never miss much."

Emma wasn't impressed. "Give one to Henny and the other to Laurel."

"All right. That leaves—"

Emma interrupted. Her smile resembled a barracuda. "The Porters."

A look of understanding passed between them. Lou Porter chattered nonstop and always with a slightly malicious slant. She worked behind the desk at the Sea Side Inn. Buddy had a car dealership, a beaming smile, and a sharp gaze that missed little.

Emma delved into another pocket, lifted out a change purse. She opened a side flap and retrieved a very bright and shiny quarter. She held it up for Annie to see. "My extra leaf Wisconsin quarter. Rare. And lucky. I'll take heads for Lou." She didn't wait for an answer, flipped the coin. The coin landed with a musical clink, rolled, turned, stopped.

Annie looked at the gleaming obverse. Why was she not surprised?

6

Max walked around the clubhouse toward the pro shop. All but three places were taken on the driving range. Max spotted several teenagers. A chubby blond. A towering dark-haired boy. A trim, athletic teenager with a mop of dark hair. Something about his build reminded Max of Vera Hurst. *Thwock.* Hitting with his driver, the teen lofted a ball to the two-hundred-thirty-yard marker.

The chubby blond hooked a drive into the woods. The biggest teen scudded a ball about ten feet ahead.

Max stopped behind the trim boy. "Jed?"

He looked around. His face was narrow and his deep-set eyes a replica of Vera's. A look of intense absorption waned. He blinked at Max and was suddenly tense, wary, alert. He hunched his shoulders in his loose polo shirt.

Max was suddenly alert, too. Was the kid always worried when an adult confronted him? Or was there something deeper here? "I want to talk to you about your stepmother's Porsche."

Jed stood frozen, his face stricken, eyes wide, lips parted. His hands clenched on the golf shaft. He stared at Max, made no reply.

Max wasn't sure what to ask, but he knew he had a live one on the hook and this was no time to let the line go slack. "What time did you see her Porsche the night of the Fourth?"

Jed let out a long breath. There was no thought, no artifice in the involuntary exhalation.

Immediately Max realized he'd made a mistake. Whatever question Jed feared, Max had not asked it. He tried again, this time speaking as if certain of his facts. "You talked to Shell."

Some of the color eased back into Jed's thin face as the flare of panic receded. His breathing came more evenly. Now his gaze was sharp. "Who are you?"

"Max Darling. I'm looking for your stepmother."

"Don't call her my stepmother." His voice was angry. "She—" He hesitated, spoke carefully, "She's married to my father. That's all I know. I don't know anything about her."

"Did you see her the night of the Fourth?"

Jed gave Max a long stare. "Why?"

"She hasn't been seen since that night."

"That's what you say. Maybe she left the island. I don't know. I don't care. And I don't have to talk to you." He turned his back to Max, stuffed the driver in his bag.

"Maybe you'd like to talk to the police. You were here at the club. You saw her."

Jed turned slowly. The hand gripping the strap to the golf bag was white with strain. "There were a lot of people around. I didn't notice her." He shouldered the bag.

92

Max felt aggressive. Sometimes a bluff worked. "You were seen talking to her after the dance."

Once again Jed exhaled. "You got that wrong." There was an odd tone to his voice.

Max had hoped to shake Jed. Instead, the question reassured him. Jed clearly knew something about Shell, but he hadn't spoken to her.

Jed moved past Max.

"Why were you looking for your dad that night?"

Jed strode away.

Joyce Thornwall balanced the box of votive candles on one hip. The sky blue of the altar guild smock was flattering to her curling white hair. Intelligent dark eyes studied Annie. "I assume you believe there is good reason to seek this kind of information."

Annie thought of a forlorn sensitive teenager, waiting for a phone call. "I do."

"Very well." Joyce's tone was brisk. "I notice if people are out of sorts at a party." A swift smile. "When you are the commanding officer's wife, it is your duty to keep everything smooth and pleasant. At the dance, it was as if there were two sets of people attending. Most of the dancers were having a lovely time, but several were not. Notably Wesley Hurst. After Shell arrived, there were four separate incidents. She joined Wesley at the bar. Shell appeared quite comfortable. She said only a few words, but when she walked away, Wesley was furious. She interrupted the Irwins on the dance floor, claimed Edward. It might have been lighthearted. Shell seemed to be enjoying herself. Edward's response was"—Joyce picked her words carefully—"unusual. Instead of being flattered or irritated or bored, he looked like a man standing on a tenth-story ledge. I don't believe I am exaggerating to say he was simply terrified." Her eyes narrowed. "It was as if she threatened him in some fashion. I glimpsed him later sitting at a table. I don't know where Eileen was. He was by himself and he was the picture of despair. Not long before the end of the dance, Dave Peterson dumped Shell in the middle of the floor. He swung away and bumped into us. It was as if we weren't there. He moved like a man in shock. So I looked past him at Shell. Before Don and I moved away, I saw her look across the dance floor. She smiled and started walking. It wasn't"—again Joyce chose words with care—"a nice smile. Rather like a card shark moving in for the kill."

"Who was she looking at?"

Joyce was regretful. "I don't like saying, but I trust you, Annie. I know you won't cause trouble for anyone if you can avoid it. Shell headed straight for Maggie Peterson." A sigh. "Maggie's decent and kind. And she's been so ill. Men . . . some men . . . are bastards. She couldn't have missed seeing Dave dump Shell on the dance floor." She stopped, finally said quietly, "Maggie looked like a woman with no hope."

Max drove toward an area of modest homes on the north end of the island. Rhonda Chase hadn't sounded delighted at his call, but she'd agreed to see him and maybe it would be helpful to know why Shell spooked Edward Irwin. But Max felt thwarted. Richard Ely wasn't answering his cell. He didn't have a landline, which wasn't uncommon these days. Max wanted to find out more about what—and who—Richard saw on the terrace during the fireworks. There had to be a reason for Jed Hurst's near panic when he'd asked him about Shell's Porsche. If Richard saw Jed going toward the overflow lot, it might give Max some ammunition for another talk with

Jed. But finding Richard might be a challenge. Maybe he didn't come to work because he was sick. Maybe he was at a doctor's office. Max had no intention of giving up. Now to figure a good way to approach Rhonda Chase . . .

E mma sniffed at the smell of sweat and disinfectant, and surveyed the health club exercise room with its apparently unending variety of machines, many equipped with TV screens. What some people considered fun astonished her. A tendril of thought imagined Inspector Houlihan on an Exercycle and Marigold insisting he immediately dash out into the cold to aid in a denouement. An emergency, no time to dawdle, turn on the siren, the inspector with knobby knees and shivering . . .

Don Thornwall, alerted by a cell phone call, dismounted from the seat of a rowing machine. He grabbed a towel and threaded his way to the perimeter of the room.

Emma noted admiringly his muscular physique. A fine figure of a man, just at six feet, black hair with touches of gray, forceful features, fit and trim as might be expected of a retired naval officer.

"Emma." He swiped at a face glowing from effort. "Nice to get in a little extra work. Already been out on the bay this morning but the heat's a little much in the afternoons. What can I do for you?"

He listened without comment until she finished, thought for a moment, said matter-of-factly, "Used to recognizing stress. I saw Shell Hurst several times. She wasn't stressed. At one point, Dave Peterson abruptly abandoned her on the dance floor. Shell was amused." He paused. "Once had a lieutenant commander who was a hothead, ready to brawl when he should have kept control. I had to give him a poor efficiency report, blocked his promotion. Dave had the same

Carolyn Hart

look as he blundered across the dance floor. He wasn't in control and he was mad as hell. I saw other evidences of stress. Wesley Hurst was also in the grip of powerful emotion. When Joyce and I were waiting for our car to be brought, Wesley was raising a ruckus, demanding a kid get his car before some others in line. He was acting"—there was a faint stress on the verb—"like a guy who'd had too much to drink. I guess one of the kids slipped away and got Jerry O'Reilly, because in a few minutes Jerry pulled up in a golf cart, all charm and bonhomie, and he and one of the kids talked Wesley into the cart, saying he should have a free ride home and one of the kids would bring his car and leave it at his house. It was a pretty slick piece of work. About that time Dave Peterson showed up and he was furious because his car was gone and one of the valets didn't help matters by saying his wife had been there a few minutes earlier and taken the keys. This took the attention away from Wesley in the golf cart, but I happened to get a look at Wesley's face as the cart left. He was a man who had suffered a shock. I don't think he was drunk." The retired captain's face reflected certainty.

Emma imagined the scene, Don Thornwall observing his surroundings, collating impressions, making a swift judgment.

"He was as sober as I was. I found that"—Thornwall's tone was dry—"interesting."

Henny Brawley stepped inside Out of the Attic, one of the island's most successful antique and collectible shops. She welcomed the air-conditioning though it was tepid, not too surprising considering the age of the shabby Victorian house. The bottom floor housed the merchandise. Roscoe and Claire Crawford lived in the upper two floors. Roscoe could have played a Southern plantation owner

in a movie, overlong white hair, a drooping white mustache and Van-
dyke beard, a white suit, but his face betrayed him, a gaze that had
a tendency to shift away from direct contact, a bitter twist to his
mouth.

The antiques included good pieces, an English Chippendale chest-
on-chest, a Georgian bowl and tea service, a japanned Queen Anne–
style secretary, a Louis XV mantel clock in exquisite porcelain,
terra-cotta urns from Italy, but there was plenty of kitsch, ranging
from a glowing Elvis velvet hanging to poor imitations of Day of the
Dead folk art. Did the odd conjunction reflect a true knowledge of
the old and beautiful paired with a disdain for products of a debased
culture? Or was he simply a businessman delighted to offer anything
that would sell?

"Henny, welcome, welcome." Roscoe strode toward her, pausing
for an instant in the pool of light from a truly glorious rococo chandelier with cut glass pendants. The light haloed Roscoe's smooth hair,
perfect mustache, finely trimmed beard, and immaculate white suit.
Satisfied with the effect, Roscoe moved forward. "What can I do for
you today? Perhaps a nice Tiffany lamp or a beautiful Coromandel
screen, eighteenth century, quite striking. You could create the perfect
retreat for reading." He gestured toward the darkly lacquered screen
with gorgeous patterns in ivory and mother-of-pearl.

Henny moved toward the screen. Drat Roscoe. He was right. In
the long open room that was her home, the screen would be perfect
to block off a portion in the far corner. "It is beautiful."

Like a shark scenting blood, he knew she was good prey. "Perhaps
you might like to take the screen with you, give it a try."

"I'll think about it. Roscoe"—her tone was confidential—"I came
directly to you because I know you notice things and you are discreet.
There are some questions about the Lady Luck dance and I just know

you can help." Actually, Roscoe loved to gossip, the more unkindly, the better.

He was instantly grave. "Of course, if I can be of assistance in any way . . ." He listened with avid attention. When she concluded, he smoothed his beard. "I saw Shell Hurst's arrival. Not a woman you miss. But"—he looked regretful—"I have no idea when she left. Claire wanted to go home early. We have a wonderful view of the fireworks from our upper verandah. We'd parked over at the golf club. Of course"—he was the quintessential Southern gentleman—"I dropped Claire off when we arrived. I went out on the terrace to go to golf parking. I'd say Wesley Hurst had a bad night." His tone was lightly malicious. "Shell accosts him at the bar and Vera gives him hell on the terrace."

"Really?" Henny wondered if Wesley remained on the terrace. Annie said Shell was last seen walking toward the overflow lot. It might be important to know where Wesley was when Shell left. "On the terrace? It's rather dark there." Henny pictured the exit from the hallway onto the terrace. "Are you sure he was talking to Vera?"

"Oh, I didn't see them. They were in the shadows of a live oak, just two figures. I heard them. I know their voices. Vera spoke rather loudly at the end."

Henny appraised his shifting eyes and sly smile and knew he'd taken his time, possibly slipped into shadow himself, curious to overhear.

"At the time"—he was full of self-importance—"I didn't give much thought to what they said, but now I wonder if their conversation might have something to do with Shell leaving."

He was parceling out the words, the better to hold her attention. Henny maintained a pleasant, most attentive, respectful expression and pictured his head on a platter with an apple in his mouth.

"Vera's voice was hard, demanding. 'You have to deal with her tonight.'"

Laurel took a deep breath as she neared the lotions counter. The thick scent of coconut oil lotion evoked memories of beaches she'd loved: Waikiki, Copacabana, Phi Phi, Natadola, Tenerife, and Cottesloe. She had a swift memory of a brawny bronzed young man at Cottesloe in an outback hat and swim trunks. She smiled. That was a night to remember. She had a quick glimpse of her image in a mirrored pillar and smoothed a tendril of golden hair cut short for the season, sleek against her head. Summer was such a lovely fashion season. She nodded approval of sparkling silver embroidery that added a grace note to an almost sheer white cotton tunic above elegant white linen slacks and strappy white leather sandals. Tiny bells on her silver earrings sounded like faraway wind chimes when she walked.

Behind the counter, Claire Crawford looked up from her perch on a tall stool. Dyed-brown hair sprang in tight curls from a long face that might have looked better on a horse. Mascara-thick lashes blinked above eyes of a curious light gold. She gave a high shriek of excitement and popped to her feet. "Laurel, we've just received a new batch of Bobbi Brown makeup. Perfect for you! Come and let me do a makeover."

Laurel felt her smile freeze. Would Michelangelo permit a preschooler to experiment? Perish the thought. But she increased the warmth of her smile. "Dear Claire. That would be such a treat, but we'll save it for another day. However, I'll purchase a makeup session for my sweet daughter-in-law. And I'll take a jar of hydrating face cream and a jar of buffing grains."

Claire almost pranced, and Laurel wondered if she received a commission on sales. "Absolutely the best. The buffing grains will do wonders for you."

Laurel managed to retain the smile. "I'm so glad I needed to replenish some of my favorites. And you can tell me all about the Lady Luck dance. I've heard so much about it." A meaningful glance. "I don't suppose you had any idea when you and Roscoe came that there would be so many exciting moments."

Claire tossed her head and the curls quivered. "I wasn't surprised."

Laurel widened her eyes, cooed enticingly, "Really. Do tell me."

Claire's golden eyes shone. "Maggie and I were in charge of decorating for the dance. Well"—Claire gave a whuff of exasperation—"she was no help. Once when I asked her which streamer, she stared at me as if she had no idea what I was talking about. Then she choked out something about going to the lounge and blundered out of the room. I thought I'd better see. In case she was ill." The golden eyes slid away from Laurel. "Sometimes people are sensitive about not feeling well and I happened to know there was an unmarked door into the lounge so I just slipped up to it like a little mouse and eased it open—I had a key because we were doing the decorating—and you will never guess what I heard." Now those golden eyes gleamed with excitement.

Laurel felt as if a cellar door had opened and out swept a rank, dark smell. "Maggie was on her cell phone?"

Claire's nose twitched. She suddenly spoke in a passable imitation of Maggie's soft voice but with a shrill edge. "'I know about the money. I know what you're planning. But there's a gun in Dave's desk—'"

Laurel drew in a sharp breath.

Claire gave a silly whinny of laughter. "Wouldn't you know! There

I was, all ears but someone walked into the lounge and Maggie cut off the call."

M ax breathed deeply. "Fresh dirt and marigolds. That's a good combination."

Rhonda Chase pushed up from the flower bed. She wore a broad-brimmed straw hat with a light blue tie beneath her chin. Her smock was clearly for gardening. She brushed dirt from the knees of her jeans. "I like the way marigolds smell. I put some out around my mamma's grave. Makes me feel good every time I go there." She closed her eyes, gave a brief nod, then opened them to look at Max with a steady gaze. "Have you found Mrs. Hurst?"

"There's no trace of her. Or of her car."

Mrs. Chase was firm. "I've told you everything I know about her."

"I have some questions about Edward Irwin. When I spoke to you at the inn—"

Her face was suddenly impassive.

"—you described Edward as 'scared to pieces' by Shell Hurst and you seemed surprised at his response to her. Why did his apparent fear surprise you?"

Her lips folded into a tight line.

Max knew there was something there, some real reason that prompted her to find Edward's reaction odd. "Is there something you know from that evening?"

There wasn't a flicker of expression in her face.

"Did you see them in conversation?"

"I suppose they talked while they danced, but I don't know what they said."

"Did you see them talking at any time? Anywhere?"

"No." Short, definitive, unyielding.

"Did you ever see them at the inn?"

"Lots of folks come to the inn."

Max had a quick memory of the hotel corridor, Rhonda Chase businesslike in her neat gray uniform. Her words danced in his mind. *I've worked plenty of parties. I know all those folks. Funny thing, they never recognize me, but I know them when I see them, know more than they'd ever guess.* Her disdain had been obvious.

"When did you see Edward and Shell at the inn?" Even as he asked, he thought the question ludicrous. Shell Hurst dallying with Edward Irwin? When did a champion skier take to the bunny slope?

"Mr. Darling, I keep myself to myself. That's all I'm going to say."

Annie walked across the blacktop of the car lot. Heat rose in waves from the pavement, reflected off the metal of cars. Puddles from the earlier rain were probably hot enough to poach an egg. She stepped inside a small building in the center of the lot, welcomed the change to frigid air. Three heads swiveled toward her. She smiled at a portly man with a round face, budding paunch, and ready smile. "Hey, Buddy."

Two twentyish-something salesmen subsided in their chairs, turning off their smiles faster than incandescent lightbulbs from China fizzle. One picked up a copy of *Ellery Queen*. The other stared raptly at his iPhone.

Buddy was on his feet. His Hawaiian shirt was loose and bright, his smile eager. "Ready for a trade-in, Annie? I can make you a deal."

Annie shook her head. "You know me, Buddy, I drive a car until it refuses to budge. Actually, I'm checking on some things about the

Lady Luck dance. You always know everything. Do you have a minute to visit?"

"Sure, sure. Slow day here. Come on back to my office."

She followed him down a short hall, settled in a luxurious leather chair. He sat behind a desk and folded thick fingers across his paunch. He knew all about Shell's disappearance. "Nobody's quite calling it that. More like, have you heard that Shell's skipped out on Wesley and who's the lucky guy?"

Annie nodded. "I guess you also know there was some bad feeling that night."

That launched Buddy. Annie made occasional encouraging comments, but there was nothing she hadn't heard before. Until . . .

". . . but Maggie Peterson got the last laugh on Dave. I don't know how he got home. It's a long walk from the club to their house."

"Walk?" Annie stared at him.

Buddy's laughter boomed. "Maggie left him high and dry."

"Maggie took Dave's car?"

"You better believe. She about creamed me in the main lot after the fireworks. She was driving like a bat out of hell, screeching that Mazda Miata out of the drive like she was heading for the stripe at the Southern 500. She was all by herself. When we drove out of the lot, Dave was raising hell with the valet boys. But how could they tell a woman she couldn't take her husband's car?"

I n the lobby of the Sea Side Inn, red wooden rockers with cane seats and comfortable sofas with a shell pattern upholstery looked summery and Southern. Potted palms afforded crannies of privacy. Sunburned tourists sprawled in comfort, enjoying tall mint juleps beneath the lazy swirl of overhead fans.

Emma stood next to a planter filled with ferns. She waited until the last of several guests checked in. When Lou Porter was free, Emma strolled to the desk, totted up a quick appraisal. Lou was tall, willowy, and might have had a certain charm if it weren't for the sour turn of too-red lips.

Lou looked toward Emma. A saccharine smile stretched the red lips. "Need to get away from it all, find solitude in the anonymity of a hotel room, escape the demands of that big old house?"

Emma recognized jealousy. She lived in a Mediterranean mansion, thanks to Marigold, while Lou and Buddy lived in an antebellum home that needed repair and likely was hard to heat and cool. She murmured, "Nice and cool here in the lobby. Perhaps my house is almost too cold. But I make do." She smiled, leaned on the counter, said almost idly, "I imagine you know that Shell Hurst has disappeared."

Lou's gooseberry eyes glistened. "I'd heard that people were looking for her. Well, she hasn't been here for at least a week or so."

Emma was instantly alert. She had a good memory. She recalled what Annie had told her of Max's interview with Rhonda Chase at the inn. Emma was intrigued by Rhonda's comment that people from the club never recognized her but she knew them. Where did she know them from other than at the club? Maybe she knew them from the inn. Had she seen someone from the dance club at the inn? If so, what did she know about them and why did she say "they all deserve each other"?

Emma was casual. "It's hard to keep things like that a secret."

"I'll say." Lou's lips curled in amusement.

At the dance, Shell had appeared at odds with her husband, with Edward Irwin, and with Dave Peterson. But it was Edward who had caught Rhonda's attention. Edward and Shell? Emma knew that six impossible things before breakfast were never out of the question. She said smoothly, "You probably noticed Edward and Shell here?"

"I'll say," she repeated. "Eileen's so high and mighty. She's a Marsh and she never lets anyone forget that her people have been here since the seventeen hundreds, like that makes them special. Everybody knows those old families have plenty of skeletons in their closets, but that's not the way Eileen sees it. She's a Marsh and they're all so fine and rich, planters and bankers and a colonel in the war." Lou was from a longtime South Carolina family as well, but her forebears were hand-to-mouth tenant farmers. "Well, she won't be so high and mighty if people find out about Edward. One of the maids told me. She didn't know what to do. I said we'd better keep out of it."

Emma longed to give Lou a shake. "Sometimes it's better not to get involved."

Lou shrugged. "It's not like he was causing a public problem, taking pictures." Her mouth spread in a malicious grin. "But it would have been fun to take a picture of him, sneaking around like a seedy PI. Wouldn't that make Mrs. Eileen Marsh Irwin sit up and take notice. Can't you just see it, Edward hiding behind a housekeeping cart with his iPhone trained on Room Two-oh-four. Course"—she nodded sagely—"I figured it out. He took a picture of whichever one arrived first going into the room, then lurked until the other one came and got another picture and then he'd have the pictures with dates and times and I suppose he probably waited until they came out and got their pictures again. That didn't prove what they were doing in the room"—salacious emphasis and raised eyebrows—"but you can take it to the bank they weren't playing bingo." Her laughter was boisterous, then abruptly her vacuous face was touched by genuine compassion. "But it's not funny." A deep breath. "My sister had to have a lot of chemo and Maggie's one of the gals who have helped her. The last time I saw Maggie, she looked like hell. I guess she really loves the sorry jerk."

7

Max's Maserati slid to a stop on the unpaved street. He'd passed some ramshackle dwellings but most of the small frame houses were well kept. Richard Ely's weathered gray wood house at 903 Black Skimmer Lane sat deep in a lot among tall pines. A glossy-leaved magnolia with huge white blossoms cast shade on the front porch. Twin ruts marked the empty drive. The overhead door to a one-bay garage was closed.

Max felt a sharp disappointment. He wanted to talk to Richard. Of course, he may have driven his car into the garage and be at home. Richard hadn't answered Max's calls to his cell phone. He might have chosen not to answer. Max shrugged. Since he was here, he might as well go up to the house and knock. He punched and the motor died.

The heat kicked Max like a mule as he slid out of the driver's seat. Steamy air pushed against him like a baked wet towel. Max hurried toward the shaded front yard. He was grateful for a respite from the sunlight when he stepped beneath the spreading branches of an old live oak with a huge trunk. As he neared the porch, he saw a fenced yard that extended from the north end of the house. Similar to many Lowcountry yards, there was more sand than dirt. Creeping lantana with lavender blooms covered much of the ground along with patches of uneven Bermuda grass near the walk.

It was very quiet.

Max stopped at the foot of the short flight of wooden steps. He'd never given any thought to Richard Ely beyond the fact that he was an excellent waiter, courteous but always impersonal. A lean man of medium height, black hair cut short, an impassive expression neither friendly nor hostile, slanted black brows above deep-socketed dark eyes, a narrow nose, long mouth, pointed chin.

There was something intensely personal about viewing a man's home.

The house was well kept, the shutters recently painted, a square of lighter-colored shingles marking an area of repair on the roof, the porch freshly swept. A garden hose was neatly coiled by an outdoor water spigot. Closed blinds in two front windows afforded no glimpse of the interior. A cane chair with a red cushion sat next to a low wooden table with a large ashtray. The unlit stub of a half-smoked cigar was carefully perched on the ashtray, awaiting Richard's return.

A faint whine sounded.

Max lifted his head, listened.

The sound came again.

Max looked to his right. He started to smile, then stopped.

Behind the links of a wire fence, a blond cocker moved unsteadily, stopping to whine, starting again, his footing uncertain. He wore a brown collar. His tags jingled.

Max moved swiftly to the fence.

The dog wavered. His head moved from side to side, much as a dazed person would look around, confused and uncertain. He plodded toward a stainless steel water bowl by the back steps.

"Hey, fella, what's wrong? Hey, guy." Max had grown up with cockers, eager, fun, boisterous, loving.

The dog paused, lifted his head, again moved it from side to side. Sluggishly, he moved to the fence.

Max knelt, looked into huge dark eyes clouded with misery. The dog's golden fur appeared rumpled and stiff. His tongue hung from a gaping mouth. Another low whine.

Max was on his feet and running. He pounded on the front door, waited a moment, pounded again. No answer. The house lay silent, unresponsive. Max thudded down the porch steps. He never hesitated at the gate. When it was open, he moved quietly to the dog, held down a hand. "Hey, buddy. It's going to be all right. Come on, buddy." He checked the tags, though there was only one veterinary hospital on the island. He saw the familiar name and picked up the dog. The cocker was heavy in his arms and his head rested against Max's chest.

Jessica Forbes, DVM, worked swiftly. "His blood sugar's over the roof. He must have missed his shot. He's dehydrated. Once I get the blood sugar down and start some fluids, he'll be fine." She fixed a hypodermic, lifted up a flap of loose skin, made the injection. "I'll take him and get an IV started." She expertly lifted the dog. Max opened the door to the interior hallway and in rushed the smell of antiseptics and the high yip of a frightened dog.

While Max waited in the examining room, he tried Richard Ely's cell number again. No answer. He had a clear picture of the weathered gray wood house drowsing in late-afternoon sunlight and silence.

When the door opened, he looked up.

Jessica's white jacket was creased and there were several spots of blood on one sleeve. She peered at Max over Ben Franklin glasses. Tawny brows drew down into a sharp frown beneath a Lauren Bacall swoop of hair. Her slender face was puzzled. "This is Richard Ely's dog. What's the situation?"

Max described his arrival at the house and the dog's whine and unsteady gait.

Jessica folded her arms. "Not much about Richard Ely would surprise me," she spoke with distaste, "but he's always taken excellent care of Sammy."

"You're surprised he'd miss a shot?"

"Very surprised."

Max looked at her steadily. "You don't think much of Richard."

She pressed her lips together, shrugged.

"I need to know about Richard. Anything you can tell me may be a help."

She shook her head. "What I know—he's a bigot and a loudmouth—won't find him for you. Let's leave it at that." But there was a ripple of raw hurt in her eyes. "It happened a while ago. He'd probably had too much to drink."

Max knew—it was a small island—that Jessica and her partner Tiffany Smith, who was a nurse at the local hospital, were a devoted couple. Abruptly, he understood. "Did he hassle you and Tiffany?"

"Nasty," she said briefly. "We used to like to drop into the One-Legged Pirate for a drink on Friday nights. Not anymore."

"But you take care of Sammy?"

"I'm the only vet on the island. Sammy's a good dog." Almost a smile, then she shook her head. "I can't imagine how this happened. Richard's a nasty piece of work, but he's really careful with Sammy."

Max sat in the Maserati, the air-conditioning on high. His cell rang. He recognized the first bars of "Deep in the Heart of Texas." "Hey, Annie."

"We're having three guests for dinner." There was a note of stress in her voice.

Max didn't have to ask. Annie had a special tone in her voice when she referred to Laurel, Emma, and Henny. He glanced at his watch. Already five thirty. If he went straight home, he could have a great dinner ready by six thirty. He had fresh flounder ready to grill. It would take only twenty minutes to oven roast sliced sweet potatoes tossed in olive oil. His Caesar salad was superb, if he said so himself, which he often did. He opted for mayo enhanced by lemon juice, fresh garlic, and minced anchovies.

"Max?"

"I'm still trying to find Richard Ely." But where should he look? Richard wasn't at the club. He wasn't home. Maybe an emergency had called him away. Yet, that didn't compute. No one knew better than Richard the importance of regular insulin shots for his dog.

"Let it go until tomorrow. You won't believe how much the ladies and I have found out. There is more than meets the eye . . ."

He laughed. "When the four of you are unleashed, that's no surprise." He made a quick decision. He'd try Richard's cell one more time. If there was no answer, he'd head home and whip up a meal to remember.

111

◆ ◆ ◆

Annie finished inputting into her laptop. "I'll print out a copy for each of us."

Laurel blew her a kiss. "So efficient." She took a dainty sip of her cream sherry.

It might have been any after-dinner gathering in their den except the conversation was limited to one topic, and the flow of information was amazing. Annie refused to feel like harried Jane Fonda in *Nine to Five*. After all, someone had to collate and organize the facts they'd gathered. She felt a trifle resentful as she hurried to their home office while everyone else reposed in comfort, sipping their drinks. Laurel, of course, had positioned herself in the golden glow of a wall sconce that emphasized the nautical jauntiness of her summer sailor blouse. Would it be churlish to murmur something about her *amazingly* youthful appearance? Well, yes. Besides, she did have an amazingly youthful appearance, blond hair shimmering like sunlight, patrician features smooth and unblemished, figure quite simply perfect, and all without artificial assistance. And she had to be on the shady side of sixty. Laurel was cheerfully vague about her birth year. On the plaid sofa, Emma sat square and sturdy as a figurehead on a Viking ship, exuding a similar attitude of power and confidence. For dinner, she'd changed into a daffodil yellow caftan that rivaled a supercharged LED in brightness. She raised her rum and Coke in a toast to Annie. "Excellent work." Henny appeared sunk in thought, a faint frown on her face as she absently drank a margarita. Max put his bottle of Heineken on a coaster and looked ready to pop up. "Can I help?"

Annie shook her head. "Back in a flash."

It was almost that quick. She passed out the sheets of paper.

Emma cleared her throat.

Annie's mouth opened, but Max gave a slight head shake. She looked at him and her eyes made the point that it was she, Annie, who had done all the work.

He repeated the motion and his eyes said that, hey, we know you put it all together, but Emma is Emma.

Annie shrugged, plopped into her favorite easy chair, picked up her Tom Collins, and prepared to listen.

Another throat clearing. "We must give credit to Annie. She certainly plucked the pertinent information from our oral reports."

Annie would have been more pleased if Emma's crusty voice had not held a definite note of surprise.

"And the headings are quite cogent. To wit . . ."

Annie looked down at the sheet as Emma read aloud:

Timetable Wednesday Evening

1. Wesley Hurst alone at the bar after dinner, apparently drinking too much.
2. Dave and Maggie Peterson danced, Dave watched the door, Maggie obviously miserable.
3. Shell Hurst arrived as band took early, short break. Approx. 8:45 P.M.
4. Shell approached Wesley at the bar, short conversation. Wesley angry. Approx. 8:50 P.M.
5. Shell interrupted Edward and Eileen Irwin on the dance floor, asked Edward to dance. Approx. 9:05 P.M. Edward appeared "scared to pieces." Eileen grim.
6. Dave Peterson danced with Shell, abruptly left her in the middle of the dance floor. He appeared furious as he walked away. Time uncertain.

7. Shell crossed the floor toward Maggie Peterson. Time uncertain.

8. Shell observed in conversation with Vera Hurst in the hallway near the door to the terrace. Shortly after dance ended at 9:45 P.M.

9. Fireworks started at 10 P.M.

10. Hayley Hurst and her brother Jed were at the club for fireworks but did not remain in each other's company.

11. Richard Ely observed Shell Hurst on the path to the overflow lot. About ten minutes after 10 P.M.

12. Ely's sighting marked the last time Shell apparently has been seen.

Observed by Witnesses

1. Don Thornwall—Dave Peterson left Shell on the dance floor, exhibited anger in his erratic progress across the room. Wesley Hurst made a drunken scene demanding his car be brought by the valet. Jerry O'Reilly showed up in golf cart, offered Wesley a ride home. However, as the cart departed, Wesley looked back and appeared to be sober.

2. Roscoe Crawford—Wesley Hurst and his ex-wife Vera were in heated conversation in the shadow of a live oak tree. Vera said, "You have to deal with her tonight." Time uncertain, but apparently between the end of the dance at 9:45 and the beginning of the fireworks at 10.

3. Claire Crawford—The afternoon of the dance, Maggie Peterson was in the ladies lounge, talking on her cell phone. "I know about the money. I know what you're planning. But there's a gun in Dave's desk—" Conversation ended when another woman entered the lounge.

4. Rhonda Chase—Refused to reveal what, if anything, she knows about Edward Irwin and Shell Hurst at the Sea Side Inn.

5. Richard Ely—Efforts to contact him unsuccessful.

6. Jed Hurst—Exhibited extreme tension when queried about Shell's car and denied talking to her after the dance.

7. Buddy Porter—After the fireworks, Maggie Peterson raced out of the parking lot in Dave's Mazda Miata. Dave was not in the car.

8. Lou Porter—Edward Irwin surreptitiously used an iPhone to take pictures of Shell Hurst and Dave Peterson entering and, after an interval, leaving Room 204 at the Sea Side Inn. Why?

A musing silence followed Emma's recitation.

Henny licked a remnant of salt from the lip of her empty glass. "An interesting exercise." She spoke with a note of finality.

Laurel nodded. "It's too bad we can't discover where Shell went, but none of those involved are likely to respond well to questions." Her smile at Annie was one of regret. "After all, how does one, for example, ask Wesley Hurst if he was playing drunk and, if so, why? I rather think he might reasonably refuse to say a word."

Emma dragged stubby fingers through her spiky purple hair, which made her look like a hedgehog after an unfortunate encounter with violet ink. "That's the trouble with real life. Loose threads. Hanging ends. But I have an idea . . ." Her blue eyes gleamed with that familiar shine of author-with-plot-burgeoning. She abruptly stood. "Good dinner. Thanks. Got to get home."

At the doorway she paused. "*Marigold's Pleasure* leaves at eight A.M. sharp, ladies."

In her preoccupation with Shell Hurst, Annie had forgotten that the Intrepid Trio, as Henny had dubbed them, were off to Nova Scotia on Emma's yacht tomorrow.

Emma glanced at Laurel and Henny. "Bring your e-book readers. I'll be working on my laptop. I think the title will be *The Case of the Disappearing Dame*." She waited for a moment, her blue eyes vivid, thoughts obviously tumbling in her authorial mind. "I have the opening sentence."

Annie knew nothing short of a trumpet tattoo imported from Edinburgh would serve as an adequate opening act for an announcement of this magnitude. But she would do her best. "Emma, you've started the book!"

Laurel placed her hands, the pink nail polish quite perfect, above her heart. "Oh, to share with us. We aren't worthy."

Annie worried for a moment. Even Emma would surely find Laurel's praise suspect.

Emma nodded in agreement.

Max's blue eyes gleamed, but he spoke in a serious tone. "This is definitely a moment to remember."

Annie slid her eyes toward Henny.

Henny smoothed back a lock of silvered dark hair. "I am sure that we shall be struck dumb."

Emma looked at her.

"In admiration." If there was the slightest edge to Henny's voice, Emma chose to ignore it.

Emma was majestic. She stood in the center of the doorway, head up, spiky hair quivering, and intoned, "Where—is—the—body?"

"Max?" Annie watched shifting shadows on the bedroom wall, the wind stirring magnolia branches in the moonlight.

"Mmmm." A sleepy murmur.

"Where is the body?" She knew her voice sounded like that of a waif on a street corner.

Max shifted. He propped up on one elbow and peered at her. "Annie, she was starting a book."

Annie wiggled her toes against the light cotton sheet. "Emma's like a sponge. She soaks in atmosphere, and something in that aberrational mind of hers picks up possibilities like vibrations from a tuning fork. She hones in on the essential point. So"—she propped up on her elbow and their faces were only inches apart—"where's the body?"

"There isn't a body. That was Emma starting a book."

"Emma said." Sure, Emma was a self-centered mess, but even Henny admitted she could outthink anybody in the room.

"Yeah."

She knew then that Emma's pronouncement had caught his attention, too.

"What are we going to do?"

He reached up, touched her cheek. "Sleep. Tomorrow we'll hunt until we find Richard Ely. He may hold the key to the whole evening. If no one followed Shell, she left the overflow lot and drove . . . somewhere. Once we know, we'll talk to Billy."

In the silence of night, Annie tried to push away images of a car driving down a road, taillights disappearing in the darkness. But the car left and that meant Shell left the lot and drove somewhere. Talk about bodies was just that, talk.

A gentle hand turned her face and Max was near. He brushed back a tendril of hair from her face.

She moved into his arms.

In a moment, there were no more thoughts.

◆ ◆ ◆

M ax turned the Maserati into the empty drive at 903 Black Skimmer Lane, coasted to a stop. This morning the weathered gray frame house appeared as it had yesterday, neat, tidy. Lifeless. He turned to Annie. "Why don't you stay in the car?" His only answer was the click of the opening passenger door.

He punched off the motor and scrambled to catch up with Annie. He admired her as she hurried up the walk, the tawny gleam of her sandy hair, the determined set of her shoulders, the swing of her hips beneath a summery white skirt. He grinned. If she saw his expression, she would shake her head and inquire, but also with a smile, "Don't you ever think about anything else?"

She knocked crisply on the door, then pushed a doorbell for good measure. There was the faint sound of a bell inside.

The early morning was already heavy with heat. A crow cawed in the magnolia. A faint breeze swayed Spanish moss in the live oak. Billowy white clouds sailed across a softly blue sky.

"His car's not in the drive, honey." He tried to sound reasonable, but sometimes women did seem to overlook the obvious.

"Let's check the garage."

The old-fashioned nonelectronic garage door screeched as Max lifted it. Like many islanders, Ely didn't bother to lock his garage. The bay was empty. The garage was as neat as the well-kept yard, a worktable along one wall, tools carefully hung. Shelving contained labeled boxes.

Max half turned, watching the house, both the front and back doors. He wanted to be ready if Richard Ely came barreling out, holding a shotgun. No doors opened. Nothing moved in the hot heavy air but swirls of no-see-ums. Max pulled down the door. After the sound died away, the silence was broken only by the rustling of the pines and the cry of mourning doves.

They turned to walk slowly toward the car.

Annie's hand gripped his arm. "Maybe he's sick." Her voice was thin.

He understood her thought, knew the eerie lifelessness of the house worried her. "Yeah. Maybe we should look. Let's try the back door."

Max wasn't surprised when the knob turned easily in his hand and the door opened to a dim kitchen. Many islanders never bothered to lock their doors when home and sometimes left them open when away. But Max didn't like the easy access. His sense of foreboding grew. "Stay here, honey."

This time she didn't object.

Max stepped into a small old-fashioned kitchen, noted dishes in a drying rack next to the small single sink. A dish towel hung askew from the handle of the stove. A red wooden table with four chairs sat next to a window. The surface of the table was bare. "Hey, Richard?" His call hung in the silence. There was no answer.

His footsteps seemed loud as he crossed the oak brown linoleum floor. He pushed a swinging door and stepped into a short hallway. If Richard had central air or window units, it was turned off. The house held the heat of several days. To his left were two closed doors, to his right a living room with a sofa, two easy chairs, a TV on a stand, a coffee table. A half-eaten bowl of popcorn was on the table and an opened can of beer. There was a musty scent, closed windows and flat beer sitting in a hot house.

"Richard?"

No answer.

He stepped into the living room but it took only a swift glance to be certain no one was there. Living or dead.

119

Dead? Maybe Emma's talk about a body had unnerved him more than he realized.

He turned back to the hallway, tried the first door. The empty bathroom was clean. A washcloth draped over the edge of an old claw-foot bathtub had dried into stiffness. The second door opened to a man's bedroom, maple bed frame, oak dresser, a worn easy chair. The closet held sheets, household supplies, clothes.

The swinging door to the kitchen sighed behind him. "Max?"

He turned, shook his head. "He isn't here." In a swift movement, he yanked his cell from his pocket, swiped a number. "Hey, Jerry, I'm still looking for Richard Ely . . . Yeah. If he shows up, ask him to get in touch with me."

On a pier in a T-shirt and jeans, holding a fishing rod, Broward's Rock police chief Billy Cameron was a good ol' Southern boy, sun-bleached hair with flecks of silver, an easy smile, a booming laugh. Behind a yellow varnished desk, tie a little askew, short-sleeve white shirt a little tight over a broad chest, he looked solid, dependable, and, at the moment, skeptical. "Two people missing from the island?"

Annie held up two fingers. "No one has seen Shell Hurst since the July fourth dance. She walked toward the overflow lot at the country club wearing this gorgeous evening dress. If she intended to leave the island, she'd change clothes."

Billy wasn't impressed. "Maybe she went someplace else and changed. Maybe she was playing 1930s Zelda Fitzgerald and wanted to leave a cool memory."

"The stepdaughter told me she doesn't think any clothes are missing."

Billy looked at Max. "The fact that the kid came to you adds a little weight to what you're saying. But deciding a server at the club's missing because he blows off work for a couple of days—"

"He wouldn't blow off his dog." Max scooted his chair closer to Billy's desk. "Unless the Bermuda Triangle's shifted north a couple of hundred miles, it doesn't make sense that two people—people with at least a tenuous connection—have disappeared from sight within the space of a week."

Billy picked up a stubby pencil, a soft lead number two. Hand poised above a legal pad, he said briskly, "You filing a missing person report? Two of them?"

Max looked surprised. "Doesn't a member of the family have to file a missing person report?

Billy shook his head. "Anybody can. Give me the particulars."

It didn't take long. Max was rueful. "I guess we don't know a lot to be helpful. Physical descriptions, yeah. What Shell was wearing when last seen. But"—he nodded toward Annie—"we've got a lot of information about what Shell did at the dance."

Annie opened her purse, pulled out two sheets of paper and handed them to Billy.

He read the timetable aloud, followed by the summary of information gained from witnesses. His tone put *witnesses* in quote marks. When he finished, his expression was bemused. "If," he spoke carefully, "Shell Hurst was a murder victim, this kind of insight would be invaluable. However, there is no evidence—none—that a crime has occurred." He put the sheets down. "As part of a missing person search, I can ask the people you mention"—he glanced down—"her husband, his ex-wife, Edward Irwin, Dave and Maggie Peterson, and Jed Hurst, when they last saw her and if they have any information about her plans, but I can't confront them on the issues you've raised."

Max leaned back in the straight chair. "So there's nothing you can do."

Billy was mild. "I can hunt for them. That's first on the agenda." He looked out of his office window at the harbor. The deep-throated horn of the *Miss Jolene* announced the ferry departure. Motorboats curved in an arc on green water. White sails glistened in the sun. "From what you've said about the lady, she may have danced right onto some Brazilian millionaire's yacht, and clothes were the last thing on her mind. I think we can be pretty sure she's off island."

Annie frowned. "Hyla—Officer Harrison—was on duty with the traffic that night. She didn't see the Porsche go on the ferry."

"Maybe she didn't leave until the next day. Maybe she left in somebody else's car. Let me see what I turn up." He swung to his computer. "Here's the vehicle registration. Two thousand eleven green Porsche Carrera, personalized plate SHELLVH. No citations or outstanding tickets." Another click. "Driver's license number 18358162; 416 Sea Crest Drive, Broward's Rock, SC, DOB: 09-23-89." He paused, raised an eyebrow. "Lots younger than her husband. But second wives usually are." His tone was dry. "License issued 10-12-11; expires 11-31-22; Class: D; Sex: female; Weight: one twenty-four; Height: five-eight. Green eyes. Brown hair. No restrictions. Now for Richard Ely"—his fingers moved fast—"2007 brown Camry, 962 SXK." His face changed. "Ticketed Wednesday morning. Overnight parking is prohibited in Fish Haul Pier parking. Car still there this morning, impounded." Billy was a cop with things to do. "I'll see what I can find out. About both of them. I'll be in touch."

8

Annie looked out at the marina. *Marigold's Pleasure* wasn't at her dock. The Intrepid Trio was at sea, heading north to cooler days. She had no doubt there would be e-mails. What were she and Max doing? What had they discovered? Where was the body? She wished Emma would drop the latter query. There was no evidence at all that Shell was dead.

Gulls cried, wheeling in the sky. Water slapped against wooden pilings. Shouts and calls behind her marked the boisterous passage of a covey of vacationing teenagers. All normal, all happy, summer at its best, but for her the day held a chill at odds with the lazy ease of a beach resort in July.

Annie turned and walked toward Death on Demand. But she couldn't fend off the question: Where was the body? Had Emma sensed evil beneath the veneer of a summer dance or was she simply taking an odd occurrence as a springboard for a new book? In any event, she and Max had done everything they could in a search for Shell Hurst. Now Billy Cameron was investigating. It was time to let a professional find the truth.

She hurried up the steps to the boardwalk that fronted the shops. Ingrid and Pamela no doubt were ready for an extra pair of hands. Annie could go back to doing what she loved. She felt buoyed as she stepped inside, taking an instant to savor the smell of books and the scent of coffee.

Ingrid waved frantically over the head of a book buyer.

Annie came around the cash desk, automatically noted the titles as Ingrid rang them up: *Night Vision* by Randy Wayne White, *Hanging Hill* by Mo Hayder, *The Thief* by Fuminori Nakamura, *The Royal Wulff Murders* by Keith McCafferty, and *The Winter Ghosts* by Kate Mosse.

Ingrid gave her a quick glance, her eyes wide with concern. "Maggie Peterson's waiting for you in the storeroom." Ingrid glanced toward the customer, pushed the credit card slip across the desk for a signature, and dropped her voice, "She looks awful."

Max clicked rapidly on the travel site. Could he persuade Annie to leave the store in the capable hands of Ingrid and Pamela so they could slip away to Ireland for a week? It might be too hot for him to hit the links in South Carolina but the Island Golf Club was only fifteen minutes from the Dublin airport. Golf holes laying in green valleys between sand dunes and cool breezes off the estuary . . .

He looked at Annie's picture on his desk. Yes, she was pretty—to his mind the prettiest in all the land—but there was character in that face, the picture of a woman with sensitivity and compassion. He sighed. She'd agreed that they should step away from the mystery of Shell Hurst's last evening, but that was as likely as Annie turning away from a stray animal. That reminded him . . . He picked up the phone. In a moment, he was connected with Jessica.

"Max Darling. How's Sammy?" He picked up a pen, sketched a cocker with droopy ears on his legal pad.

Jessica's voice was pleased. "Ready to go home. Will Richard pick him up?"

Max thought of an impounded Camry in the lot next to the police station. "I'm not sure. Let's board him for a few days. I'll take care of the bill. Or hey, could one of your techs run him over to Playland for Pooches, tell them I'll pick up the tab?" The doggy day care center was new to the island. "If they have someone who can give him his daily shots?"

"That'll work. He'll be fine there." A pause. "Are you sure you want me to bill you? Richard won't mind paying for Sammy."

"I'll take care of it." He'd picked Sammy up, saved his life. For now, that life was his responsibility. He replaced the phone in its cradle. He clicked off the vacation site. The sooner Billy—maybe with some help from him and Annie—figured out what had happened to Shell and Richard, the sooner he might feel the caress of Irish breezes and possibly the caresses . . .

The phone rang.

Billy Cameron didn't waste time. "A shrimp trawler's coming into dock. Got more than brown shrimp. Man's body. Fits the general description of Richard Ely's height and weight. Or would if a hammerhead hadn't taken out some chunks. Got some queasy fishermen on the way. Got more info on the Hurst woman. Don't have time to talk right now. I'll get back to you." The connection ended.

◆ ◆ ◆

Annie opened the door to the storeroom. The only light came from a torchiere floor lamp in one corner. Annie flicked the switch for the overhead florescent panels, which threw into stark relief the sorting table, desk, computer, rows of metal shelves filled with books, unpacked boxes, and the woman huddled in a shabby wing-back chair next to the desk.

Maggie Peterson turned.

Annie's breath caught for an instant. Maggie had always been lovely and vibrant, glossy dark hair, deep-set brown eyes, a rounded kind face with a trace of dimples, and a faint indentation in her chin. She dressed with flair, the newest cut of blouse, the season's fashionable colors. Now she was haggard, hair dull, face sunken, eyes filled with dread, wearing a too-large top that hung on too-thin shoulders.

"Maggie, what's wrong?"

Maggie made an effort. She forced her face into a semblance of a smile. "I just wanted to see you, catch up on things."

The social response was in such evident contrast to her demeanor that she seemed to shrink against the cushions. She took a deep breath, hurried. "Eileen called me. About her shawl." Maggie looked frightened. "She said you came by. Is it true that Shell's missing?" Her eyes held, fear, uncertainty, and a flicker of panic.

Annie slid into her seat at the worktable and felt the terror of the woman who sat across from her. "No one has seen or heard from her since the dance. That's more than a week ago. There's been an official missing person file opened."

Maggie's face looked even thinner. "She may have left the island."

"She doesn't answer her cell phone."

Maggie's fingers closed on the silver chain of a summer necklace, a pendant with a lavender starfish. The necklace was perfect for the sunny days when it seemed summer would never end. Now the chain quivered because Maggie's hand trembled.

"The last time anyone admits seeing her was on the terrace during the fireworks. She was walking on the path to the overflow lot."

Maggie hunched her thin shoulders. "I wonder," she spoke as if the words were painful, "where she went."

Annie felt a wave of pity for the woman who stared with lost and hopeless eyes. Annie steeled herself and asked a question that had to be asked. "When you talked to her Wednesday afternoon, did she say anything about her plans?"

Maggie's lips parted. Her haggard face stiffened. "How did you know?"

Annie didn't feel any triumph that she had been right in guessing that it was Shell on the other side of Maggie's cell phone conversation in the ladies lounge Wednesday afternoon.

"What did she say?"

Maggie's eyes shifted away. "We just had a talk." Her voice was numb.

"About Dave?"

Tears slipped down Maggie's face. "Does everyone know? I suppose they do. She laughed, that's what's so awful."

"You told her"—Annie remembered Laurel's report of Claire's eavesdropping—"you knew about the money and you knew what she was planning but there was a gun in Dave's desk."

Maggie folded her arms tight against her chest.

"I understand he was selling out and putting half of everything in cash accounts."

Maggie's face looked stricken, her face slack from shock. "How did you know?"

"People talk about things." Or people's wives talk. Annie left that unsaid. She didn't want to set up a confrontation between Dave and his banker. Dave was big and powerful and a bully, and the banker, Leon Bailey, was a mild-mannered man who deserved a wife who could hold her tongue. "Was Shell planning on leaving with Dave that night?"

Maggie's head jerked up. "No." She gave a wild laugh. "She was just—" One thin hand covered her mouth.

"What did she say to you in the hallway after Dave left her on the dance floor?"

That thin hand slid to her throat.

"Maggie, it's important to know what Shell said that night."

Maggie shook her head back and forth. Her eyes were filled with fear. She came to her feet. "She was hateful. Hurtful. The way she always was. I can't remember"—she seemed to gain strength, repeated the words louder—"I can't remember what she said. Anyway, I don't know where she went. Dave doesn't know." But her voice sounded hollow. "Oh, God, everything's so awful." She started for the door.

Annie stood, too. "Why did you leave the club in Dave's car by yourself?"

The storeroom door slammed and Annie was alone. And she hadn't found out whether the gun was still in Dave's desk.

Max stood a few feet behind the official party on the pier, watching as the shrimp trawler docked. The breeze riffled whitecaps across the bay, tugging at his shirt, pleasant despite the heat. Billy Cameron was in the lead. Lou Pirelli, looking hot in his khaki uniform, talked to Hyla Harrison. Billy's wife Mavis carried an evidence kit. Mavis served as both dispatcher at the station and a crime tech. In repose, Mavis's long face often had an aura of uncertainty and wariness. She had escaped an abusive husband and found refuge on the island with her little boy, Kevin, and eventually a fine second husband and new father for Kevin in Billy.

Light steps clipped on the pier behind him.

"Hey, Max." Marian Kenyon, the *Gazette*'s star reporter, skidded to a stop next to him. A bony whirlwind, Marian moved, thought, and wrote fast, her gamin face often scrunched in concentration beneath a mop of unruly dark hair. She brushed back a tangle of hair and snapped a series of shots on her Leica. "Scanner. A body in a shrimp net. I called the cop shop. Two missing person reports with your name and Annie's all over the place. What's up?" Her eyes never left the group now boarding the *Julie Joy*. Several crew members stood as near the stern as possible, staring out at the harbor, men used to tough labor but not to bloated bodies.

"Nobody knows for sure yet. It may be the body of Richard Ely."

"One of the missing person reports is chock-full of detail. Somebody talked to Ely's ex-wife, Clarissa." She recited crisply. "Five foot ten. Approximately one hundred sixty pounds. Caucasian male. Surgically fused left ankle following high school football injury. Ex-wife says she left his house about nine o'clock Tuesday, hasn't seen or talked to him since. Ely's thirty-three. Divorced. Native of Hardeeville. Broward's Rock resident since 2008. Waitstaff at the country club. So what's your connection?"

Max was saved from answering when heavy footsteps sounded.

Marian turned to watch burly Doc Burford stomp past with a jerk of his head to acknowledge them. For a big man, he was agile as he swung onto the shrimp boat. He was there for about two minutes, then on his way back to shore.

Marian darted toward him. "Hey, Doc, what can you give me?"

He never slowed. "Dead. Been immersed in seawater for at least a couple of days. Visible trauma from shark bites. Won't know more until the autopsy's done."

Marian took a deep breath and turned back to Max. Even brash Marian was a little subdued. She wrinkled her nose, looked more than ever like a street-smart waif. "Probably not a pretty sight. No point in going closer for pictures." She brightened. "But, hey, I can get pics of the *Julie Joy*. Everybody loves shrimp boats, and someday we may not have any if they keep flooding the market with those nasty, limp, farm-bred shrimp." She clicked a series of shots. "Like it, like it. The arms with the nets up, men huddled at the stern. Striking but not gross. As Vince always says, we put out a family newspaper. No gore, no overt sex, no nasty photos. Wonder if there's enough skin left on his fingers for prints?" She turned her bright brown eyes on him. "Okay, you didn't show up here to sniff the sea air. What's the deal?"

S hrimp creole's our special today. Got an extra flair with a dash—" Ben Parotti broke off. "Something wrong?"

Annie had no idea how Richard Ely's body looked when the net brought him up, but she knew it had to be awful. "Not shrimp. For a while."

Ben's grizzled face was grave as Max described the scene at the dock. Ben, as always, was forthright. "Richard Ely was bad news. Clarissa worked for us until she went back to school to get a pharmacy tech certification." Ben jerked a thumb at the big old-fashioned room behind him. "She handled the tables along the wall. Richard treated his wife like dirt, ran around on her. Sometimes he was slow paying on the child support. Richard played poker for pretty high stakes with folks who want their money when the cards are down. After she got a divorce, she was working as a pharmacy tech, but I hear she lost her job a little while ago. The kid has asthma and he's sick a lot and she missed too much work. How'd Richard get in the water?"

"Probably from Fish Haul Pier. His car was in the lot."

Ben frowned. "Must have been some weird time. That pier's busy night and day in the summer. Nobody saw anything?"

"We think maybe he was on the pier Tuesday night during the storm."

Ben looked like a coon dog sniffing a scent. "Out on the pier in a thunderstorm? Must have been a babe or money. Babes don't like to be wet and they scare easy. The lightning was pretty fierce. Sounds to me like he was out there to meet somebody on the sly. You can figure the reasons for that. Drugs. Selling something hot. Maybe hush money. Never heard he was part of the drug scene. As for stolen goods, wouldn't surprise me. Or maybe he knew something somebody didn't want anyone else to know, made a few threats. What goes around comes around." Ben looked pontifical. "Anyway, we're here and I got good food. That'll perk you up. How about spinach quiche with a green salad?"

As Ben walked away with their orders for the day's special spinach quiche, Annie turned to Max. "'He knew something somebody didn't want anyone else to know.' Max, I think when Richard was on the terrace, he saw someone with Shell. He avoided saying who else he saw on the terrace. After I talked to him, I think he called up the person he saw with Shell."

"He may have seen someone with her or he may have seen some-one follow her. But Billy knows all about Shell and everything that happened at the dance and you told him about Richard. He can find out what happened."

Annie made a shooing gesture. "That's not what I'm worried about. I'm worried about Maggie." She recounted Maggie's visit to Death on Demand. "She ran out before I could ask her about the gun in Dave's desk. I called her cell a couple of times but I didn't get an answer. I'll bet she saw it was me calling and she didn't want to talk to me. So"—she gave him a determined look—"I'm going to go see Dave."

Max's frown was quick and intense. "I don't like that." His tone was flat. "We don't know what happened at the club that night but they hauled a dead body out of the water. If Richard died because of something he saw on the country club terrace, that raises the odds that Shell's dead. Murdered. Dave was furious with her. Maybe he's behind her disappearance. Let Billy talk to him about that night. If Shell was killed, the murderer got pressed by Richard and now he's dead. This is no time to confront someone who may have killed twice."

Annie lifted her shoulders, let them fall. "I have to do something. Billy's busy with Richard Ely. If I called him, he'd just say he'd get to Maggie when he could. I have to talk to Dave. Is there a gun in his desk? What if Maggie got the gun?"

Max looked grave. "Do you think she shot Shell?"

Annie turned her hands up in uncertainty. "I don't know what she meant when she told Shell she had a gun. Was she threatening Shell? Or was Maggie saying she might"—her voice thinned—"shoot herself?"

"This is no time to screw up Billy's investigation. Back off, Annie. Billy's the one to ask Dave about that night and Shell."

Annie shook her head with finality. "I'm not going to ask Dave about Shell. I want to know about the gun in his desk. You didn't see

Maggie. She's desperate. If she has a gun, somebody's got to get it away from her."

Max looked at her steadily. "Desperate? Or dangerous?"

Max reassured himself. Nothing could happen to Annie in Dave's office with a secretary in the anteroom and people going up and down the hallway. He wished he'd insisted on going with her. He well knew how successful that attempt would have been. Annie would have shaken her head with finality. But there were other ways to take care. He lifted the phone, called. "This is Max Darling. My wife's dropping in to see Mr. Peterson in a little while. Tell her I'd appreciate it if she'd come by my office after she leaves there."

When he'd hung up, Max's smile was rueful. He didn't know Dave's secretary, had no idea how much thought she gave to calls, whether she simply did as instructed or whether she was quick to note anomalies. If the latter, she might well wonder why, in the smart phone world, Max was requesting that a message be passed along. Whatever, he had reinforced the secretary's awareness of Annie's visit.

There was one other call he needed to make. He called the residence of Vera Hurst. The phone rang several times. When the answering machine took over, he made a quick decision. The time for subterfuge was past. He'd hoped to speak personally to Hayley Hurst, though no matter how he couched the message, she was likely to be upset. But she deserved to know. "This is Max Darling. This message is for Hayley Hurst. I filed a missing person report with the police this morning in regard to the disappearance of Shell Hurst. The police will contact the family or may have already done so. So far as I know, no trace of her has been found. Again, this is Max Darling at Confidential Commissions." He left his number, hung up.

Max pushed up from his leather chair, wandered across the room, plucked the putter from his golf bag. But he stood at the edge of the indoor green, staring at nothing. He felt somewhat reassured. Billy was hunting for Shell, alive or dead, and he was investigating Richard's death. Everything was under control. Like he'd told Annie, this was no time for them to get in the way.

The offices of Peterson Construction occupied the second floor of a brick building two doors down from Parotti's. Annie walked up a flight of stairs that opened into a welcoming reception area with several comfortable sofas and a broad window that overlooked the harbor. When she reached the counter, a heavyset woman with stiff gray hair, oversized glasses, and a square chin rose from a desk and stepped up to the counter. "May I help you?"

"I'm Annie Darling. I would like to see Mr. Peterson."

"I'll see if he's free. I have a message for you, Mrs. Darling. Your husband called and asked you to come to his office when you leave here." There was no curiosity or interest in her tone.

Annie understood. Max wanted her to be safe. She felt a warmth inside even though she would have to chide him for being overly protective. Nothing bad was going to happen to her in a daylight visit to an office. "I'll do that. Thank you."

The secretary was as uninterested in her response as she was in the message she'd delivered. She rose and moved unhurriedly through a swinging gate at the end of the counter and turned to her right down a broad hall.

Annie thought it interesting that she had to check in person. Apparently Dave had rules about how and when he could be interrupted.

In a moment, unhurried steps returned. The receptionist gestured. "If you will go to the third door to the left."

When Annie reached the door, it stood open. That must be the signal. Open door, visitors welcome. Closed door, no.

Dave rose from behind a huge steel desk with neatly arranged stacks of papers and a rack of folders. A green folder lay open, a pen next to it. "Come in." He looked as he always had, obviously an old football player, a big beefy face red from hours in the sun, blond hair cut short, dark eyes that often challenged, an expensive soft-weave polo, tan summer slacks. He exuded masculinity and toughness. He looked at her with curious brown eyes. "Hey, Annie. What can I do for you?"

Annie hesitated, then closed the door behind her.

Something flickered in his eyes, but he gestured toward the small sofa to the left of his desk, returned to his chair, and swung it to face the sofa.

"I came to see you because I'm worried about Maggie."

"Maggie? Why?" He raised an eyebrow.

Annie felt a sweep of relief. She wasn't sure what she had feared. That Maggie was afraid of Dave? That she was afraid for Dave? That Maggie had killed to keep him and was now wracked by guilt? But Dave's reaction seemed genuine. He appeared surprised and puzzled, but not threatened.

"It's awkward." She stopped.

His eyebrows drew down and his big face hardened. "I wouldn't have thought you were one of those women who meddle in other people's lives. I don't know what kind of gossip you've heard"—his eyes shifted and she knew he had a very good idea of what kind of gossip she might have heard—"but you need to butt out. Now, if that's all, I've got work to do."

135

"Is the gun still in your desk drawer at home?"

His eyes widened. "What the hell are you talking about? Of course it is." He pushed up from his chair, moved around the desk, stopped a foot away. Face flushed, he glared down at her, big, overbearing, and angry. "Why are you asking about my gun?"

Annie eased to her feet, backed away nearer to the door. "Someone overheard Maggie talking to Shell."

His big hands clenched into fists. "You better tell me and tell me quick." His voice was hard.

"Maggie was on her cell phone. She told Shell that she knew all about the money and what you and Shell planned but she told Shell there was a gun in your desk. Then she broke off."

"Maggie said the gun . . ." He looked like a big man who had taken a blow to his gut. His face mirrored shock, uncertainty, and, finally, fear. He turned and bulled toward the door, opened it, plunged into the hall.

Annie stared after him. Fear rode him like a spur to a maddened horse. Was he afraid of what Maggie might do with his gun? Or what she might have done?

Max came to his feet at the sound of the bell at the front door. But the rattle of footsteps wasn't right for Annie. Hayley Hurst skidded into his office. Instead of a tight blouse, short skirt, and high heels, she wore a chambray top, very short shorts, and leather thongs that revealed toes with flaming nail polish. Too much makeup still made her face garish, but this afternoon she looked much more like a teenage girl than a twentyish bimbo.

"Mr. Darling." Her voice wobbled. "I got your message. My mom's really mad. She wanted to know how come you called to tell me you'd filed a report on Shell and I had to tell her I'd asked you to find Shell. Mom's . . . scared." The word hung between them. Hayley's eyes were huge and dark with worry. "I know something awful's happened to Shell. I was over at Dad's this morning. He wasn't there so I checked out his computer. I keep thinking maybe she'll send an e-mail. If I saw an e-mail to him, I'd know she was somewhere. Today the bill from her credit card came. I got it open. Nobody'd ever know I opened it. I wiggled a table knife under the flap. I saw the charges. She hasn't bought anything since July third. And everything's weird at home and at Dad's house. Nobody will talk to me. Not Mom or Dad or Jed. And Jed's crazy nuts. He doesn't sleep at night. I hear him in his room, walking back and forth, back and forth. But I guess you can't do anything. Nobody seems to be doing anything." She jumped up, trying not to cry, and raced toward the door.

Max decided it was his day for distressed females. Hayley's departure had been as precipitous and emotional as her arrival. Annie wasn't distraught but he knew she was worried to the bone when her rebuke about his call to Dave's secretary was delivered almost absentmindedly.

Now she held his putter and worried with her thumbnail at a slight tear in the leather grip. "I don't know what's going to happen. After Dave left, I went outside and called Maggie. No answer. I left her a message and told her what I'd done." She turned huge eyes wide with uncertainty toward him. "I was trying to protect her. That's what I told her. She could have taken the gun because she was afraid of him. Do you think she's in danger?"

"No." He made his answer crisp, definite. "If Dave intended harm to Maggie, he would have played it cool, told you not to worry, he'd seen his gun that morning, whatever Maggie said, you didn't need to give it a thought. He wouldn't storm out, obviously on his way to see her. You said he seemed upset, maybe scared. It sounds to me like he was afraid of what she might do with a gun. You can rest easy about Maggie."

Annie looked relieved. "Still, we can tell Billy. He can check on the gun."

Max had no doubt Billy could ask Dave, but Dave was under no compulsion to answer, not until and unless Billy had an official reason to investigate the people who'd been among the last to see Shell. "I haven't been able to talk to Billy. I left a message. I said you'd gone to see Dave about Maggie and the gun and that Hayley Hurst opened Shell's credit card statement. And," he spoke without pleasure, remembering too clearly the scared look in Hayley Hurst's eyes, "I told him to ask Jed Hurst why he can't sleep at night."

M ax peppered two salmon filets, added lemon juice. As he placed the dish in the oven and set it at three fifty, the back door opened.

Annie clattered into the kitchen from the back porch, waggling a copy of the *Gazette*. "The new delivery boy has a talent for tossing the paper right in the middle of a rosebush." She unfolded the afternoon paper and settled on a tall chair behind the granite island. "Lead story." She read the headline first.

SHRIMP BOAT CATCHES BODY;
ISLANDER MISSING SINCE TUESDAY
APPARENT DROWNING VICTIM

She looked surprised. "I don't see how Doc Burford could already have done an autopsy." She read the story aloud:

> Police Chief Billy Cameron announced today that shrimpers in the bay hauled up the body of missing islander Richard Ely this morning. Cameron said medical examiner Dr. T. W. Burford made definite identification on the basis of dental records and a fused left ankle from a previous injury.
>
> Cameron said the cause of death will be established when a formal autopsy is completed. The police chief said Dr. Burford made a preliminary judgment that Ely's death resulted from drowning. The chief said the autopsy will determine if there were contributing factors.
>
> Cameron said a concerned citizen filed a missing person report this morning after being unable to locate Ely. Ely did not report for work at the country club Wednesday morning, where he was employed as a server. Club service manager Gerald O'Reilly said that Ely had been a reliable and conscientious employee. O'Reilly declined to speculate upon what may have happened to Ely.
>
> The concerned citizen also filed a missing person report regarding Shell Hurst, wife of islander Wesley J. Hurst. According to the report, Mrs. Hurst, 23, has not been seen since the night of July 4 when she was observed during the fireworks display as she walked toward the Island Country Club overflow parking lot. Attempts to contact Mr. Hurst have not been successful. O'Reilly had no comment about the report linking her disappearance to the country club.

Mrs. Hurst was driving a 2011 green Porsche Carrera. She is five feet eight inches tall, weighs 124 pounds, has chestnut-colored hair and green eyes.

Cameron said efforts to locate Mrs. Hurst have so far been unsuccessful but authorities have been alerted statewide and the search continues. Anyone with information about Mrs. Hurst may contact the police or the family.

Cameron declined to say whether the missing person reports are linked.

Cameron said the *Julie Joy* pulled up a net at shortly after ten o'clock today and the catch included a body later identified as that of Richard Ely. Captain Bo Woodson immediately contacted police and brought the body to shore. Cameron said Ely's car had been found in the Fish Haul Pier parking lot and had apparently been left there between 7 P.M. and midnight Tuesday. A patrol checks the lot at 7 A.M., 7 P.M., and midnight. No parking is permitted between midnight and 7 A.M. The car was ticketed Wednesday morning and impounded Thursday morning.

In the police report, an unidentified neighbor reported seeing Ely at approximately 9 P.M. Tuesday. A *Gazette* reporter contacted neighborhood residents. Harold Bates, who lived next door to Ely, reported that Ely's former wife visited him Tuesday evening. She left the house shortly before Ely departed. Bates said it was raining heavily at the time. Bates said that on several occasions this summer he'd heard them quarreling over child support payments. The *Gazette* has been unable to contact Mrs. Ely.

Max stirred pickle relish into mayonnaise, added a dash of mustard. "I'll bet Billy's not happy the neighbor spilled everything he saw to Marian."

Annie shrugged. "You know Marian. She's not going to stop with one source. I'll bet she knocked on all the doors on Black Skimmer Lane." Her eyes dropped again to the newspaper. "Cameron said the neighbor may have been the last person to see Ely. He is asking anyone with information concerning Richard Ely's activities to contact his office or leave a message on Crime Stoppers. Cameron emphasized the search for Mrs. Hurst and the investigation into Ely's death are being handled separately."

Annie dipped a piece of salmon into homemade tartar sauce. "Divine." The dinner was one of Max's finest: succulent salmon, steamed asparagus with a mustard and butter sauce, a salad that sang of freshness with a delicate peach vinaigrette dressing. She felt relaxed for the first time since they'd started their search for Shell. They had done everything they could do. Billy Cameron would find what could be found. Tomorrow she would once again move among books and happily guide readers to new pleasures, the nostalgic charm of Susan Wittig Albert's Darling Dahlias series, the heartfelt emotion in Earlene Fowler's Benni Harper series, the always fascinating and often touching entries in Lee Goldberg's quirky Mr. Monk series.

She lifted her glass of chardonnay. "A toast."

Max obediently picked up his glass.

Annie looked across the table. "To Billy's success."

A sudden harsh knock sounded at the kitchen door.

9

Max opened the door.

Wesley Hurst looked like a man whose world had collapsed around him. "I got a message for you." Gone was the affable, easygoing, trust-fund, late-thirties rich kid. He was still prep perfect, sandy hair cut the right length, a Billy Reid plaid linen shirt, Brunello Cucinelli pants, Moncler suede boat shoes, but his face looked pummeled, purple smudges beneath his eyes, cheekbones jutting. "I'm telling you"—his voice was husky with emotion—"keep away from my kids."

Max spoke quietly. "Your daughter came to see me because she was worried about Shell."

Wesley hunched his shoulders. "You had no business talking to her. Hayley meant well. But she doesn't understand"—an appreciable pause—"what Shell's like. Part of it was just kid stuff. She resented her brother trying to tell her what to do, keep her from hanging out with Shell. Hayley made a mistake."

"Did she?" Max was abrupt. He stood with his hands loose at his sides, prepared for whatever might happen. "Shell hasn't been seen or heard from since the dance."

"Shell called me." Wesley looked from Max to Annie, back again. "A couple of days ago. But I don't tell all my business to the world like you've done. I saw the *Gazette*. A concerned citizen, hell. You're butting into my life. I talked to the mayor. He told me you're always poking your nose in where it doesn't concern you. I'm telling you to leave me and my family alone. Now everybody thinks something's happened to Shell." His stare was straight. And unconvincing. "There's nothing to this. She left the island."

Annie took a step forward. "Where is she?"

Wesley's tone was harsh. "She wouldn't say. She told me she's off having fun and it's for me to wonder and she doesn't plan on coming back. I told her I'd get a divorce. Abandonment. Whatever. She can't do this to me."

Max stared at Wesley, saw his eyes shift away. "Did she call you on her cell?" There would be a record of that call. Billy could find out.

Wesley blinked. "I don't know. I just answered. All I know is, she called me a couple of days ago—"

"Exactly when?"

Wesley's chin jutted. "What difference does it make to anybody but me? She's my wife. What she does is none of your business. And I told that cop he better not hassle me. Yeah, Shell and I are through. I'm getting a divorce. Want to put that in the paper? I'll get a lawyer. From here on, you better not cause me or my kids any more trouble."

"Why was Jed frightened when I asked him about Shell's Porsche?"

Wesley sucked in a breath. "You got to stop badgering him. He's just a kid. He got in trouble because he scraped the side of her car backing out of the driveway and it made Shell mad and he thought that's what you were asking about." As he talked, he seemed to gain confidence, but his eyes had a hollow, desperate look. "Like I said, leave my kids—and me—alone." He turned, moved heavily toward the back door. He pushed the screen, thudded out onto the porch.

As his steps receded, Annie looked at Max and shook her head. "Shell didn't call him."

"Billy will find out." Max closed the door with finality.

Max eyed her shorty pajamas admiringly as he placed an omelet on her plate. "Nice legs, Mrs. Darling." He dropped a hand and slid warm fingers along her thigh.

Annie smiled, patted his hand, firmly lifted it, her eyes saying, *Thank you, but not now.* "Another beautiful morning in paradise and thou, along with an omelet, sausage, and the best Colombian coffee north of the border."

He grinned as he slipped into his chair. "Can't blame a guy for trying."

She tilted her head. "Do you like cold omelets?"

"No, but I like warm women. Uh, warm woman," he amended hastily. "What border?"

She airily waved a hand. "Colombia has borders," she said vaguely.

The cat door flapped and Dorothy L's round white head poked inside. In a moment, after one quick glance at the kitchen table, she strolled casually toward the counter.

Max put down his fork. He reached the electric skillet in time to remove the cord, swipe out grease with a paper towel.

Annie laughed. "She has you well trained. Cat in, skillet wiped."

The morning ritual complete and Max back at the table, Dorothy L settled on the counter behind Max's shoulder. Her purr indicated she harbored no ill will though her blue eyes held fond memories of the occasional times when she scored and enjoyed lapping up remnants of butter.

Annie was determined to keep their morning untroubled for as long as possible. They didn't talk about Wesley Hurst or Shell or Hayley or Jed or Richard Ely or Dave Peterson or Maggie. They talked about a revival of *The Pajama Game* currently running at the Island Playhouse and a discovery of a ribbon-tied packet of WWII love letters at a flea market in Beaufort and how Barb would look in black hair since a vacation e-mail hinted she would return to the island in Hedy Lamarr mode after seeing *Tortilla Flat* on Turner Classic Movies.

"Speaking of e-mails." Max pointed at several printouts on the counter near Dorothy L. "A long one from Laurel and two shorter ones from Henny and Emma. I suppose we'd better take a look." He removed their plates, picked up the sheets, and refilled their coffee mugs.

Annie admired the way his T-shirt and boxer shorts fit, but she kept her face carefully schooled. This was not the time to distract him. He was easily distracted.

He settled at the table, arranged the sheets. "Emma first. Two sentences, short, succinct, far from sweet. *Where's the body?*" His lips folded into a tight line.

Obviously, Max took offense at Emma's brusque tone. Annie

offered a defense. "You know how she is when she gets involved in a book."

Max raised an eyebrow. "Obnoxious? Or maybe I ought to say, more obnoxious than usual?"

Annie grinned. "Lacking charm."

Max's tone was sour. "Second sentence: *Get off your duffs and look for it.* Assuming there is a body, and that's still a big leap for me, where does she suggest we start? Does she remember this is an island? Just because a shrimper found Ely, it doesn't mean Shell's dead or, if she is, whether a body will ever be found. Ely was found because he went off Fish Haul Pier and the currents took him where they did."

Annie was thoughtful. "Do you think Shell could be in the ocean?"

Max looked discouraged. "She could be. If she isn't in Rio. But that still leaves the Porsche. I don't know why it hasn't turned up. It's too bad we didn't know she was missing earlier. If somebody drove the car into the ocean, Tuesday night's rain washed away any tracks in the sand."

Annie frowned. "There aren't many beaches on the island where you could access the beach by car without messing up the dunes. The rain would wash away tire tracks on the sand but not damage to dunes." She carefully avoided thinking about the heat and what would have happened since last week if a body was left in a car. "The car must be in the woods somewhere."

"I'm sure Billy has officers checking all the back roads for any evidence a car was driven off track. Since Ely's body was found, Billy has plenty of reason to investigate." He picked up another sheet. "Here's from Henny. *The shadow in the hall haunts me. Why did Edward Irwin eavesdrop when Annie came to see Eileen? Why didn't he come in the living room?*" Max looked at Annie.

Annie remembered the odd chill that swept her in the immaculate living room when she saw that splotch of shadow on the shining wood floor. "Henny has an instinct. There was something off-key about that whole episode. Somebody was afraid. I don't know whether it was Eileen or Edward." She had a clear memory of Eileen's severe features framed by white gold hair, a tall woman with a commanding presence. Of course, Annie hadn't seen Edward, only his shadow. Funny, he was always a shadow compared to Eileen. She was not a woman one would miss seeing. Edward, on the other hand, was unimpressive, thinning gray hair, a round face with slack lips, somewhat portly.

Max looked at the next sheet. "This one's from Ma." His face was suddenly bemused.

Dearest Ones, how to phrase this? Perhaps, dear Max, it might be best if Annie were to peruse this communication.

He stopped, raised a blond eyebrow.
Annie held out her hand.
He surrendered Laurel's e-mail.
Annie scanned the sheet.

Dearest Ones, how to phrase this? Perhaps, dear Max, it might be best if Annie were to peruse this communication. Annie, though you are so deliciously unworldly, I know you will understand when I mention that moments of the heart often obscure reason. Or perhaps not. You do rather think things through. However, I digress. Once upon a love affair—my dear, doesn't that phrase have a ring to it?—I became involved with, dare I say it, a young man who turned out to be a cad. Though he danced beautifully. Especially the tango. I think even you—

Annie's eyes narrowed.

—understand the romantic excesses of the tango. Suffice to say, I was indiscreet. Tony thought perhaps I would be willing to finance a villa in Bermuda for him in exchange for his silence concerning our fling. Silly boy. He didn't realize that I am not concerned about gossip. *C'est la vie.* And my divorce from Reginald—

Annie could never quite keep Laurel's men straight in her mind. Was that her second husband or her third?

—was final. Moreover, Reginald had agreed to a very reasonable prenuptial agreement. The cogent point is this: When you have nothing to lose, it's quite easy to dismiss a blackmail attempt. Of course, not being vindictive—my dear, he danced divinely—I let the matter drop. But think of Edward skulking about the Sea Side Inn. It does bring intriguing pictures to mind. Clearly, he was stalking Shell and Dave. To what end? Not just curiosity. One doesn't go to such lengths. There had to be a purpose. I've heard several interesting stories about Edward's financial ventures. I know because I discreetly inquired. You see, he thought I was a rich woman just waiting to be lured into investments. I discovered he'd been careless about money in other instances. What if he's been careless recently? What if he was desperate to come up with a goodly sum of cash? What if Edward tried to blackmail Shell? Perhaps, she, too, was impervious to such threats. What if she threatened to report the attempt to the police? There are serious penalties for blackmail. What would Edward do to avoid the prospect of criminal charges, a trial, certainly a scandal that would rock the island, perhaps prison?

Annie folded the e-mail. It was not necessary to explain to Max what prompted his mother's conclusions. "To sum up"—Annie thought it was a lovely turn of phrase—"what if Edward tried to blackmail Shell and she turned the tables and threatened to go to the police?"

◆　◆　◆

Annie glanced at her watch. In half an hour, she and Max would leave their respective places of business to keep an appointment at the police station. She'd been surprised when she'd received Billy's text. She would have thought he was too busy to spend time with them. He knew everything they knew, including the contents of the e-mails from Emma, Henny, and Laurel. Of course, Annie had shared her sanitized version of Laurel's e-mail. Max viewed his mother's romantic interludes in a softer light perhaps than was warranted but everyone clings to some illusions. As he often said, a trifle defensively, "Ma can't help it that she's attractive to men." No, but . . . However, a wise wife doesn't go down fruitless paths.

At the coffee bar, Annie checked the glass shelves on the wall. There was time for her to have some strong, fresh brew. She looked up at mugs decorated with mystery inscriptions and a dagger with a bright spot of red at its tip. She ordered ceramic mugs in bulk, and a local artist painted them in exchange for books.

Annie reached for *Consequence of Crime* by Elizabeth Linington, shook her head, chose *No Lady in the House* by Lucille Kallen, filled the mug almost to the brim.

Rushed footsteps thudded in the central corridor. Marian Kenyon, dark eyes glittering, black hair tousled, stormed to the coffee bar, slapped a notebook on the counter. "The Great Kibosh. Finis. Kaput. Crime? Why, someone smashed a ceramic frog in Betty Bingham's garden. Probably that incorrigible kid with a slingshot who lives next door. Get out an APB." She slid onto a stool, pointed at the second shelf. "Double shot of espresso with a dash of chocolate in *Fear Walks the Island.*"

Annie poured two ounces of the thick black brew in the mug with the Hugh Desmond title, added two tablespoons of chocolate syrup, placed the mug on the counter.

Annie spoke soothingly. "You seem upset."

Marian grabbed the mug, drank, blinked her eyes. "Upset? Oh hey, why should I be upset? You know, Max knows, I know, and Billy Cameron knows that we may be dealing with two murders. As far as I'm concerned, only an idiot—as in our porcine mayor—can believe Shell Hurst ended up anywhere but dead on the Fourth. As for Richard Ely, maybe he went out in a deluge to meet the tooth fairy. I don't know. Stranger things have happened. According to our got-my-eye-on-the-buck mayor, after a chummy confab with richer-than-Croesus Wesley Hurst, who'll be a good campaign donor next year, the police have no business hounding kindly Mr. Hurst because his soon-to-be ex-wife Shell called him and she is clearly off island, and their separation and ultimate divorce is of no concern to the constabulary. As for dead-as-a-mackerel Richard Ely, why, these things happen. The autopsy report states drowning as the cause of death and that pesky wound at the base of his skull—"

Annie now understood the reference to contributing factors in the news story.

"—could easily have been caused by a fall. In the unlikely event foul play occurred, remember the first rule of homicide, look at the spouse. However, the ex-wife's a kindly single mom now so heaven forbid we suspect her. Therefore, Chief Cameron is instructed not to waste department time and energy asking questions about matters that do not require investigation. And the *Gazette*, compliments of yours truly, will have a truly touching story this afternoon about Wesley Hurst's struggle to combat unfortunate rumors about him and his wife." For an instant, Marian looked bleakly amused. "Hard for a rich guy to pander to the press, but a man does what he needs to do. You know what that tells me? This guy's desperate to shut everybody up."

The harbor view through Billy Cameron's office window was in idyllic summer mode, sailboats, catamarans, and powerboats plying placid green water. Two shrimp boats rode on the horizon. Porpoises curved up and out and down into the water in a graceful ballet.

Annie tried not to sound accusatory. "Billy, is there anything you can do?"

Billy's face was somber. "Not much. The autopsy report on Ely doesn't afford reason to launch an investigation. He drowned. Assuming he ate dinner between six and seven, death likely occurred between eight to twelve P.M. according to the stage of digestion. That was during the height of the thunderstorm. That's the long and short of it. There's a contusion at the base of the skull but nothing to show he didn't have an accident. Since his car was parked in the pier lot, it's reasonable to assume he was out on the pier when he went into the water. As to why he should have been at the end of the pier, the mayor points out that we don't have to know why he went there. The fact that he left his house during a huge storm and so far as we know never returned doesn't faze the mayor. The storm lasted most of the night. It seems almost certain Ely went out on the pier during the storm. Why? No matter, the mayor says. He went, he slipped, he fell, he drowned. End of story. Picking up gossip about what he saw or didn't see at the club during the fireworks is immaterial." He looked sour. "The mayor loves the word *immaterial*. He used it at least five times."

Max shared Billy's disgust. "Did he also think it was immaterial that Shell Hurst hasn't used her credit card since July third?"

"Like a French movie."

Annie and Max stared at him.

Billy's lips curled. "Yeah. He said it was like a French movie, a loose woman on the make leaves with some guy who's picking up the tab. That explains why she hasn't used her cell phone either. No calls made since July fourth. But no problem. It's obvious, he said. She's using lover boy's cell." He turned his big hands palms up. "The hell of it is, he may be right. I don't have a body. Wesley Hurst can claim Shell called, the mayor can write a script, but until I have some kind of evidence of foul play, there's nothing I can do."

Annie understood his frustration. "There's lots Max and I can do."

Billy's gaze was somber. "I don't have proof of any crime, but things are screwy. There may be a killer out there. You two better leave it alone. You may get more than you bargained for."

Max glanced at his iPhone. His eyes narrowed. "I wonder if anyone's ever told Emma to take a hike."

"Not in this lifetime." Annie grinned. "Harassing you?"

He handed over the iPhone. The text was clear: *WTB?*

Max glared at the offending message. "If she's so smart, why doesn't she tell us?"

Annie pushed up from her perch on the edge of Max's desk. She walked to one of a pair of comfortable webbed art deco chairs she'd helped him choose when they'd redone his office and sank down with a sigh. "Okay, let's give Emma her due. She may be right. So, where's the body?"

Max didn't answer. He stared at a print of a Mark Rothko painting, a swath of luminous gold above a block of intense orange. Finally, slowly, he began to speak. "If there's a body, someone knows. That's what we have to remember. Someone knows. When people are under pressure, they can make mistakes. It's up to us to apply pressure."

Eileen Irwin opened the door at Annie's first knock. She was summery in a light blue hand-embroidered blouse and a blue linen peasant skirt with gathered ruching at the hem. There was a quizzical expression on her narrowly planed face. "You sounded most mysterious over the phone." An amused smile. "I gather everything's still up in the air about Shell." She led the way into the living room.

Annie sat again on the plaid sofa while Eileen sank into what was clearly her chair.

Eileen was at ease, her light blue eyes curious. "I've heard so many different stories. Shell left on a yacht. Shell called Wesley and won't say where she is. Shell's in Tahiti. Shell's moved back in with Bucky." Her face expressed distaste. "Wesley is such a fool. Imagine taking your brother's leftovers. But the Hursts were always crude." She spoke from the safe pinnacle of an old Southern family.

"No one knows where she is." Annie's eyes lifted to the mirror. This morning there was no shadow on the hall floor. Annie lowered her voice. "There is some suspicion she might be dead."

Eileen's air of supercilious amusement vanished. She looked shaken, a woman confronted by possibilities she'd never envisioned. "That's dreadful. Why, she's so young." She bent forward. "Surely not. Who thinks that?"

Annie evaded the question. "She was last seen walking on the path to the overflow parking lot on the night of the Fourth. No one has seen her since. She hasn't used her cell phone. She's made no charges on her credit card. She's vanished. That's why I wanted to see you."

Eileen lifted a hand to her throat. "Me?" Her voice was thin.

"You were on the terrace during the fireworks."

Eileen's pale eyes never left Annie's face. "Yes."

"Where did you stand?"

Eileen's hand dropped to her lap. She looked puzzled. "I don't know exactly. I was a few feet away from the French doors. The grandstand was on my right, the pool to my left."

Annie felt a flicker of excitement. "You had a clear view of the path Shell took."

Her thin face creased in thought. "I suppose I did, but I don't think I looked that way. I was watching the fireworks."

"Was Edward with you?"

"For a bit. But he left soon after the fireworks started."

So Eileen was on the terrace and Edward was walking home. Annie pictured the layout of the golf course. From the terrace, Edward would have headed across the parking lot for the golf clubhouse. He could as easily have skirted the lot and darted onto the path Shell took.

"Did you see him walk toward the clubhouse?"

"I didn't look after him. Why should I?" Her tone was sharp. "Edward doesn't know anything about Shell. Neither of us do."

"You were on the terrace and you may have seen something that will help. Did you see Shell take the path past the grandstand?"

Eileen shrugged. "It was dark except for the fireworks. People milled everywhere. I suppose I may have seen her but it didn't register."

Annie felt frustrated. Eileen had been there. Surely she knew something helpful. "Who was standing near you?"

"It's hard to say. People came and went. The terrace was shadowy. There was some light from the French doors but the lights on the terrace and around the pool had been turned off. It was hard to identify anyone. I saw the Thornwalls over near the pool. Vera Hurst came past me at one point and she didn't even say hello. I suppose she was looking the other way. I saw her face in a burst of white fireworks. She didn't look like she was having a good time. Some teenage girls were near me." Eileen's eyes narrowed in concentration. "Then there were some perfectly marvelous fireworks, a huge blue constellation. You should have heard everyone cheer. That was later so I don't suppose it matters. About the time the fireworks ended, I saw Jed Hurst next to the grandstand and he looked upset. He was watching his dad. Wesley was walking fast toward the back entrance to the club."

Annie knew a treasure hunter's glee at uncovering a glint of metal. She was careful to keep her tone casual. "So the story that he'd had too much to drink is just nonsense." This was more confirmation that Wesley was sober despite his behavior at the valet stand. Was he trying to establish that he was in no condition to be associated with any harm to Shell?

Eileen looked surprised. "I don't know who said that but they're mistaken. Wesley was walking quite purposefully." She shook her head. "That doesn't sound right, like he was showing that he was sober. It wasn't that at all. You can tell. People who have had too much to drink may manage to go in a straight line, but it takes effort and they move slowly. Wesley was in a hurry, walking fast. I would say he was absolutely sober."

◆ ◆ ◆

Max remembered a church committee meeting one winter evening at Edward and Eileen Irwin's home. Eileen was the kind
of woman who naturally rose to power on church committees, a
lifetime member from a well-respected island family. She'd served
sherry trifle. Max had admired the lightness of her Madeira cake. He
contrasted the elegance of the Irwin home with the hollow slam of
the downstairs door of the thin-walled building where Edward Irwin
Investments was housed in a second-floor office. The stairway was
narrow. The office directory showed only two occupants listed
upstairs. Edward's office was midway along the hallway. Most of the
office doors were blank. Not a thriving hum of commerce.

Max had decided to take a chance that he would find Edward at
his office. He was pleased to see light shining behind the frosted glass.
He pulled out his cell to turn it off, saw a new message: *WTB?* He
deleted the text with an irritated tap. He opened the door and stepped
into a cramped anteroom with a tired-looking rubber plant in a
ceramic pot, an unoccupied desk with a plastic-shrouded computer,
two easy chairs with a small table between them, and a stack of
magazines, a copy of *Southern Living* on top.

"Hello?"

A chair squeaked in an inner office. Edward appeared in the
doorway. Max looked at a small, worried, tired man. The incongruity
of his suspicions in relation to the reality of Edward's appearance made
his quest seem absurd. Especially when eagerness lighted Edward's eyes.
Did Edward see a rich man who, if he could be lured to invest, might
stave off debtors for another day?

Edward bustled toward him, plump pink hand outstretched.

"Max, good to see you." His eyes flickered toward the empty desk. "My secretary had to take a leave of absence. I've been handling things myself until she gets back." His shifty gaze told Max that the lack of a secretary reflected a salary in arrears from a man who had his back to the financial wall. Obviously, Eileen was parsimonious with her own holdings. "Keeps me pretty busy but I always have time for friends."

Max couldn't see this middle-aged, defeated man committing murder and doing it so cleverly that there was no trace of a crime or a body. But there was no doubt what he had done at the Sea Side Inn. Max stood with folded arms, his stare hard. "How much money did you want from Shell for the pictures?"

Edward froze where he stood, hand outstretched. His puddly face sagged. His eyes rounded in shock.

"She threatened you, didn't she?"

Edward struggled to breathe. His chest rapidly rose and fell, rose and fell.

"You'd better tell me your side of it." Max never took his gaze away from Edward's stricken face.

"I don't know what you're talking about." The words were scarcely audible.

"Someone saw you taking the pictures at the Sea Side Inn."

Edward turned and walked blindly into his office.

Max followed. He disliked bullying this hapless man, but cornered creatures could be dangerous.

Edward sank into the chair behind his desk. He swallowed repeatedly, breathing fast.

Max remained standing. "When did she tell you she was going to the police?"

158

Edward looked even more shrunken. "I don't know what you're talking about."

Max recognized dull, stubborn, hopeless denial. Max never doubted that Edward had attempted blackmail, but Edward wasn't going to admit anything. Was that because he knew the person who could send him to jail was safely dead? Max looked at a weak face and shifting eyes and considered how to attack. Edward had been obviously disturbed when Shell insisted he dance with her. That had to mean she threatened Edward before the dance. She must have talked with him. Max bluffed confidently. "Her call to you was overheard."

Edward lifted his head, looked at him straight, a liar's posture. His words came fast now. "There was a misunderstanding. That's all that it was and she knew it was just a joke. That's right, a joke. She wouldn't listen when I apologized."

Max gave him an incredulous stare. "Let me see if I've got this right. You threatened—"

"It was a joke."

"—to tell her husband about her trysts at the inn with Dave and then said you'd keep quiet for a payoff."

"It was a joke."

"I didn't know you were on joking terms with Shell Hurst."

Edward pressed his thin lips together.

"When was she going to file the police report?"

Edward clasped his pudgy fingers together. "She knew it was a joke."

"She broke in to dance with you. Did she say she hadn't decided to make a report yet? Did you offer her money? I'll bet she thought that was hilarious. First you wanted money from her and then you offered her money. But you don't have any extra money, do you?"

"It was a joke." Edward's voice was defiant.

"What did she say when you danced?"

Edward hesitated, eyes shifting. Finally, he looked at Max with a craven earnestness. "You've got to understand. She thought everything was funny. She said she hadn't made up her mind what she'd do to make the evening a real blast. She said, 'Maybe I'll make a public announcement, go up on the bandstand, borrow a trumpet.'"

Max realized with a shock that Edward was now quoting Shell, that this was what she'd said as the swing music played and dancers laughed and chatted in the background and, no doubt, Eileen watched them with a grim stare. Eileen would have found that moment in the middle of the dance floor when she surrendered her husband an incredibly public affront.

"'I can blow a few notes, get everyone's attention. People love reality TV. I'll do *Reality among the Rich on Broward's Rock*. Trumpet trill and I share the trauma of a wife betrayed, the man she thought loved her sneaking around, cheating on her with his ex-wife. Messy, you know. But I will proclaim my love, insist that I will never leave his side no matter how he has treated me. Everyone will love it. Then there are the rumors about me and Dave. Am I going to run away with him? Stay tuned. Hint: I don't like self-important men. Then—'" He broke off.

Max didn't doubt there had been more. Shell wouldn't have let him off the hook. No doubt she'd included Edward and his attempt at blackmail. He looked into Edward's watery eyes and knew he was right, but Edward now sat with his lips pressed tightly together.

"And that's all?"

Pale brown eyes flickered back and forth. Edward talked fast again. "Then she said she'd been thinking about things and she'd decided to accept my apology and not cause any trouble. She said"—

and now his voice was stronger—"that she was going to leave the island."

Max's stare was level and hard. "Where's the body?"

Edward's eyes flared in panic. "She left the island. That's what happened. She left."

10

The juke box played "Mack the Knife." Annie shivered. "I've never liked that song. That's what I feel like. If Shell's dead, someone out there"—she waved a hand toward the big oak door of Parotti's Bar and Grill—"is dangerous. It may," she spoke slowly, "be Wesley Hurst. Eileen thinks he was sober. Sure, he stood at the bar through most of the dance, but maybe he was only nursing one drink. Maybe he played drunk later to make a scene so everybody'd remember him leaving and wouldn't associate him in any way with Shell. Eileen's observation confirms what Don Thornwall told Emma. Eileen said Wesley was walking fast toward the back of the club with no indication he'd drunk too much. That also tells us he was coming from the direction of the path to the overflow lot. And Eileen saw Jed near the grandstand, right by that path."

"Jed knows something. I've been sure of it ever since I talked to him." Max spooned a generous helping of chicken potpie.

Annie's fried flounder sandwich was, as usual, superb. She wished she could concentrate on its flavor and the generous splash of tartar sauce and a bun with just a hint of onion, not enough to detract from the fresh whitefish. She wished the music would change. "Eileen saw Vera, too. All of the Hursts looked upset. Did Wesley go to the lot? Jed and Vera were both on the terrace. One of them could have followed him."

Max looked grim. "They'll never admit it."

Annie put down her sandwich. "If we ask, it will get their attention."

Y ou and your husband have caused a lot of trouble." Vera Hurst's voice dropped with venom. "I'm warning you, Wesley and I have had enough and the mayor agrees. Wesley can't help what Shell does. Leave us alone or we'll sue you for slander."

It had taken Annie several calls to track Vera to the pool at the club. She kept her voice even, but forceful. "We intend to find Shell."

"We'll see you in court. You've been warn—"

Annie interrupted. "You and Wesley were overheard at the dance."

There was no answer, except for a quick intake of breath.

"I'm coming to the club. Wait for me." Annie clicked off the line. Before she could put the phone in her purse, a text arrived: *WTB?* She compressed her lips, shot back: *Looking.*

It was hard enough to hide a body, but how did you hide a Porsche? Shell had left the overflow lot in the Porsche, either alive or dead. Where was the car? Impatiently, she shook her head, slid onto the hot leather seat of her Thunderbird.

By the time she reached the club, the car's air-conditioning had lowered the temperature from sauna to just baking. In the main parking lot, Annie started to look for a slot, changed her mind. Instead, she drove through the main lot to exit onto the blacktop that led to the overflow lot and skirted the perimeter of the golf course.

The overflow lot was empty of cars on a drowsy hot Friday. Sunlight glanced through the filigree of Spanish moss, turning the gray epiphyte a shimmering silver. Beneath the canopy of the tall pines, the air was still and heavy. Annie left the windows down. She gazed at empty parking spaces. Somewhere here on the night of July fourth, Shell Hurst parked her green Porsche. There would have been visibility enough from the occasional lights strung in the trees. Slowly Annie walked toward the gap in the trees that marked the path to the club. Shell came this way in her lovely dress with its startling cleavage. Was she at all worried about the trouble she was causing?

What had been her mood? That morning she had taunted Edward Irwin over the phone, threatened him, surely frightened him. Max had described Edward's gray face, his refusal to make any admissions. Edward was accustomed to comfortable surroundings, to wealth even though the money was his wife's, not his. Annie thought of Eileen, so self-possessed this morning, taking a malicious pleasure in what she had seen and what she knew, but how would she feel if she ever found out what Edward had done? Eileen would not be pleased to see her husband accused of blackmail, possibly brought to trial, convicted. Annie hoped, for Edward's sake, that she would never have to know. But wasn't that reason enough for Edward to do whatever he had to do to keep Shell quiet?

Annie walked more slowly. Eileen had been open about Edward's early departure from the fireworks. He'd claimed a headache, presumably walked home on a golf path, but he could have seen Shell on her way to the overflow lot and followed her.

Annie reached the oyster-shell path. She moved carefully in the exact center of the path. Although the club kept undergrowth at a minimum, she never doubted that beyond a rotten log there might be a sunning rattlesnake, and dank green water near a stand of cane very probably offered a haven to alligators. Annie had a healthy respect for alligators and if one chose to take up residence in the middle of the path, she was ready to grant the scaly beast immediate property rights. She subscribed to the if-you-don't-bother-them-then-maybe-they-won't-bother-you school of island residents.

She was relieved when she came around the last cluster of pines to reach the paved area. The silence of the wooded parking area was in marked contrast to the cries and shouts and squeals from the swimming pool to her right. Straight ahead was the terrace. The grassy area between the pool and the golf pro shop that had been used for temporary bleachers to view the fireworks was once again a sweep of green.

The night of the dance when she and Max slipped outside to step into the shadow of a honeysuckle arbor, the milling throng of guests had been the last thing on her mind. In Eileen's recollection, the lighting had been dim and people came and went, but she had seen the Thornwalls, Vera, Wesley, and Jed Hurst. Annie felt a spurt of exasperation. She should have asked Eileen whether Vera was walking toward the terrace or toward the path. Then she shook her head. It didn't matter. What mattered was that Vera had been on the terrace at or near the time Shell was seen on the path.

Annie kept to the walk, didn't try to wend her way through the clusters of chairs and stretched-out beach towels on the apron of the pool. It wasn't hard to spot Vera. The club had a bit of paradise for everyone. Teenagers splashed to music near the deep end with occasional forays to the diving boards. Toddlers in swim rings and floats enjoyed their own pool with watchful mamas in nearby deck chairs. Preteens splashed and squealed, ran and jumped, played tag and bounced in the shallow end. Beneath a jasmine-covered pergola, those seeking a quieter venue read and drowsed on cushioned pool chairs.

Vera Hurst was at the far end of the pergola. Her ivory swimsuit was beautifully cut, a perfect accompaniment to her long-limbed grace. She rose and waited, tall, slim, with the regal air of a woman who would have her way. Dark-tinted sunglasses hid her eyes. She might have been the picture of summer ease except for the taut line of her jaw, the unsmiling line of her coral lips, the stiffness of her pose.

Annie approached, unsmiling as well. She stopped and looked at the unrevealing dark glasses. All around them was the cadence of summer and play and evanescent happiness, but they stood in a separate, tight, tense pocket of silence.

Vera turned a hand in irritation. "I started to leave, but I don't intend to let you arrange my schedule."

"You don't care whether Shell is ever found?"

Vera's lips twisted in what might have been a sardonic smile. "Frankly, my dear, no."

"Not even if you and Wesley can't remarry? Everyone assumed since you're having an affair—"

Vera's lips parted in shock.

"—that he would leave Shell. Did he change his mind? Even if he didn't, I don't think he can get a divorce if she can't be located."

"If you don't mind"—her voice dripped sarcasm—"we'll manage our lives without your assistance. It was a mistake to wait. I'll gather up my things." She started to turn away.

Annie felt a hot flick of anger, decided she had nothing to lose. "You waited for me because you're worried. Are you scared for yourself or for Wesley? You and Wesley quarreled on the terrace at the club. You told Wesley he had to deal with Shell that night. She hasn't been seen since."

The rigid face with the unrevealing sunglasses swiveled toward her. "What are you suggesting?"

"Where's the body?"

Nothing moved in Vera's still face.

The lack of response was an answer in itself. Vera, too, thought— or knew or feared—that Shell was dead.

Annie's throat felt tight. "You think she's dead."

Vera spoke slowly, as if carefully choosing her words. "I have no reason to think anything of the kind. That's all I intend to say." She turned and walked away.

Max admired Jed Hurst's stance. There was ease and confidence as the teenager addressed the ball. His swing was smooth, without a hitch. He had the untroubled arrogance of a young golfer with steady nerves who had never known the yips. If his putting game matched his long game, he would be formidable. *Thwock.* The golf ball curved up in a beautiful trajectory. The drive completed its arc, landing near the two-hundred-forty-yard marker.

"Good shot."

Jed hunched his shoulders. He turned slowly, one big hand wrapped tightly around the shaft of his driver. The mop of dark hair that dangled down into his face made him look young and vulnerable, but his narrow face had the same strong jawline as his mother's. He jutted out his chin. "My dad says I don't have to talk to you."

"There are witnesses. You and your dad were on the terrace."

Jed's mouth opened, then shut. He drew a breath. "If people know so much, what happened, then?"

Max spoke as if certain. "Your dad followed Shell."

Jed stared at him, his dark blue eyes wide and strained. "Is that what he says?"

"He was seen."

Jed yanked a cell from his pocket, called. "Hey, Dad, that guy, that creep's here on the range, bugging me. He says somebody saw you go on that path to the back lot." He listened, then handed the phone to Max.

"Get away from my boy. I'll swear out a complaint. Stalking, harassment. I'm on the phone to the cops right now." The call ended.

Max returned the cell to Jed.

Jed folded his lips tight, jammed the cell in his pocket. He moved toward his bag, stuffed the club inside, hefted the bag by the strap, gave Max a dark glare, and strode away.

Max drew a _U_ to represent the main parking lot at the country club. A thin line led from the base to a thicker streak, the blacktop road. He shaded stacked triangles for pines, made a rectangle for the overflow lot. More quick strokes created the curving blacktop as it passed the boundary of the golf course, ending when it merged into a residential street in the housing development where homes backed onto the golf course.

Annie looked over his shoulder. "The first thing we have to decide is whether Shell drove the Porsche out of the overflow lot."

"I don't think she was driving. Or she had someone with her." Max's answer was decisive.

Annie moved around the end of his desk, settled in one of the webbed chrome chairs. "I don't disagree but why are you so sure?"

"She left before the fireworks ended. If she'd driven out toward the front of the club, Ross Martin would have noticed the car. He likes sports cars. He saw her arrive. She left during the fireworks and the valet boys weren't busy then. Ross couldn't have missed seeing the Porsche. It would pass very close to the valet stand. That means the Porsche was driven away from the club on the back road. Shell had no reason to use the back road. That's not the way she would drive home. If she drove on the back road, there had to be a reason. Perhaps someone was with her and they were headed somewhere other than her house."

Annie looked discouraged. "If the car went on the far side of the golf course and into the residential area, it could be anywhere on the island."

Max tapped the thicker line on his drawing. "If the Porsche took the back way out, she was taking someone somewhere or she was dead and the murderer wanted to get rid of her and the car."

Annie tried to picture a faceless driver. Was Shell smiling seductively at her passenger? Or was a murderer, hands clenched on the wheel, a dead woman slumped in the passenger seat or tumbled into a backseat, seeking somewhere to leave a body and a car? If the latter, no wonder the back road was taken.

For that moment, Annie looked at the overflow lot as if it had been a crime scene and Shell the victim. Had Shell died as she sat in the driver's seat? If so, her body had been dumped over into the passenger seat. If she had been killed outside the car, perhaps standing alongside it, perhaps caught unaware as she turned to open the door, again the body must have been dragged to the opposite side, possibly heaved into the backseat, her evening purse tossed inside. The grisly task would be done quickly, heart pounding. At any moment, someone might come. Perhaps someone did come. Perhaps there were cheerful voices and the crunch of oyster shells scarcely heard above the crackle and boom of fireworks. The murderer heard because life depended upon hearing. If dark figures moved toward a car, the murderer slipped into deeper shadow, waited, perhaps dropped to the ground to avoid being seen in passing headlights. When silence returned, had there been a moment when the murderer considered returning to the terrace? Or had the departing car planted a seed? Would it help to take the Porsche, place it somewhere else, delay the discovery of Shell's body? Was there a desperate search for the keys or had the killer been savvy enough to think it through, her keys must be in her evening bag, the bag was on the floor of the passenger seat, it was only necessary to punch the push-button starter.

Thinking of bodies . . . "If she's dead, the murderer must be a man. How would a woman handle Shell's body, especially if she was killed outside the car?"

"Adrenaline. Shell wasn't big or heavy. I wouldn't count out a woman."

Annie was definite. "A woman couldn't carry a gun in an evening bag. A man could manage in a tuxedo."

Max looked at her curiously. "Why a gun?"

"Maggie talked about the gun in Dave's desk. A shot wouldn't be heard because of the fireworks."

Max drew a gun on the pad. "If Maggie shot her, she didn't have much time to drive the Porsche away before she was seen leaving in Dave's car. Or maybe Dave did the deed. We don't know where he was during the fireworks." Abruptly, Max reached in his pocket, pulled out his cell. "Vibrating." He looked. "Cute." He didn't sound amused.

Annie raised an eyebrow.

"Three texts in a row from Emma, Henny, and Ma. Same old, same old."

"WTB?" Annie asked.

171

"Right. But"—there was a considering expression on his face—
"we may surprise them with an answer one way or another pretty
soon. If Shell was murdered, I don't think someone came out of the
blue and just happened into the overflow lot and just happened to
murder her and just happened to drive her body away in the Porsche.
And we know who had reason to follow Shell into the lot and kill her."
Max pulled the pad close and sketched with quick, sure strokes. He
handed the pad to Annie.

She recognized each face with features and emotions exaggerated:
a thin-haired Maggie with staring eyes, Dave's heavy features set in
anger, Wesley's patrician good looks marred by a scowl, Vera's straight
gaze that revealed nothing and thereby revealed much, Jed's young
features stony but scared, puffy-cheeked Edward with shifting eyes.
"There wasn't much time. The Porsche had to leave the lot before
the fireworks were over and people started streaming out to get into
their cars."

Max stared at her. Suddenly his face was excited. "Annie, that
tells us everything. Now we know where to look."

Annie wished for a heady little dose of ESP. She had no idea what
Max meant. Then, abruptly, she did. He realized that those who had
reason to kill Shell were observed very soon after the end of the fireworks. If she died shortly after leaving the terrace at perhaps five
minutes after ten, there was less than twenty minutes for the murderer
to get rid of the car and return to the club. Once the car was left, the
murderer was on foot so the car couldn't be more than a few minutes
drive from the overflow lot.

"Almost all of them were seen after the fireworks ended. Edward's
the only one we don't know about." Annie pulled out her cell, called.
Eileen answered. There was an undercurrent of interest in her voice.
No doubt she enjoyed being a part of the ongoing drama about Shell

since, so far as she knew, it didn't affect her personally. "Eileen, Annie Darling." Though, of course, she knew. Cell phones made it easy to find anyone at any time, but caller ID revealed your identity. "Max and I are still sorting out where people were during the fireworks. Eileen, when you got home, did you and Edward talk about the dance or Shell? . . . Maybe you could ask him when he gets home . . . Yes, thanks." Annie clicked off the cell. "Eileen said he had an ice pack on his head and she brought him some milk with a Tylenol and they didn't talk about the dance at all. Now we know Edward was at their house when she walked home after the fireworks. That means he, too, only had a short time when he could have driven the Porsche—"

The front bell to Confidential Commissions sang. Purposeful steps sounded in the anteroom. Billy Cameron, big and imposing, stood in the open doorway.

"Hey, Billy—" Max broke off.

Billy's face was furrowed in a tight frown. He folded his arms, stood with his feet apart, like a man at the bow of a boat. "Heads up. Wesley Hurst's sworn out a complaint, accusing you and Annie of stalking, harassment, defamation of character, slander." Billy looked disgusted. "The mayor's all over it. The message to me is back off, stay off, leave it alone." He took a deep breath. "'Private citizens'"— it was clear he was quoting—"'have to respect the rights of others. There is no crime. There never was a crime.'" Billy pressed his lips together, then concluded heavily, "The safe thing for you two is to play ball. The last thing Wesley Hurst yelled as he went out the door was that he'd see you both in court and he hoped you went to jail. I'm pretty much stymied, but I've got people looking for the Porsche." He turned, strode briskly away. The front door bell signaled his departure.

Annie was puzzled. "Why didn't you tell him what we've figured out?"

"Because he would set wheels in motion, the mayor would hear about it, and Billy would probably be put on leave for complicity in harassment of that fine upstanding Broward's Rock rich guy Wesley Hurst. There's no point in making Billy go out on a limb until we have more than a theory." Max turned to his computer, clicked several times. He picked up a sheet of paper from the printer. "It may take us a while, but when we figure out the area that's within a few minutes drive from the overflow lot, surely we can find the car if it's out there. If we don't find it, we can almost be sure that Shell drove on her merry way, the Porsche's hidden in a forest somewhere, and she's having a ball thinking about Wesley trying to explain where she is. But if somebody killed her, there was very little time to get rid of the car and make it back to the club and be seen. Here's a map of the golf club and the surrounding area. We know we can pinpoint everyone during the fireworks and not too long after. That means, a murderer had maybe twenty minutes to kill Shell, move the Porsche, and show up again."

"It could be that Shell set it up to look like she'd gone missing, knowing talk would start." Annie kept her voice steady. "But if someone killed her, that would take at least a couple of minutes, maybe more. Then the body had to be placed in the passenger seat. That's another three minutes, maybe four." There was something hideous about figuring the time it took to quench a life, struggle with a corpse.

Max's eyes narrowed. "So the Porsche was driven somewhere and hidden is less than five minutes."

Annie never felt confident about math but she thought Max's estimate made sense.

"If Shell wasn't the driver, if she was dead, the murderer drove the car somewhere, left it, then had to walk, maybe run, back to the club or, in Edward's case, his house. There was very little time." Max came to his feet. "Come on, Annie."

Max turned into the overflow lot, stopped the Maserati midway between the entrance and the oyster-shell path to the terrace.

Annie looked around the overflow lot. At least there were a half-dozen cars now as afternoon drew on and the crowd at the pool increased. Would she ever see these spangles of silvery Spanish moss and palmetto shrubs and tall pines without wondering, Did she park there, between those two big pines, or there, near that camellia shrub? When Shell reached the Porsche, young, lithe, beautiful in a striking gown, was she on her way to leave the island with a lover? Or did death walk at her elbow?

Max looked at the map. "The Porsche went out of this lot, turned right. If the car had gone left, that took it through the front lot and one of the valets would have seen it. So, I figure the car had about six minutes to reach a destination and be hidden well enough that no one could find it." The Maserati purred onto the blacktop road. Max lowered the top, despite the heat, making it easier to look. "Watch for broken vines, anywhere that looks like a car went through."

Twice they angled off on rutted side roads, but the growth was impenetrable on both sides of the car and showed no evidence anyone had been into the brush. Max winced as spears of palmetto shrubs scraped along the side of the car. Both roads finally narrowed to paths, forcing him to back the car out to the blacktop.

The heat pressed against them. To her right through the pines, there were glimpses of the golf course. Of course, that land was manicured and even the rough afforded no sanctuary for a Porsche.

A yell of anguish indicated a shot gone wrong. Annie looked at the golf cart trail. "Max, stop!" She reached out, gripped his arm.

The car jolted to a stop.

Annie pointed. "There's where that boy said the colonel's MG got onto the course that night. Max, if someone wanted to get rid of the Porsche, it could be driven on a golf cart path."

Max stared at the path. "Quick. Call the pro shop." He was backing and turning the car. "Ask how deep the lagoon is at nine."

Annie got the pro shop. ". . . about fifteen feet, eighteen right in the middle."

"That's deep enough." She knew her excited comment puzzled the girl in the shop. "This is Annie Darling. Reserve a cart for me and my husband. We'll be there"—the car roared around a curve—"in about four minutes."

They made it in three, piled out of the car, and ran toward the rank of waiting carts. As they started off, a boy yelled, "Hey, that's the wrong way."

Max waved a hand. "An emergency." Twice Max eased the cart off the golf path to yield to carts heading toward the back nine. Several of the golfers knew him. A Korean vet and active pilot in the Confederate air force called out, "Looking like Wrong Way Corrigan, Darling." A humorless banker said acidly, "Reprehensible. It's one way that way," with a forceful gesture.

Max pushed the cart to its maximum twelve mph. When they reached the wooden bridge over the lagoon by the ninth green, Max stopped the cart on the bank.

A foursome approached the green. Red flags marked a swath in the center of the green where sod, not yet deemed playable, had been placed in the ruts left by the colonel's MG the night of July fourth. If a ball landed in the repaired area between the flags, a golfer could drop the ball without penalty.

A new railing, not yet painted, was near the center of the bridge. Their footsteps echoed on the wooden bridge. Max looked at the new railing, then pointed at the stone post. "There's a streak of yellow midway up. That's probably where the front fender of the MG hit. Damn clever to hide the first damage."

Annie stared at the murky brown water. If her conclusion was right, Shell's car careened onto the golf cart path, driven by someone who knew this course well, plunged through darkness to the bridge over the lagoon, then, carefully, a door open, one hand on the wheel, the car was guided over the edge of the span to plummet into the lagoon, taking with it the top railing. Somewhere in the depths, mucked into mud, the green Porsche, no longer elegant, was touched by wavering reeds.

That night either a laughing Shell exulted in leaving no trace of her departure or a desperate murderer fled into the night. Shell could have walked across the course, taken the keys to the MG, staged the cover-up on the bridge, then left in another car. Or the driver left death behind and ran across the course to grab the colonel's key from the valet stand. Fireworks burst above as the finale came nearer and nearer. There would have been a sweet sweep of relief when the MG wheeled onto the golf cart path. It wouldn't have taken long to trench the fairway between nine and ten, gouge turf from the green at nine, and finally, to end on the bridge, the MG crumpled against the post. Out of the car then and a last sprint into the darkness.

Max looked down at the muddy water. "There's one way to tell." He started to pull up his polo shirt.

Annie grabbed his arm. "If the car's down there, it can wait a few more minutes." She yanked her cell from her pocket. "Billy—"

Max frowned. "He's been warned off. Let me find out if there's anything there."

Annie gave him a look of sheer panic. "Go in that water? Are you out of your mind? Do you see that thing"—she pointed across the lagoon at a seven-foot alligator basking on the bank—"over there? That is not a toy. Contrary to what tourists think, that is not a dear adorable creature to be fed, especially not with your body." She looked around. The far side of the lagoon bordered private property. A well-kept lawn sloped up to a cream-colored two-story stucco home. "Over there. There's a canoe on the bank. We can borrow that." She was extraordinarily proud that she used the plural. To be on water in the proximity of a scaly beast was not in her job description, but she had no intention of letting Max go out on the water by himself. He was just idiot enough to think he could take a dive.

Max held the canoe steady while Annie climbed in the stern. He settled in the bow, picked up a paddle. Annie's nose wrinkled at the smell as they moved away from the reeds and into a patch of algae toward open water. "I hope it's not blue green algae."

Max spoke over his shoulder as he paddled smoothly into open water and headed toward the bridge. "Has anyone ever told you that you worry too much?" His voice was mild with an undercurrent of amusement.

"Blue green algae can make people really sick—" She broke off at the sound of low laughter. "Well," she said finally, "maybe."

The canoe glided to a stop next to the pillar nearest the newly restored railing. Max looked up. "The Porsche could have nosed almost straight down right there." He used the paddle to point. The muddy brown water was opaque. "I'll maneuver the canoe out a couple of feet. Bend over the side and put your paddle as far down in the water as you can."

Annie tilted as far as she could, holding tight to the side, while Max leaned the opposite direction, a countervailing weight. Annie knew only too well how easily canoes tipped . . . Blue green algae . . . She didn't look toward the opposite bank where she'd last seen the alligator sunning. If there was a ripple in the water and the alligator headed toward them, as well he might, this, after all, being his domain, she didn't want to know. She concentrated on her task, felt the oddly warm water on her hand, up to her wrist, reaching her forearm. She held the paddle firmly and poked down straight.

She lifted the paddle to avoid a drag as the canoe moved perhaps a foot or two at a time. Each time the canoe stopped, she eased the paddle down to its full extension. The bridge was about four feet behind them now. She didn't want to think about the contortions necessary for Max to lean and maneuver the canoe at the same time.

The downward thrust of her paddle abruptly stopped.

Annie loosened her grip on the side, held up a hand. "Keep us here." She lifted the paddle, again pushed down. When the tip met resistance, she raised the paddle, lowered it in a jabbing motion. There was no give, her hand jolted by the contact. "Whatever I hit, it's hard."

11

Four police cars and a forensic van lined up on the road. Billy Cameron and several officers watched from the bank. A blue tow truck was backed to the lagoon's edge with its flatbed upended and tow lines loose and ready to attach. Max stood talking to the driver.

"Hell might be cooler." Marian Kenyon shot a longing look across the lagoon at watchers in the shade of a towering live oak.

Annie agreed. Five o'clock on a July afternoon on the unshaded side of a steamy lagoon sent rivulets of sweat down her legs. She knew her face was as red and moist as Marian's.

Abruptly, Marian lifted the Leica that hung on a strap around her neck as a masked figure in a wet suit broke the surface of the lagoon. "Here he comes." *Click, click, click.* "Yeah, spray of water, nice. I can see the caption now: From the depths . . . Poor Lou. He must be even hotter than we are in that outfit."

Athletic Sgt. Lou Pirelli, who'd grown up as an island kid, was at home in any kind of water anytime, anywhere. He trod water, shouted. "There's a car. I can hook up the lines." He stroked to the bank, maneuvered through the reeds.

Annie hoped he was wearing rubber swim slippers to protect his feet from sometimes razor-sharp reeds and broken mussel shells. He was too good a swimmer to need flippers in an area of water as small as a lagoon.

The tow truck driver relayed the lines to Lou. He swam out, disappeared into the depth, resurfaced, once, twice. When he bobbed to the surface the third time, he stroked quickly to the bank. "Ready."

Max moved away from the tow truck, joined Annie and Marian.

Marian was oblivious now to the heat, the Leica aimed and ready as the winch moved the cables and the muddy water swirled. As a car roof lifted above the surface and Marian snapped one shot after another, an old black coupe jolted to a stop next to the tow truck. Doc Burford, his white shirt wrinkled and his brown trousers shabby with one droopy cuff, climbed out to stand and stare at the water, face heavy, arms folded.

After one last click as the cables pulled the muddy car up onto the hoisted flatbed, Marian scrabbled for her notebook, flipped the pages, then eased up to fluttering Do Not Cross tape for a look at the back of the rescued car. She came back to Annie and Max, waved her notebook. "License matches. Not that there are likely to be many Porsches gigged from a lagoon, but this is Shell Hurst's car. And Billy must think there could be foul play or Doc Burford wouldn't be here."

Water streamed from the Porsche, likely draining from the engine and the trunk.

Marian stood on tiptoe, squinting. "I can't see through the windows."

Despite the heat, Annie felt cold. They had found Shell's car.

Where was Shell? Annie tried to picture Shell dancing the night away on the deck of a yacht moored in Rio.

Billy Cameron stood to one side of the tow truck, talking to Lou Pirelli, who also streamed water. Lagoon muck scummed his wet suit from the knees down. In a moment, Lou nodded. He waited until Mavis Cameron hurried to him with a pair of latex gloves. He slipped them on. She handed him a foot-long length of leather cord.

A grinding sound marked the slow descent of the flatbed. When the flatbed was horizontal, Lou scrambled up one side. He approached the front window of the driver's seat, bent forward to peer inside. With a shake of his head, he looped the leather cord around the door handle, moved to one side, pulled. Water spewed from the interior.

Using all his strength, Lou prevented the door from swinging wide. A stream gushed through the six-inch passage, murky green water and a bloated blue gray hand with no nails on the tips of swollen fingers.

The door to the break room opened.

Hyla Harrison stepped inside. She held up several sheets of paper. "Your statements. After you check them over and sign, Billy wants to see you." She placed stapled sheets in front of both Annie and Max. "Some iced tea?" Hyla's face was uncommonly pale, emphasizing a sprinkling of freckles across her nose.

Annie was thirsty, but the police station break room's vending machine carried canned tea, which ranked only a tad better than roach poison in Annie's view. "Maybe a Coke." At least cans were a natural habitat for soft drinks.

"Pepsi?"

At their nod, Hyla brought each of them a chilled can, pulled out a chair at the end of the table, and sat down, her posture straight.

Annie felt disheveled from the long hours at the lagoon. She and Max both looked sweaty and wrinkled. His seersucker shirt had some dried brown splotches from the splash of lagoon water. When they'd rowed back to the bank, she'd stepped in mud up to one ankle, and that light blue canvas espadrille would never be the same. Tonight she'd have to dig out the calamine for both of them. Her cheeks were hot and Max's face was much too red. Usually they were equipped with hats and sunscreen, but this afternoon's vigil hadn't been planned.

Thoughts skittered like confetti, her defense against images that would be seared in her memory for a long time, though Max had tried to shield her from the moment that the swollen, foul-smelling mass that had been Shell's body was removed from the mud-stained Porsche after Doc Burford officially pronounced that life had ceased to exist.

To fight the queasy unease in her stomach, Annie flipped the tab, took a long drink of the Pepsi, welcomed the quick uptick from sugar. It took only a moment to check the statement. Hyla was good and careful and she'd transcribed the recordings accurately.

Annie signed with a feeling of relief. As soon as she and Max spoke with Billy, they would be free to go and they could leave behind them the uncertainties that had driven them since Hayley Hurst enlisted Max's help to find Shell.

As soon as Max signed and dated, Hyla was on her feet. She took the statements, held the door for them. They followed her down the beige-walled hall to Billy's office. Annie knew that Hyla recognized they could find the office on their own, but that wasn't proper protocol. She was an officer discharging her duty.

Hyla tapped on the door, opened it. "Mr. and Mrs. Darling are available, sir."

Billy's answer was grave. "Thank you, Officer. Please show them in."

They settled in the wooden straight chairs opposite his yellow oak desk. Through the window on the Sound, the sunset blazed vivid orange. Lights sparkled on boats heading toward the harbor. Black skimmers flapped inches above the darkening water on their search for menhaden.

Billy gestured at two brown bags sitting on the edge of his desk. "Figured you guys were hungry. Cheeseburger with chili for Annie." He pointed at a sack with an *A* on it. "Fried flounder on an onion bun for you, Max."

Annie spread a couple of napkins on her lap and ate, surprised at her hunger, as Billy tapped a sheaf of papers and talked. "Good stuff in your statements." He glanced at Max. "I get the picture that Edward Irwin was afraid Shell Hurst planned to publicly expose him at the dance. That didn't happen, but she may have told him she'd contact the police the next day. That certainly would have given him a motive to silence her." Billy's broad face folded in thought. "From what Edward said about the phone call, she probably gigged the others ahead of time, too. We have her cell calls that day. She talked to Wesley. If she threatened to announce at the dance that he was running around on her with Vera, you can bet Wesley told Vera. Or Shell may have told him to go whistle for a divorce; she wasn't going to play."

Annie licked a smear of mustard from one finger. "Vera told Wesley he had to deal with her 'tonight.' That put Wesley right in the middle, Vera demanding that he do something to shut Shell up and arrange for a divorce, Shell laughing and refusing to agree."

Billy made a couple of notes. "One of them—or both of them together—could have decided the only answer was murder." He shook his head. "Shell intended to cause as much misery as possible at the dance. We know she talked to Dave Peterson. It looks like he planned to split from his wife, run away with Shell, but we didn't find a suitcase in the trunk of the Porsche and she and Dave had a dustup at the dance. What's your take on Dave's reaction if she blew him off?"

Max spoke quickly. "You don't make it as a big-time highway contractor unless you're one tough dude."

Annie remembered Dave's flushed face when she confronted him about the gun Maggie said was in his desk drawer at home. "He wouldn't like being played for a fool. Billy, can you find out if there's a gun missing from Dave's desk at home?" She paused. "Do you know yet how Shell was killed?" She didn't want to ask about the bloated mass that had to be explored.

"Not a gun."

Annie felt a welling of relief. Now she didn't have to picture Maggie with a gun, slipping through the summer night in pursuit of Shell.

Billy wasn't forthcoming. "The cause of death isn't being publicly released." His face creased. "I got hold of the sister. Damn tough to tell someone that kind of news over the phone. I told her we'd do our best to find out what happened. We told her what we knew, but for now we're keeping forensic facts under wraps."

Annie understood. They weren't family. Billy was comfortable discussing with them only information they had provided. He wasn't sharing details of his investigation.

As if to underscore that intention, he turned another page. "From your statements, we know the following persons were present at some point on the terrace during the fireworks: Edward and Eileen Irwin, Wesley and Vera Hurst, Jed Hurst. We know Maggie and Dave Peterson were at the club. We need to find out where Dave went when he left Shell on the dance floor and why Maggie Peterson left the club in Dave's car, alone and apparently in a hell of a hurry."

Billy straightened the sheets. "I think that takes care of everything." He gave them an approving look. "Good work finding the Porsche."

Max didn't take a victory lap. "I should have tumbled to the location of the car a lot earlier. The connection between the smashed railing of the bridge over the lagoon at nine and the missing Porsche seems obvious now. The murderer knew the layout of the golf course, knew the lagoon was fourteen or fifteen feet deep with plenty of room to hide a car. Shell's body was dumped in the passenger seat, the Porsche driven along the back road to the golf cart path, up the path with lights off to the bridge over the lagoon. The next part was tricky. I'd guess the car was stopped right by the railing, angled to go in, then started. The murderer jumped out and slammed the door as the car moved forward. The car took out a post and part of a railing. The car sank out of sight, but it would have been pretty obvious what had happened and there would have been a search of the lagoon Thursday morning. The next part's brilliant. The murderer hiked back across the course, slipped around to the front of the club, snagged the colonel's car keys from the valet stand, drove out the back way to the golf cart path, trenched the greens on nine and ten, and ended up on the bridge. This time the car was butted against the broken post. That explained the damage to the bridge. Some vandal messed up some holes, then lost control on the lagoon bridge. Nobody was going to look in the water when there was a ready-made reason for destruction sitting there. I should have known from the first that there were too many out-of-the-ordinary deviations from normal that night, the theft of the MG, Wesley Hurst making a scene at valet parking, Maggie

Peterson whipping out of the lot in Dave's car. My guess is that all three are tied up with Shell's murder."

Billy stood. "I'll check everything out."

Annie gathered up the trash from their hamburgers, tossed the sacks in Billy's wastebasket. "Have you talked to the mayor?"

Billy's big face remained stolid, but there was a glint of satisfaction in his blue eyes. "I reported the discovery of the car and body to His Honor. I told him a homicide investigation was under way and I would keep him informed." A slight pause. "I was concerned about his health for a moment. Some strangling noises, but I assume he choked on a piece of cake. Or something."

Dorothy L jumped up onto the kitchen table, her white fur gleaming in a bright swath of sunlight.

Before Annie could shoo her down, Max intervened. "We've finished breakfast. Look, she's not going to bother anything."

As if to proclaim innocent intent, Dorothy L settled at the end of the table and regarded them with shining blue eyes.

Max ended with a hearty, "Good girl."

Annie knew when the stars were aligned against her. She wasn't altogether sure if the choice had to be made whether Max would first rescue her or Dorothy L from peril on the high seas or a dank dungeon. Some questions were better left unasked. And, fair was fair. When she and Agatha were alone at the store, Agatha delighted in sprawling on her back atop the coffee counter, four paws elevated. It was not a graceful pose, but, to Annie, utterly endearing.

She smiled at Max, who was endearing in another fashion entirely. He also sat in the sunlight, relaxed in a T-shirt and boxers, blond hair tousled from sleep, blond bristle on his face very sexy. He refilled their mugs from the carafe on the table, looked hugely satisfied as he pushed his iPhone toward her. "That should stir up the Intrepid Trio."

Annie read the three identical text messages he'd sent: *WTB? ITL.* Snap, crackle, pop, three responses arrived in order:

From Emma: *Cute. What's ITL?*

From Henny: *ITL? Elucidate.*

From Laurel: *ITL? A union?*

Max looked even more satisfied as he tapped: *In the lagoon. Where else?*

Three further responses.

From Emma: *Should have realized. Marigold would have figured it out sooner.*

From Henny: *Skype alert.*

From Laurel: *I2IRequr.*

Annie raised an eyebrow. "What the heck does your mom mean?"

Max deciphered. "Eye to eye required."

"Tell them we aren't dressed."

Max tapped. Then laughed. "Mom says dishabille is never an excuse."

Annie was intrigued. "Excuse for what?" she murmured, but Max was already fetching the laptop. Armed with coffee mugs, they settled on a sofa in the den with Dorothy L snuggled between them.

In a moment, thanks to the webcam, they viewed the magnificent saloon aboard *Marigold's Pleasure*, mahogany decor, soft leather settees, and cane furniture, and knew they were equally visible. Emma's seersucker blue caftan was the same shade as her spiky hair and inquiring eyes. Henny sported a red-and-white-striped blouse, red slacks, and red dock shoes. Laurel was elegant in a soft yellow blouse and white slacks and yellow espadrilles.

Laurel beamed at them. "If everyone saw others in their night-clothes, the world would surely be a better place."

Annie tugged a bit on the hem of her shorty nightgown. Was Laurel saying that an unaffected appearance in intimate garb was the solution to world peace? Possibly. She pictured the president and secretary of state in dishabille. It would alter perceptions.

She yanked her mind back to *Marigold's Pleasure.*

Henny frowned. "It's too bad Billy can't look further into Richard Ely's death. I know it was stormy that night but you'd think someone might have observed him out on the pier."

Max shook his head. "Lots of lightning. I doubt if there were any casual strollers on the boardwalk."

Emma was disdainful. "The mayor's obtuseness reminds me of Inspector Houlihan at his worst. Obviously only something of great importance drew Ely out on the pier under those circumstances. However, there are other avenues to explore." She waggled a cushion with four squares within a square. On a diagonal, the squares were yellow one way and black the other.

In the saloon, each occasional cushion represented a maritime flag. Emma, always majestic, sat on the central settee.

"L," Max interpreted. "The signal means: *You should stop. I have something important to communicate.*"

Annie forced herself to maintain a look of bright interest. How like Emma to use a maritime signal to increase the drama. Emma, of course, believed her every thought to be important. What could she know on a yacht moving steadily northward?

Emma cleared her throat, signaling that her inferiors should listen up. "It is no doubt unfortunate that sometimes in the throes of creativity, I lose sight of the world beyond the page. Mea culpa." Her deep voice dove down like a hound's bay. "I regret that once drawn into Marigold's struggles with that exceedingly tiresome Inspector Houlihan—"

Annie kept a straight face. Barely. Emma was a victim of her own success. She'd created the hapless inspector as a foil for Marigold and readers loved him, which necessitated his appearance in many scenes. Unfortunately Emma found it increasingly difficult to be original. Just how many different ways could the inspector hinder Marigold?

"—I lost sight of other matters. I realized this morning when we received Max's report—"

Annie's eyes narrowed. The missive had been a joint effort. Was she an afterthought?

"—that I failed to communicate a fact that may be of great importance."

There was respectful silence. Henny turned her thin, intelligent face toward Emma, her gaze attentive. Laurel gave a soft sigh, clasped her hands together in anticipation.

The pause continued.

Frosty blue eyes turned toward the undoubtedly informal tableau of Annie and Max in their jammies.

Max stroked Dorothy L. "Emma, you always amaze." His tone was light.

The demanding gaze moved to Annie.

Annie's voice quivered as she suppressed a giggle. Emma assumed Max was laudatory and in fact Annie knew he was simply stating the awful truth that Emma's self-regard was quite simply amazing. However, Annie hastened to join the chorus. "Taking time from Marigold and the inspector is splendid of you, Emma. Splendid." Annie decided it was fun to talk like a John Buchan character even if she was indulging the old battleaxe's lust for attention.

Satisfied, confident she was center stage, Emma announced grandly, "To avoid the congestion, I took the back exit from the club on the night of the Fourth. As you know, the road is bordered on one side by the golf course, on the other by thick woods. I saw a man, walking fast. He wasn't strolling. Had I described him in a scene, I would have said"—her voice dropped—"'In the headlights a burly man strode through the night, head poked forward, shoulders hunched, a man in a hurry.'" A pause. "Or something like that."

"Powerful," Laurel breathed.

Henny's dimple showed briefly and then she was appropriately grave. "Riveting."

Emma nodded, accepting her due. "As I came nearer, I slowed. He glanced around and I recognized Dave Peterson. I saw him fully in the headlights. His face was flushed. He was clearly in the grips of great emotion." Now she was crisp and succinct. "The time was nine minutes after eleven. The fireworks ended at ten forty-four. I stopped and asked if he'd had car trouble. He slowly approached my car. I don't think I exaggerate when I say he looked like a man who had suffered some kind of mental trauma. Finally he took a deep breath and said that there had been a mix-up with the car, that Maggie had left before him. I thought that was quite interesting but you don't ask a man if he and his wife have just had a quarrel. I said something about sometimes we all get mixed up about things and I'd be happy to give him a ride. He blurted out no, then realized his response was rude. He gave a kind of odd laugh and said he'd spent too much time inside, he was ready for a walk, but thanks, anyway. He turned and walked away. I drove past him."

Max gave Emma a thumbs-up. "Your testimony may be very important. The killer drove the Porsche from the overflow parking lot onto the back road and took the golf cart path to the lagoon. Then he—or she—ran to the front of the club, took the MG keys from the valet board, drove the MG out the back way, and followed the same route to the lagoon. If Dave smashed the MG into the bridge post, he would have reached about that point on the back road when you saw him. Send Billy an e-mail."

Annie looked thoughtful. "I wonder if Maggie hunted for Dave before she left."

Laurel was sympathetic. "They said she was driving fast and obviously upset. She may have known that he was intending to leave with Shell. Or"—a blond brow arched—"perhaps she knew he wasn't leaving with Shell."

Annie blinked. As often happened, Laurel's comments contained more substance than might seem apparent at first. There were several layers here. Maggie knew Dave was leaving with Shell, and Maggie killed Shell out of jealousy. Or Maggie knew he was leaving with Shell so Maggie fled the club alone in his car. Or Maggie knew he wasn't leaving with Shell and hurried from the club to try to find him because she was afraid what might happen if Dave confronted Shell. Or Maggie knew he wasn't leaving with Shell because Dave had killed her.

Henny said quietly, "That would explain why Maggie left in his car. She may have suspected Dave was desperately trying to hide evidence of murder."

Emma nodded in agreement, her spiky blue hair quivering. "However, we shouldn't forget that Maggie told Shell there was a gun in Dave's desk."

Annie remembered Maggie's distraught appearance. "It may not have been a threat to Shell. She may have thought of using the gun on herself."

Emma shot the question. "What basis do you have for that assumption?"

Annie felt a moment of confusion. "Because Dave was upset when I told him about that conversation. He rushed out of his office. I think he was afraid about Maggie."

Emma raised a sardonic eyebrow. "I'd suggest Dave has given very little thought for Maggie's well-being. Instead"—she pressed stubby fingers against each temple, a signal of creativity arising—"let us delve into the mind of a murderer. You come to his office, ask about Maggie speaking of the gun in his desk, thereby revealing you are aware that Maggie was distraught over his involvement with Shell. If he murdered Shell, he instantly realizes this is an opportunity to act in a manner that will deflect suspicion from him. He hurries out, giving the appearance of a man concerned that his wife might have taken his gun and possibly committed a crime. The deduction would be that, of course, he could not have committed the crime."

Annie continued to appear interested though she considered Emma's suggestion just this side of preposterous. Her interpretation was both too generous and not generous enough to Dave Peterson. Dave was a swaggering, bluff, hearty engineer with all the subtlety of a rampaging bull moose. He was also a man who had evidenced kindness and care when his wife was ill and had surely, perhaps still, loved her very much. That he had succumbed to Shell's sex and beauty didn't mean that he cared nothing for Maggie. The other faces watching Emma were equally bland.

Laurel broke a rather strained silence as Emma scowled, correctly sensing a lack of acceptance. "You have marvelous insight, Emma, discerning motives where others might be led astray by surface observations. It does rather seem to me"—a diffident smile—"that we should focus our energies on one basic question." Laurel beamed at each of them in turn. "Toy soldiers." Her tone was assured.

Annie shot a worried glance at Max. Had Laurel finally slipped the bounds of reality? Laurel's mind often appeared to hover in a world of her own imagining. Toy soldiers?

Laurel's smile was chiding. "My dears, everything depends upon location. And"—a nod of her golden locks toward Annie—"since Annie introduced me to the amazing wonders of mysteries and mystery writing, I follow the lead of the masters." A flutter of impossibly long eyelashes. "In this instance, America's revered Mistress of Mystery, Mary Roberts Rinehart. You will recall in her autobiography, *My Story*, how when writing a play, she used her sons' toy soldiers to play the characters on the stage. We—and dear Billy—cannot determine who could have committed the crime until we know the location of each person during the critical period."

Max applauded. "Ma, you put your finger on it. We know Shell left the terrace midway during the fireworks."

Emma was didactic. "The fireworks began at nine forty-five, ended at ten forty-four. Therefore, Shell walked toward the overflow lot at approximately ten fifteen."

Laurel murmured, "It isn't a long distance. Perhaps two minutes, three at the most to reach her car. I think we can assume she was dead five minutes after she left the terrace. Otherwise, she would simply have slipped into her Porsche and driven away. She didn't. That puts the time of her death at ten twenty." She turned her limpid gaze toward Annie and Max. "Determine the location of those involved at ten twenty."

"Good advice. But"—Henny looked at Annie, then at Max—"even if you delete some names, several will have had opportunity.

What matters is motive. Wesley Hurst wanted his freedom and he must have been humiliated by Shell's affair with Dave. Vera Hurst very likely hated the woman who had taken her husband, and Shell's refusal to agree to a divorce would have added to her fury. Jed Hurst made some kind of threat to his sister about Shell on the day she died. Maggie Peterson was about to lose her husband and, whether he went or stayed, he had been unfaithful with Shell. Dave Peterson has a quick temper and Shell apparently blew him off that night. Edward Irwin faced not only embarrassment to be revealed as a blackmailer but possibly prosecution and prison. Eileen is a very proud woman. How would she respond to people sniggering about Edward and his surveillance with an iPhone? She saw Shell leave the terrace. Eileen could have slipped into the shadows and followed her."

Annie absently stroked Dorothy L, loved the feel of her warmth and soft fur. "Eileen's obsessed with her missing shawl. She doesn't have a clue about Edward trying blackmail."

Henny was thoughtful. "Eileen is very attuned to those around her. Not much escapes her notice. I would be amazed if she didn't know everything there is to know about Edward. At the same time, I wouldn't underestimate the danger Shell took in provoking Edward. Sometimes a weak personality can be the most vicious."

Laurel's smile was dreamy. "Everything comes down to people. Wesley Hurst is a rich man, spoiled, accustomed to having his way. Vera Hurst has an iron will. Jed Hurst is young and sometimes the young don't count the cost of their actions. Maggie Peterson is a passionate woman who had everything to lose. Dave Peterson is tough, not a good man to anger. Edward Irwin faced the specter of prison, which would terrify him. Eileen Irwin is proud and formidable."

Max looked fondly at his mother. "Good analysis, Ma. Billy will be interested in hearing from you three. He already knows everything we know. The best news is that he's in charge and we can leave the investigation to him." He grinned. "Bon voyage, ladies. Annie and I are planning on a happy weekend here at home." With a click, he turned off Skype, gave an admiring look at a long length of shapely leg. "As for you, Mrs. Darling . . ."

12

The newspaper sheets rustled. "Oh my."

Max was stretched out on an orange-and-green-striped beach towel. His drowsy voice murmured, "Can't stop there."

"Lots of innuendo. Marian does that really well." Sunday afternoon at the beach was their summer tradition, unfurled blue-and-white-striped umbrella punched deep in the sand, two low-slung beach chairs, a cooler, coconut oil sunscreen, and the Sunday *Gazette* to share. Today was a bit different because they both sported preventive patches of zinc oxide on sun-reddened faces. Annie was wearing a big-brimmed raffia-straw hat in addition to sunglasses. She rattled the paper. "Lead story, of course."

"Why the 'oh my'?"

"Listen to this: 'Chief Cameron declined to say whether there is a "person of interest." However, the chief explained that the dead woman had been observed in a series of confrontations at the Lucky

Lady dance at the country club the evening of her death. Anyone with knowledge of Mrs. Hurst's encounters with persons present at the country club is requested to contact the police. The chief emphasized that the investigation is also interested in information about Mrs. Hurst between the beginning of the fireworks and perhaps halfway through the show. Chief Cameron went on to say there is some confusion about the approximate time of Mrs. Hurst's murder and he has been unable to speak with Mr. Hurst about his claim that he received a call from Mrs. Hurst several days after July fourth, which has now been determined to be the night Mrs. Shell Hurst died. The chief said he is sure the matter will be resolved. However, Chief Cameron admitted that the autopsy is consistent with death occurring sometime the evening of July fourth because of the state of digestion of stomach contents. As to cause of death, Chief Cameron revealed that Mrs. Hurst died of asphyxiation but he declined to suggest the manner in which the death occurred other than to say she was definitely a victim of foul play.'"

Max rolled to one side and propped up on an elbow. A ball cap shadowed his face, emphasizing splotches of zinc oxide. "Asphyxiation. As in strangling or did somebody hold something over her face?"

Annie turned the page. "Chief Cameron said reports have been received that Mrs. Hurst and a lover held several trysts at a local hotel." She looked up. "I'll bet Billy starts getting calls about Shell and Dave at the Sea Side Inn." She began to read again. "'Chief Cameron revealed Mrs. Hurst's cell phone records included several calls made on July fourth that police will be investigating. The chief said that Mrs. Hurst's credit card was last used on July third.'" Annie closed the paper. "That pretty well knocks down Wesley's claim of a phone call several days later."

Max fished a Bud Light from the cooler. "Billy's putting pressure on Wesley. That was the point of every word of that interview. Tomorrow he may name Wesley as a 'person of interest.'"

Annie knelt to shelve four copies of Denise Swanson's *Little Shop of Homicide*, the first in a clever new series set in a five-and-dime store. She reached to a higher shelf to straighten the Mary Stewart titles. Which was her favorite? She adored the opening line in *My Brother Michael*: *Nothing ever happens to me.* The reader felt a quick electric jolt and enjoyed the sure knowledge that a lot was going to happen.

If Death on Demand enjoyed a slow day, Annie could slip away home to the hammock in their gazebo and reread *My Brother Michael*. Her hand hesitated at the long line of Stewart's reissued suspense novels. Maybe she'd choose *Madam, Will You Talk?*

The front bell sounded. Hurried steps sounded in the central corridor. Eileen Irwin jolted to a stop beside her. Eileen's face was pale, her white blond hair straggly, evidence of a cursory brushing. She had dressed too quickly, a lime green blouse that looked odd with tan slacks. She called out, her voice shaky. "Thank God you're here. You know something about the police and I can't get anything out of that redheaded policewoman. 'Yes, ma'am, no, ma'am, I'm sure I can't say, ma'am.' And it's sickening." Her blue eyes held a look of horror.

Ingrid was a few paces behind Eileen. She watched anxiously. "Can I help?"

Eileen ignored Ingrid, spoke to Annie. "She wouldn't tell me what happened. They just sent a car for me, took me to the police station, to a room with tables and shelves and cabinets. She brought out a metal tray—" Eileen shuddered.

Annie glanced at Ingrid, nodded toward the coffee bar.

Ingrid slipped around her, moved swiftly down the central corridor.

Annie gently touched Eileen's arm, found it rigid. "Come sit down, Eileen. You've had a shock. Ingrid will bring us some coffee."

Eileen followed her as obediently as a child, dropped into a chair at the nearest table.

"What was in the tray?"

A light tic jerked Eileen's left eye. "My shawl." Her voice wobbled. "You know it's made of silk and silk discolors so easily. I wouldn't have known what it was, it was so dirty and stained, but I could make out the dragon even though the red was almost gone. After I identified it, the policewoman nodded and turned to take the tray away. I asked her where it was found, why it looked so awful. She didn't really answer, just said it was a material piece of evidence in a crime and"—Eileen's tone was almost a wail—"that's all she'd tell me. Then she wanted to know exactly when I last saw the shawl and where and who could have taken it. Anybody at the dance could have taken it or one of the staff. I left it on my chair when we went out for the fireworks. If someone took it, what did they do with it? But everyone knows about Shell and that car in the lagoon. My shawl looked like it had been in that nasty water and dried out. Annie, what does it mean?"

Ingrid brought mugs of coffee, placed them on the table, then circumspectly walked toward the front of the store.

Annie was afraid she knew only too well why the wrinkled, stained shawl was in an evidence bin. In the *Gazette* story, Shell's death was attributed to asphyxiation. If the shawl was material evidence in the commission of a crime . . .

Eileen reached out, gripped Annie's arm. "You know something. Tell me."

"I don't know anything for a fact, but Shell died from a lack of air. Did you see the story in the *Gazette*?"

"I read the story." Eileen was impatient. "It didn't say anything about a shawl."

"The police revealed that Shell died from asphyxiation. She could have been suffocated. Or strangled." Annie spoke quietly. "Someone could have rolled up the shawl into a sort of cord and used it to strangle her."

Eileen stared at her in disbelief. "My shawl?" Her voice was almost a whimper.

Annie spoke quickly. "I could be wrong, but If the police are holding the shawl as evidence, that means the shawl is connected to the crime."

Eileen eyes looked huge in an even paler face. "If she was killed by my shawl, someone took it from my chair in the dance room." Eileen lifted a trembling hand. "That's dreadful."

Annie's thoughts had already moved past the shawl and its condition. She pictured the dimness on the periphery of the dance floor and a swift figure stopping just long enough to snatch up the shawl. "Premeditated."

Eileen frowned. "What do you mean?"

"You left the shawl inside, right?"

Eileen nodded. "On the back of my chair. It was too hot on the terrace for a shawl."

Annie didn't know who had picked up the shawl, but there must have already been a thought of murder. The shawl grabbed, perhaps folded into a small square that could be slipped inside a tuxedo jacket or held between a woman's arm and side, hidden from view on the dark terrace with the only light from occasional torchieres. Had an angry, vengeful person seen the shawl, picked it up, and followed Shell onto the terrace, standing in the shadows, waiting and watching until she started for the overflow lot? A murderer stalking prey could easily have skirted the shadowed edge of the terrace, slipped into the woods, and kept pace with the woman on the path walking to her death.

"When I went inside"—Eileen's voice was faint—"after the fireworks, I looked everywhere. I wasn't nice about it. I thought one of the waitstaff had stolen my shawl. Instead, someone took it and . . ." She closed her eyes as if to shut out pictures of struggle and terror.

13

Max tried to decide which was his favorite quote about golf. High on the list was Phyllis Diller's *The reason the golf pro tells you to keep your head down is so you won't see him laughing.* Or maybe Peter Dobereiner's *Half of golf is fun, the other half is putting.* Putting . . . He tried to erase a memory of a six-putt debacle on Hole Four. He stood by the indoor golf green, waggled the club. All right. Knees bent . . .

The bell sang. Footsteps clattered. He turned and had an instant of déjà vu as Hayley Hurst burst into his office. Her face was mottled from crying. She reached his desk, glared at him as he stood. "It's all your fault. You found that car and now they've taken Jed away. Jed wouldn't hurt anybody. Sure, he was mad at Shell, but to hurt someone . . ." She shook her head violently, like a dog plunging out of surf, her tight blond curls quivering. "Dad and Mom are at the police station but they wouldn't let me come. You've got to do something." With that she burst into tears.

"Hey, kid." Dismayed, he hurried to his golf bag and pulled out a towel. He stepped closer, held it out to her. "Hey, wipe your face. Come on, take some deep breaths." He pulled up a webbed chair for her.

Hayley sank into the chair, scrubbed her face, stared at him woefully. "The police found Jed's fingerprints on the steering wheel of Shell's car. They were the last prints on there. Hers were underneath." Tears welled again. "They're saying he drove the Porsche and sank it in the lagoon, then took the colonel's MG and wrecked it on the bridge. Somebody"—she gulped—"wiped off the MG's steering wheel, but they found one of Jed's prints on the inside of the driver's door."

Max leaned against the edge of his desk. "Had Jed ever been in the colonel's car?"

Her lips quivered. Her silence was a sad answer. "He may"—she struggled to get out the words—"have driven the Porsche. He didn't kill Shell. He wouldn't. He never, never would." She looked up at Max with reddened eyes, her face drooping with misery. "You'll help us, won't you? You figure things out. I can get money. Mom will pay, I know she will."

"The police—"

"They've got Jed. He's in jail. They say he stole the MG and destroyed property and he ob-ob-ob—something justice."

"Obstruction of justice." Max was grave. Billy had plenty of grounds to make the charges, hold Jed as a juvenile, while the investigation continued. There could, likely would, be later charges. Murder.

"They're saying Jed strangled Shell. It's so awful. Like he could do something like that. But they've made up their minds. They won't hunt for anyone else."

Max wished he could wipe away the fear in her eyes, knew she felt empty and scared and desperate. Billy Cameron was a good man. He followed evidence. "The chief doesn't make mistakes about fingerprints. If Jed's prints were on top of Shell's, he was the last person to drive the car." He knew every word he spoke was like a blow. "Shell's body was in the car. That has to mean—"

"He didn't kill her. He didn't!" She jumped up and rushed from his office.

When she saw the familiar number on caller ID, Annie automatically computed the time difference between the Lowcountry and the Hawaiian resort where Rachel and the family were staying on their vacation. It was the middle of the night there, but obviously the heartbreak and trouble on Broward's Rock had reached Rachel.

The connection was amazingly clear, not a crackle or a hiss. Annie would have needed an almanac to figure the distance between Broward's Rock and Poipu Beach on Kauai, but it was a long darn way.

". . . Jed never, never, never in a million years would hurt anybody." Rachel's voice quivered with distress.

Annie jerked her mind away from images of a once elegant silk shawl now crumpled and stained and resting in a gallon-sized plastic bag in the evidence bin at the Broward's Rock Police Station. "I hope you're right."

"I know I'm right. Hayley texted me they're saying Jed drove that car into the lagoon—"

Annie heard the shock and fear in her voice.

"—and I told her I'd call you. You and Max can help him. I know you can. You can figure out what happened. Please, Annie. Promise me you'll help."

◆ ◆ ◆

Max wiggled his way through a clutch of waiting customers to the Death on Demand cash desk. "Annie?"

Ingrid finished ringing up a sale, jerked a thumb toward the back. "Storeroom. Rachel called her from Kauai. She's threatening to come home early if you and Annie don't do something about some boy."

At the other register, Pamela Potts paused in her description of the Alan Bradley series. ". . . this girl is the most original detective ever . . . Max, Annie's upset. A call from Rachel. Some boy's in big trouble."

He edged his way through readers clotted near the bookcases. At the storeroom, he tapped on the door.

The panel opened in a jerk, but Annie's frown at the interruption was replaced with a sigh of relief. "Rachel called—"

"Pamela told me. Hayley just left my office. She's frantic." Max knew his description of the shaken girl with reddened eyes was inadequate. "She swears Jed couldn't hurt anyone."

"Rachel's terribly upset, too. She cares about this boy. Rachel said you and I can find out the truth. We have to do something." She looked down at the worktable, which was covered with brown wrapping paper taped to the edges. "I'm trying to place everybody at the club that night when Shell started for the overflow lot. Maybe it will help figure out what happened."

Max wished he could be persuaded that someone else was guilty. "The facts are bad. The police said Jed was the last person to drive the car. They found Jed's fingerprints on top of Shell's."

Annie was skeptical. "The car was in the lagoon for more than a week. How could they find prints?"

Max made an effort to keep his expression unchanged even

though he felt a wrench deep inside. He had learned more than he ever wanted to know about fingerprints when he was suspected in the murder of a voluptuous beauty killed by a tire tool from the trunk of his car. He spoke in a level tone. "Fingerprints can survive a lot, including water. Especially if there's no current. There wouldn't be a current in the lagoon. The water is still." Still as death. "If the police told the Hursts that Jed's prints are on top of Shell's, that's a fact."

Again that inward lurch. His fingerprints had been on the tire tool and he had been innocent. Was Jed sitting in jail now, scared and innocent, waiting for the DA to certify him as an adult to be charged with homicide? But, Max felt like he slammed up against a wall, Jed got rid of the body. Why would he dispose of his stepmother's body if he was innocent?

"Lagoon water . . ." Annie shivered. "Eileen Irwin was here a few minutes ago. Hyla took her to the station and brought out an evidence bin. Eileen said they had her shawl and it was all crumpled and stained, like it had been wet. They must have found the shawl in the Porsche. Since they have the shawl as evidence, I told Eileen I think that means someone used the shawl to strangle Shell. Otherwise, there wouldn't be any point in having Eileen come in. The shawl wouldn't matter."

"The shawl as a rope, a garrote?" Max concentrated, then said abruptly, "Wait a minute."

Annie started to speak, but he held up his hand. He yanked out his cell, called. He spoke fast. "Mavis, Max Darling. Can I talk to Billy?" He held, then talked fast. "Billy, was Eileen Irwin's shawl used to strangle Shell? . . . I understand that you haven't released that information. Billy, give me a break. If the shawl was the murder weapon, I think it clears Jed . . . Right. I understand about the prints. But the shawl may make a difference . . . Thanks, Billy." He clicked off.

Max felt his face break into a smile of relief. He knew suddenly that he didn't want a skinny kid who played good golf to be a murderer. "Jed may have driven the Porsche into the lagoon, but I don't think he killed Shell." Max hoped he wasn't swayed by his own near escape from circumstantial evidence and the tearstained face of a terrified sister. He didn't think he was. He was taking a fact—the fact of the missing shawl—and basing Jed's defense upon that fact. "The shawl was embedded deep in Shell's neck. How," he asked simply, "would Jed Hurst get his hands on Eileen's shawl?"

Annie started out confidently. "He went inside, found the shawl." She stopped, frowned. "That doesn't make sense. Even if he went inside, say he was looking for his dad, and happened to see the shawl, I can't imagine a teenager thinking about strangling somebody with a shawl rolled into a rope."

"No one's mentioned Jed going anywhere near the dance room. If he didn't go in there, he didn't get the shawl. Plus, the timing's wrong." Max looked excited. "Eileen left the shawl on her chair when she went out to see the fireworks. At that point, the dance was over. Jed had no reason to go inside to look for his dad. Nobody was in there except waitstaff. They would have seen him. You can bet when they were asked about the shawl in the beginning, they would have mentioned a teenager coming in there. Besides, why would Jed wander around looking for Wesley? If Jed wanted to talk to his dad, he'd have called him on his cell."

"Does that mean only someone attending the dance could have murdered Shell?"

"Vera Hurst wasn't at the dance but she could have seen Eileen in the hall at some point. Otherwise, yes. I'm sure the murderer is among those at the dance or possibly Vera. It would have been easy for one of them to grab the shawl."

Annie looked at him steadily. "You know what that means."

He did. Whoever took the shawl had already decided on murder, picking up the shawl, likely folding it or concealing the length of silk in some fashion, then moving out onto the terrace and watching and waiting until Shell walked toward the overflow lot. He continued his thought aloud. "Wesley Hurst. Dave or Maggie Peterson. Edward Irwin. Or Eileen. Maybe Vera Hurst. One of them."

"They are all longtime club members."

Max raised an eyebrow. Was Annie having another Pam North moment? That observation was a classic non sequitur.

A trace of a smile touched her face. "Members know how parking is jammed on the Fourth. Shell didn't arrive until eight forty-five. By that time, she had to use either valet parking or park in the overflow lot. It was clear that she parked in the overflow lot because she made her grand entrance from the terrace. If she'd used valet parking, she would have come in through the front of the club and entered from the center hallway. Anybody at the dance would know her car was in the overflow lot and could have taken the shawl and reached her car before Shell took the path to the lot."

He mentally apologized. "Or one of them may have spoken to her during the evening and they agreed to meet at Shell's car and she could have said where she parked."

"Someone met her as prearranged or someone was waiting for her or someone followed her." Annie took a breath. "With the shawl rolled into a rope."

"I'd guess Shell was dead within a couple of minutes after she reached the Porsche. Around ten fifteen. All this time, we've tried to figure out how the murderer killed her, then drove the Porsche along the back road and onto the course, then raced to get the colonel's MG. Instead, the murderer only had to slip away to the overflow lot for a very short time. The murderer could have returned to the terrace to watch the fireworks or gone to get a car or, if it was Dave, started to walk on the road that runs along the golf course or, if it was Edward, hurried on home across the golf course. Meanwhile Jed found her dead, got the body into the Porsche, and drove to the lagoon."

"If Jed is innocent."

"The shawl." That was all Max said, but it sealed his conviction. Jed might have picked up a broken limb or a rock and smashed Shell. But it was ludicrous to imagine him choosing a shawl as a murder weapon. Moreover, there was no evidence at all Jed ever stepped into the dance room, so he could not have stolen the shawl. "The murderer isn't Jed Hurst."

Annie frowned. "Why did he get rid of the body?"

"Scared." Max knew that kind of fear, the heart-stopping, panicked fear that twisted up your guts, made you feel empty inside. "Maybe for himself. Maybe for his Dad. Or Mom. Impulsive. Kids act first and think later."

Annie's gray eyes brightened. "That makes all kinds of sense. All right. We think Jed's innocent. But the evidence against him is overwhelming. We have to find some new facts. Like *The Court of Last Resort*."

Max knew the story, too. Erle Stanley Gardner not only wrote the Perry Mason books and Donald Lam and Bertha Cool books, he tried to help people he believed had been wrongly convicted. "I'm hoping it doesn't come to that." He didn't want the kid with the beautiful swing to pace a prison floor.

Hi, Annie." Joyce Thornwall was cheerful and pleasant. Caller ID simplified connecting these days. "Sorry to bother you, Joyce."

"Not a bother. I'm in the cheese aisle, trying to decide between Havarti or triple crème brie." There was a smile in Joyce Thornwall's cultivated voice.

Annie imagined her as the captain's wife at innumerable dinners and parties, effortlessly charming, genuinely kind, always perceptive. "Joyce, you know about Shell."

"The news is dreadful." Joyce's voice was grave.

"Max and I are trying to help the family." Certainly that was true. "It's important to know who was on the terrace during the fireworks. Do you mind thinking back?"

"I'll do my best." Thoughtfully, Joyce recalled this person and that.

Annie scribbled notes. "You didn't see Dave Peterson. Or Maggie. Did you notice anyone standing near the bleachers?" The east end of the bleachers abutted the path to the overflow lot. Annie listened, made more notes. "Right. If Don remembers anyone else, let me know. Thanks, Joyce."

Annie called club members whom Joyce had recognized on the terrace, took more notes. As she spoke to various members, she marveled at the willingness of people to respond to a purported survey. No one was questioned why the country club was collating information about the location of guests during the fireworks, specifically at the midpoint of the fireworks. When she was done, she moved purposefully toward the table covered with brown wrapping paper.

Max sat in his Maserati, air conditioner on high, hands on the wheel, frowning. It was all well and good for Annie to try to locate suspects on her sheet of wrapping paper. Suspects . . . That's how he thought of them now. Not as friends or acquaintances. Suspects in the murder of a young woman who had been foolhardy and careless about how others felt. But Shell hadn't had much welcome on the island.

If Max had known her, he might have found her fun and lively, as her sister remembered her. Did she enjoy watching porpoises at play? Was she interested in sports? Probably she knew every tidbit about the glitterati in Hollywood. Whatever mistakes she'd made, she'd been very young and she deserved the chance to change and grow, know love. Perhaps she would always have been selfish, thoughtless. But perhaps not. Instead, life ended abruptly, harshly, and her beauty was destroyed in the still waters of a lagoon.

Shell had perhaps intended only to taunt those she disliked. She had misjudged one of them.

Max knew everyone involved. He'd seen them smile, heard them laugh. Now faces touched by unfamiliar emotions—fear, anger, despair, jealousy, resentment—flickered in his mind. Wesley Hurst, the once amiable rich husband who was unfaithful to his new wife and she to him. Dave Peterson, the burly, strong-willed man with whom Shell shared a bed at the Sea Side Inn. Maggie Peterson, haggard and worn, a betrayed wife. Edward Irwin, a back-to-the-wall failing businessman unwise enough to threaten blackmail. Eileen Irwin, an imperious woman proud of herself, her family, her social preeminence.

Did Shell resent them because they had made clear their disdain after she destroyed Wesley's marriage and became the second Mrs. Hurst? When she learned that Wesley was having an affair with Vera had she felt humiliated, scorned? Or did she care so little for him that his adultery didn't matter? Was her affair with Dave striking back at Wesley? Or did she find Dave exciting and perhaps take malicious pleasure in injuring Maggie, who was Vera's friend? Did Shell really intend to take a charge of blackmail to the police or was she simply punishing Edward for daring to threaten her? Eileen would have been stricken at the possibility of her husband facing trial with all the likely media and tabloid attention. Nothing in Eileen's demeanor indicated she knew about Edward's dilemma, but Henny insisted that very little escaped Eileen's notice. Was there any way to find out?

As for Shell, she might simply have been young and reckless, incapable of empathy, more a creature of carelessness than malice, perhaps finding amusement in her detractors' discomfort, never imagining that she was evoking a rage that would culminate in murder.

Max felt sudden brotherhood with a gerbil on an exercise wheel as his thoughts went around and around and around. Ever since Shell's murder, they had focused on the dance club members Shell singled out for attention. Maybe it was time to try something new, something different. Hadn't they discovered everything there was to know about Shell and the people around her?

Richard Ely . . . No one was trying to find out about Richard's last evening. There would be no investigation because his death had been deemed accidental.

Max put the car in gear and peeled out of the parking lot.

Annie's sketch of the country club and its grounds lacked proportion but everything was there, the main building and front parking lot, the golf pro shop, golf parking, the path from the terrace into the woods to the overflow lot, the temporary grandstand for fireworks that bordered the path to the overflow lot, the overflow lot, the exit to the back road that ran between woods on one side and the golf course on the other. She absently wiped her fingers with a napkin. Ingrid had popped in with lunch from the coffee bar on a tray: chicken salad, fresh fruit, and Tazo tea.

Now to use the information she'd gathered, pinpointing the locations of those angry with Shell between ten fifteen and ten twenty P.M. during the fireworks. Taking her time, she placed letters at various points: *VP* for valet parking at the front of the club, *MG* for the colonel's car in the main lot, *E* for Eileen, *V* for Vera and *W* for Wesley on the terrace, *J* for Jed near the grandstand. According to Eileen, Edward had started home, walking on a golf path. Arbitrarily she put *EI* for Edward on the golf path near the seventeenth hole. Below the sketch, she placed question marks after Dave and Maggie. No one mentioned seeing them on the terrace. If either was present, they'd taken care not to be seen. That wasn't an impossible task in the dimness. Maggie had been somewhere at the club because she was seen tearing out of the main parking lot in Dave's car after the fireworks. Dave was at hand after the fireworks because he'd berated valet parking for giving the keys to Maggie, and later Emma Clyde saw him walking on the back road behind the club. There was no witness to his location when Shell started toward the overflow lot.

However, there was no doubt that Wesley and Vera and Jed Hurst had been on or near the terrace. Annie hesitated, then with a determined nod, flicked a number on her cell.

Max didn't hold out much hope but maybe the observant neighbor in Marian's story knew something more about Richard's last night. It was worth a try. However, as he turned into Black Skimmer Lane, he saw a red Chevy parked in the drive of Richard's house. In the side yard, a boy around seven or eight kicked a soccer ball. Was Clarissa Ely at the house with her son? Max hurried up the walk and once again stood on the front porch of the neat frame house. He knocked.

The door opened. Barely. The interior was dim. "Who are you?" A woman's voice, wary and uncertain.

"I took Richard's dog to the vet—"

The door swung wide. Hazel eyes beneath short black bangs studied him from a rounded face that might have been pretty if it weren't for lines of worry and fatigue. "Do you have Sammy? I was afraid he'd run away." She glanced past Max.

Max spoke quickly, reassuringly. "I don't have him with me. He's at Playland for Pooches. He was sick but the vet fixed him up and I put him there until the family could be found. Are you Clarissa?"

Her brows drew down in a tight frown. "How do you know my name?"

"Ben Parotti thinks very highly of you. Are you staying here?"

Her face was a mixture of sadness and regret. "Richard hadn't changed his will. The house is mine. I wouldn't want it but Kyle is excited to be home. And maybe," she spoke as if to herself, "I can remember when things were good. Kyle and Richard used to go out in the yard and toss a tennis ball for Sammy to fetch. Those were happy times. Sometimes Richard drank too much and that's when he got involved with . . . people. He was always sorry but he was sorry one time too many. Anyway . . ." She sighed. "I wish things could have been different. He was a sweet dad except sometimes he was slow on child support. But he loved Kyle." Then a brief smile. "Sorry. That's not why you came." The worried look returned. "If Sammy's at that fancy dog place, it'll cost a lot of money to get him."

Max shook his head. "No charge. After he was discharged from the vet, he was put there until he could be returned to the family. I'll run over and get him and bring him here."

"No charge?" Clearly the expense worried her.

"Sammy's a good dog. I left him there. I was glad to be able to help him."

She looked puzzled. "Were you a friend of Richard's?"

"We were acquainted. But that's not why I came today. I'm trying to find out why Richard went out the night of the storm. You were here for a little while. Can you tell me if he said anything about going out?"

"Why do you want to know? Are you a reporter?" Her tone was sharp. The hand on the door clenched, ready to slam the panel shut.

"No." His reply was quick.

She still looked poised for flight.

"Mrs. Ely, you love your little boy. There's another boy, a few years older than your son, and he's in big trouble. I'm trying to help him. Will you let me come inside and explain? My name's Max Darling. You've probably seen the story about the woman's body found in a car sunk in a lagoon on the golf course. I've been helping the family. My questions have nothing to do with you or anything that happened between you and Richard that night. I'm looking for information about someone who contacted Richard, asked him to come to Fish Haul Pier. I know the police spoke with you. The autopsy can't prove that Richard was murdered but I think he knew something that was dangerous to someone. You may not be able to help me. But I know you wouldn't want another boy to go to jail for a murder he didn't commit."

She looked at him gravely, a plain woman in her early thirties with lines of sadness fanning out from her eyes and mouth.

"Hey, Mom!" Footsteps thudded in the hall behind her. "Can I have some Kool-Aid?" The dark-haired little boy skidded to a stop next to his mother. He saw Max. "Oh. I'm sorry, Mom." He looked shyly at Max. "Would you like some Kool-Aid?"

218

Max smiled. "That would be great."

Clarissa suddenly smiled, too. "Please come in." She led him into a living room transformed by a thorough cleaning and brightened by a green pottery vase filled with red hydrangea blooms. As she gestured toward the sofa, she said, "I have iced tea instead of Kool-Aid. Let me bring you a glass."

"That would be nice. Thank you."

He could hear mother and son in the kitchen. "You can take your Kool-Aid outside, honey."

In a moment, she brought a chilled glass of iced tea topped by mint.

When the back door slammed and a little boy was safely beyond earshot, Max described the dance at the country club, Shell's fateful walk toward the overflow lot, and Annie's conversation with Richard the next Tuesday.

Her face changed, drooped, emphasizing the fine lines at her eyes and mouth, old lines on a young face. "I should have known."

Max waited, watched as she struggled with inner turmoil.

Finally, she gave a deep sigh. She didn't look at him. Instead, she stared past him. "Richard sometimes picked up extra money. He'd see someone from the country club, somebody rich, out someplace he shouldn't have been, maybe with a girl. Not his wife. Richard said guys like that like to keep the peace at home. He'd say a little something and mention he could use an extra hundred bucks for some expense and the guy would hand it over. Richard never pushed it, just a little extra every once in a while. Richard used to laugh about it, say he knew not to make it a hassle. When I was here that Tuesday night—I came because he was behind again with the child support— his cell rang. He looked excited and said he needed to take the call and maybe he could catch up with child support. It made me mad.

219

If he didn't spend so much at the casinos, he wouldn't owe me money. I thought there he was again, up to no good, and I turned and started out the door."

Max kept his tone even, hoping, hoping. "Did you hear any of his conversation?"

"Enough to think I was right. He was smooth as butter like he always was when he was up to no good. He said something like, 'I always try to accommodate club members, help them avoid any . . . trouble. It's often been my pleasure to serve members above and beyond my duties and I've been generously rewarded. I was out on the terrace near the French doors when you and Shell Hurst spoke. I heard you plan . . .' I didn't like the look on his face. He didn't look . . . nice. That's when I left. He was leaning on somebody and I didn't want to hear it. I slammed out the door and I made up my mind I wasn't going to take any more money from him. My mom's coming to live with me to help with Kyle and I can go back to work. That night I left all disgusted. And now he's dead." Tears slipped down her face.

"I'm sorry." Max knew she grieved for the Richard she had once loved, not the Richard who leaned on people. She knew the man who had been her husband. He was accustomed to getting payoffs for silence about discreditable activities. This time he couldn't have known how shocking his words were to his caller. Richard didn't know Shell was dead, but he knew she hadn't been seen since the night of the dance and that people wanted to know who talked to Shell. Richard knew the answer. He heard Shell and a club member talking on the terrace in the shadows near the French door. *I heard you plan . . .*

Something planned . . . To meet? To leave together?

Richard overheard Shell speak to someone. He didn't see someone follow Shell. Perhaps what he heard was more damning than that.

Perhaps Shell said, *I'm parked in the overflow lot. I'll talk to you there.* If so, someone could have left the terrace before Shell walked toward the path and been waiting near the Porsche. "Did Richard mention a name?"

Clarissa shook her head. "Not while I was here. After the shrimp boat found Richard, I got a call from an officer who said Richard must have fallen from the pier. I wondered then about the call that night. I thought he was going to set something up, meet someone. Get money." Her voice was tired. "That's what I thought. I was going to tell the police, but when they got back to me, an officer said the autopsy revealed he'd died from drowning and the police didn't plan an investigation."

Annie frowned, clicked off the phone. Vera Hurst wasn't answering her cell, which was understandable. She and Wesley might be in a tense discussion with Billy Cameron or they might be with Jed as he fielded questions from Billy. They would have contacted a lawyer by now. Possibly Jed had declined to answer questions without a lawyer and was being held in a cell pending arrival of counsel. Whatever the circumstances, Annie was sure Vera and Wesley would stay at the station, hoping for Jed's release. If Vera and Wesley were in an office, Vera might have looked at the phone, seen caller ID, and deliberately ignored Annie's call.

Annie tapped another number.

Mavis Cameron answered. "Broward's Rock Police Department. How may I help you?" Alerted by caller ID, her formal tone segued into recognition. "Hey, Annie. What's up?"

"Mavis, I need to talk to Vera Hurst. I know she's there." Annie felt unspoken resistance on the other end of the call. "Mavis, she's a mom. She's terrified. I can help her. I know Billy has good reason to question Jed, but Max and I think he's innocent. Jed's folks want to help him. Please tell Vera I'm sure Jed is innocent and I'm working to find a way to clear him. Give that message to Vera and ask her to call me on my cell."

Silence.

"What harm can it do for me to speak to her?"

Mavis was a mom, too. Her son, Kevin, likely knew Jed at school. "I will if I can."

M ax stood on the boardwalk and looked the length of Fish Haul Pier. On this bright July afternoon, fishermen crowded the pier, some standing, some on camp stools, coolers beside them, clean for the catch, messy and stained for bait. A few had beach umbrellas to fend off the sun. Straw hats and ball caps offered some protection. Heavy humid air pressed against him. Mixed with the salty scent of the sea was the stench of a dead fish rotting on the shore.

No one had been on the pier on the night of July tenth. Rain pelted the wooden planks. Lightning zigzagged across a heavy sky. Clarissa said someone called Richard Ely at shortly after nine and set up a meeting.

Everyone was savvy about phone records now. Max knew that if he planned a murder, made a call to his victim, he wouldn't use a home or cell phone. That meant the call had been placed from a public phone. Pay phones were almost a relic of the past now, rare and hard to find. The island had two pay phones not far away. One was attached to a wall of the ferry building. The other was an old-fashioned booth on one end of Main Street, maybe a block from the pier.

Max turned and walked fast. He reached the beginning of Main Street. A small shabby hotel sat in a weedy lot opposite the harbor. A second-story screened verandah held a half-dozen rocking chairs. Max squinted against the sun. A small elderly woman occupied one of the rockers. She had her choice of vistas. Straight ahead the *Miss Jolene* sat at the ferry dock. To the left, Fish Haul Pier jutted into green water. Down and to the right plate glass windows marked a row of small shops. An old-fashioned phone booth nestled between a butcher shop and a florist.

Max approached the wooden phone booth. The paint had long vanished, the glass panels in the folding door were scratched and dim, almost opaque. Max turned, shaded his eyes. The pier was not more than a block distant. Maybe, just maybe . . .

He pulled out his cell.

Mavis was brisk. "Broward's Rock Police Station. Max, I've already given Annie's message to Mrs. Hurst."

Max had no idea what Annie was doing, but finding out could wait. "This is a different matter. I have information for Billy."

"I can switch you to his voice mail."

"It's urgent." Max stared at the pier, so clearly visible from the phone booth.

Mavis was reluctant. "He's in conference."

"A quick call. It's important."

The line went on hold. Max stood in the broiling sun, sweated, waited. But the connection held. Mavis wouldn't cut him off. Max moved his shoulders, felt his damp shirt sticking to his back. One minute, two, three . . .

Billy's voice was gruff. "Cameron."

Max didn't waste time. "Richard Ely talked to Shell's murderer at nine P.M. July tenth. Here's what his wife heard on Richard's end."

Max was precise, repeating Clarissa's words. "Two facts jump out: Richard said he liked to save club members from trouble. He wouldn't talk to a kid like that. Richard expected his caller to be willing to meet him and pony up some cash in exchange for silence."

Billy was still gruff. "For starters, we're not investigating the death of Richard Ely. If it's homicide, we'll never prove it. But let's give you Richard as a blackmailer. You may be right. You got to remember, the kid's from a rich family. God knows how much ready cash he has around. And the kid dumped the body."

"Nobody's going to schmooze a teenager about going out of his way to save trouble for members and how generous members have been in response."

Another silence. "Yeah. Not what I'd expect him to say."

Max felt a twinge of hope. Billy was listening. "You'll have to convolute like Houdini to convince me Jed Hurst used a woman's shawl to strangle somebody. Plus he didn't have access to it. If you check the waitstaff that was clearing up, nobody saw Jed Hurst." Maybe this would prod Billy to ask that question. Max felt confident of the answer. It wasn't Jed Hurst who picked up a length of silk with murder in mind.

"Maybe that Irwin woman dropped the damn thing on the terrace. That woman's a basket case. She stared at me like a goggle-eyed fish with a spear in her chest. Whatever, the kid dumped the body. We know that. He won't say a damn thing. And I got a call from a club member who read Marian's story, saw the bit about us hunting for information concerning Shell and people she talked to. The member saw Jed stop Shell on her way across the terrace when she first arrived. They had some kind of set-to. She laughed and walked on to the French door. The kid looked mad as hell, according to the witness.

But I don't get any answers from Jed Hurst. He stares at the floor and acts like he doesn't hear me."

Billy's words landed like a punch in the gut. Max remembered his hard days of August when questions came at him and he was a grown man and a lawyer and they still struck panic inside. Jed was a kid. Jed stared at the floor because he was scared and bewildered and had his back against the wall.

Billy continued, his voice hard. "We're waiting for the lawyer. We're holding him on vandalism, car theft, obstruction of justice. More to come. He isn't going anywhere."

Max knew too well the quiet and isolation of the two cells at the end of a corridor at the station. Jed had probably never seen a jail cell except in a slam-bang movie. He wouldn't have his iPhone in there. "Billy, will you do me one favor? Maybe it will turn out to be a favor for you. Check the outgoing calls from the public phone booth on Main Street a block from Fish Haul Pier at nine P.M. the night of July tenth."

"Can you give me one good reason?"

"The murderer called Richard Ely at nine P.M. I'm betting the call came from that booth."

A considering pause. "Say the numbers match. The kid could have used the phone booth."

Max almost grinned. "I doubt Jed knows what a public phone booth is."

A grudging chuckle. "You got a point. Kevin thinks the world began with an iPhone. Okay." His voice was abruptly remote, obviously his mind moving beyond this conversation. "We'll get the phone booth records. Not that it will matter a damn." The connection ended.

14

Annie grabbed her cell. "Vera?"

"How can you help Jed?" Vera Hurst's voice was thin, reedy, desperate.

Annie leaned against the storeroom worktable, glanced down at the drawing paper that covered the surface. "Someone waited for Shell at her car or followed her on the path. You and Wesley and Jed were on the terrace. You've got to tell me what you saw."

"I thought you knew something." Vera's voice rose in disappointment and anger. "I thought—"

"If you want to save Jed, hear me out. What did Shell say when you talked to her on the terrace?" If Vera had slipped through the night to wait for Shell by the Porsche, the unexpected question should shock, constricting throat muscles, affect her voice.

Instead, Vera answered easily, without constraint. "That wasn't me. I talked to her earlier in the hallway outside the dance. But I saw her on the terrace. She was in a shaft of light and that dress was so damn sheer she might as well have been naked. Slutty. But that's what she was."

Annie tried to keep her voice level. "Who was she talking to?"

"I don't know. Does it matter? She was laughing. She looked at her watch and said something, then she turned and walked across the terrace. She came past me and said . . . It doesn't matter now. Nasty. She went to the middle of the terrace and stopped to talk to that poisonous Lou Porter." Vera's words were clipped, anger evident.

Annie had a good idea of Shell's intent. She was exacting revenge that night. More than likely she paused to talk to Lou simply to taunt Vera, knowing Vera would wonder if Shell was offering a juicy tidbit to Lou, something like, *I suppose you know about Wesley and Vera* . . . That didn't matter now. All that mattered was Shell's conversation that had been overheard by Richard Ely, Shell talking to her murderer.

"At the French door was Shell talking to a woman? A man?"

"I couldn't see. The other person was in the shadow of a pottery vase."

Annie pictured the terrace windows. Between each window stood tall earth-filled vases with honeysuckle spilling down the sides.

Disappointment swept Annie. That was the critical moment, Shell's encounter with the person who planned to meet her in the overflow lot. "Did you see anything that could identify that person? A hand? A shoe? Anything?"

"I didn't even get a glimpse. It was dark there."

Once Shell turned away, Vera's gaze had turned as well, following her across the terrace, watching her talk to Lou. Shell's conversation with Lou gave the murderer time to slip down the terrace, staying in shadow, and move on the far side of the temporary bleachers to slip

ahead of Shell to the overflow lot. Or the unseen person waited and
followed Shell.

"Was anyone else standing near the terrace windows?"

"I don't think so." But Vera's voice was uncertain. "I wasn't paying much attention. Oh . . . I saw a waiter near them. I think his
name's Richard. I don't know his last name." Personal contact with
waitstaff wouldn't be a priority for Vera. "Maybe you can ask him."

Perhaps Vera never bothered to read the *Gazette*. Or perhaps
the fate of a drowning victim brought in by a shrimp boat wasn't of
interest.

"You were watching Shell. She took the path. Did anyone follow
her?"

Annie had sensed no constraint earlier. Now the silence throbbed
with wariness, tension, and fear.

Then there was no connection.

D ust motes swirled in a lazy current of air from a creaking ceiling fan. On one side a staircase rose in gloom. The front desk
had likely been in place since the Mermaid Hotel's first day. A plaque
proudly proclaimed: Mermaid by the Sea since 1907. Max stood at
a narrow wooden counter marked with stains and gouges. No one sat
at an old swivel chair next to a deal table beneath a wooden case with
slots for keys. More than half the slots held keys.

"Hello?" His call emphasized the quiet in the postage-stamp lobby.

A Persian cat jumped to the top of the counter, gazed at him with
limpid green eyes.

"Are you in charge?" Max smiled and reached out, smoothed
well-brushed hair. "Somebody takes good care of you."

A narrow door next to the deal table squeaked open. A tall woman with a thin, bony face stepped into the cramped space behind the counter. "Tell him you are brushed morning and evening, Lydia."

Max once again stroked the cat. "Lydia. That's a nice name."

The sharp features softened. "Of a noble sort. The name is perfect for her. Don't you think she has a regal air?"

"Definitely. Persians are always beautiful. How long have you had her?" Max didn't hurry the proprietor, Miss Beatrice Barton, as she traced Lydia's lineage. But soon enough they were on very good terms as he described Dorothy L. As for the rooms that opened to the second-story verandah, she had her regulars who came every summer, had done so for years.

"I'm interested in the occupants of the rooms fronting the second-story verandah on the night of July tenth. The night of the big storm."

Miss Barton placed long, thin fingers flat on the counter. Her face was abruptly wary. "May I ask why?"

"I want to find out if anyone was on the verandah during the storm. To be exact, at nine P.M."

"That is an odd question." Wary brown eyes studied his face.

Max made no effort to cajole. This was a woman of intelligence who had no intention of revealing the names of guests. "Miss Barton, I am not from the police. I am a private citizen trying to help a young man who is in danger of being arrested for a murder he didn't commit. I can't promise I'll discover anything that will help him. But it's possible. From the porch, a guest could easily look down and see the telephone booth. Will you call the occupants of each of those rooms"—he thought quickly—"the four rooms that front on the porch and ask these questions: Were you on the porch the night of July tenth at nine P.M.? Did you see anyone using the public telephone? Can you describe that person?" He pulled his billfold from a back pocket, slipped out a business card. "Here is my cell phone number. Miss Barton, he's a good kid. He's innocent." And his golf swing was a thing of beauty and his sister and a friend on faraway Kauai believed in him.

Annie flashed a smile at Dave Peterson's secretary. "No need to announce me. I know the way. Dave's expecting me." She walked fast, expecting at any moment to hear a stern challenge. But sometimes brashness carried the day and the secretary's silence meant Dave was in his office. Annie moved swiftly down the hallway. The door was closed. She took a deep breath, tapped twice, turned the knob.

Dave looked up with a frown that turned into a scowl. "What the hell do you want?"

She stepped inside, closed the panel behind her. "The police are holding Jed Hurst on suspicion of murdering Shell."

The scowl faded. "That's nuts. He's one of the best junior golfers in the state. He's not that kind of kid."

She felt a wave of thankfulness that men cherished athletes. "Max and I are sure he's innocent. We know someone either waited for Shell in the overflow lot or followed her there from the terrace. Did you see Shell leave the terrace?"

He looked grim. "I didn't hang around to see the fireworks. Shell—" A deep breath. "We had a disagreement." His gaze shifted away from her.

Annie knew he'd stormed off in a fury after Shell—surely at what he would see as the last moment—announced she wasn't going to flee the island with him for a new life. But antagonizing Dave wasn't part of her plan. If he killed Shell, he would have a smooth story ready. If he was innocent of murder, he might know something useful.

"What happened after you left the dance?"

"What business is it of yours?"

"I'm trying to find out everything that happened that night. I don't think Jed's guilty either. You may know something useful. You have no reason not to answer if you're innocent."

The combativeness eased out of his face. "You've got a point. I might have wanted to kill her but I didn't. So I'll tell you what I did. I wasn't"—his tone was laconic—"in a hell of a good mood. I took the golf path, then started up the fairway on nine. About halfway to the green, I decided I was going to give her an earful. I turned around and headed for the overflow lot. The fireworks weren't over and I figured I'd catch her after they ended."

Annie pictured the golf course. He was midway up the fairway to the ninth green. "How did you get to the lot?"

"I cut across the fairway to one, came through the pines to the path."

"How did you know she'd parked there?" Annie watched him carefully.

Dave didn't appear to attach any significance to the question. His beefy face looked impatient. "She came late. Where else would she park? Besides she came in from the terrace. Anyway, I headed for the lot. I got there and I got mad all over again." He seemed oblivious to her. His face corrugated in a frown. "But I was too late. She was leaving. All I thought about was how I wished I'd been there two minutes sooner and caught her."

"You saw the Porsche leave?"

"Yeah. I was too late."

"How'd you know it was her car?"

He sounded impatient. "You know how cars park there. A winding road curves around under the pines and people pull up in cleared spots between the trees. She'd parked in the last row. I saw the Porsche heading for the exit. There's a light pole there. I ran. But I couldn't catch up. The Porsche turned right. I thought that was odd. I decided maybe she had a new guy on the string, was going to somebody's house."

The Porsche went to the right, Jed driving fast to get to the golf path.

Annie was suddenly breathless. "Did you see anyone in the lot?"

"Not in the lot."

"On the path? Did you see anyone, hear anything?" Jed found Shell dead, decided in a panic to do away with her body, afraid the police might suspect him or his dad. By then the murderer may have regained the terrace or headed behind the bleachers to walk across the golf course. But it was possible that the murderer was still nearby, escape to the terrace blocked by Dave's presence.

The urgency in her voice caught his attention. He sat at his desk, big, burly, thinking, just like he might figure a job, taking this figure and that into consideration. "Let me get it straight. Shell walked to her car. She left. So what difference does it make?"

"Her body was in the Porsche. Somebody strangled her in the lot and drove away."

He looked momentarily shocked. "You mean she was dead when the car pulled out of the lot?"

"Yes."

He took a quick breath. "Then . . ." He paused, swallowed. "When I came through the woods to the path, I waited in the pines for a few minutes. I sure didn't want to talk to him."

"Who did you see?"

"Wesley." Dave's voice was subdued. "He was walking fast back toward the terrace. He looked like hell. I thought he'd had a dustup with Shell. He rushed past. I gave him time to get to the terrace. I was about to step out of the shadows and here came Jed, running toward the lot."

Annie imagined Jed's shock when he found Shell's body. He couldn't have missed seeing his dad return to the terrace, obviously upset. No wonder Jed decided to get rid of her body.

Dave shook his head. "I didn't know what was up. I let him get ahead of me. And then when I got to the lot, the Porsche was leaving. That's when I took the back road to the front parking lot. I was going to get my car. That was a bummer, too. Maggie got there first, left without me." He sounded aggrieved. "I guess she thought . . . Anyway, I was stuck. So I took the back road again and walked home."

Max watched the harbor through the window in Billy Cameron's office. Another day in paradise, white sails brilliant in the late-afternoon sunlight, the *Miss Jolene* moving out on a run to the mainland, a shrimp trawler a distant speck against the horizon. But not for a kid hunched in a chair, Billy there, a lawyer, maybe his folks. Not looking at anybody. Saying what?

The minute hand in the big round clock that reminded him of a schoolroom made another jerky move. He'd waited almost a half hour. But he counted himself lucky because Billy could have left word that he was unavailable. Period. At least Max was in a straight chair in front of the yellow oak desk Billy's stepson had crafted in a summer carpentry class. The varnish was sticky, never seeming to dry completely, and one front leg was a little short. Billy was proud of that desk.

The door opened. Billy stepped inside, his face creased in a tight frown. He had an end-of-the-day, wrinkled appearance. He gave a nod as he settled behind the desk. "Lawyer's busy rousting out the judge, insisting the kid be charged or released. I got the circuit solicitor's support on holding him. We've got too much to let him roam around, I don't care how rich his folks are." His mouth turned down. "The mayor's on my ass."

"The phone booth?" Max reminded him of his promise.

"Yeah, yeah, yeah. Lou was going to see to it." He turned to his computer, clicked.

As Billy clicked, Max described his visit to the Mermaid Hotel. "We may get a heads-up on who used the phone booth that night."

Billy muttered, "I'd like an eyewitness. Be helpful." His tone was wry. He clicked again.

Max watched Billy's profile, saw a sudden intensity.

Billy's face was thoughtful when he swiveled to look at Max. "If you got a crystal ball, I can use it. Looks like you nailed this one. A call at nine oh-three P.M. July tenth from the phone booth to Richard Ely's cell." A shrug. "There's no proof the call wasn't made by Richard's ex-wife. If she bumped him off the pier—"

Max broke in. "Come on, Billy. Why would Richard meet his ex-wife at the end of a pier in a huge thunderstorm? I mean, she was already at the house. That's really reaching."

Another shrug. "We don't know why Richard went there."

"Money."

"If we take her word for what he said."

"Let's start with the fact that somebody called him from the phone booth close to the pier. He went to the pier. A shrimp trawler brought his body to shore. He was murdered, Billy. That phone booth may tell us who killed him and Shell Hurst."

"A talking phone booth?"

"Fingerprints. Even if someone's used the phone since July tenth, there will be all kinds of fingerprints around. On the interior panel when you push to get out. On the wall. On the counter below the phone where there used to be a phone book."

Billy leaned back in his chair, his expression disdainful. "Whose fingerprints?"

Max named them one by one. "Wesley Hurst. Vera Hurst. Shell wouldn't agree to a divorce. Maggie Peterson. Shell was destroying her marriage. Dave Peterson. Fury over Shell dumping him. Eileen Irwin. A woman who would be appalled by scandal if Shell brought blackmail charges against Edward. Edward Irwin. Threatened with disgrace and possibly prison."

Billy's stare was steady. "I haven't had a perp leave fingerprints in years."

"Let's say the murderer wore a raincoat, maybe just plastic game rain gear. But what are the odds there are gloves in those pockets in July? Besides, the murderer had no reason to think anyone would try to trace that call."

Billy almost managed a smile. "You have an answer for everything. There's one little hitch in your plan. On what basis do I request fingerprints from people who are not officially suspects in a crime?"

Max had one more answer. "Mavis can take her kit, visit each one, and be sweet as honey. You and the circuit solicitor anticipate attacks from the defense when you file charges against a suspect currently under investigation. All of those people know they aren't that suspect. You can say it's essential to prove that there are no unaccounted-for fingerprints in the colonel's MG and this is an effort to prove to the defense that every avenue was explored. None of them will be worried about prints in the MG. None of them were ever in it. But one of them made a phone call the night of July tenth."

Max leaned back in the storeroom's extra chair, looked satisfied. "Hyla Harrison is on her way to the phone booth."

Annie felt sure that if there were fingerprints, Hyla would find them. She was a police officer with a dogged determination never to overlook any possible bit of information. That doggedness had served Annie well in the recent past.

"You know how thorough she is. She'll pick up every latent print inside and out. I saw Mavis pull out of the station lot so she's making the rounds of the suspects." Max sounded relaxed. "That's what I've been up to. How about you?" He glanced toward the worktable with its sketch and notations.

Annie wanted to talk to Maggie and Edward before she and Max called Billy. It was only fair to try to place all of them the night of the murder. It was possible that Wesley may have run back to the terrace, a man shocked by what he'd seen, that he was not a murderer leaving behind a body. To think he would let his son be accused in his stead would make him monstrous.

Why hadn't he spoken out if he found the body? Annie knew the answer. Shaken and scared, he didn't want anyone to know he'd ever been near Shell in the overflow lot. In murder, the spouse is always the first suspect, especially a spouse involved in an extramarital affair. Perhaps his hope was to get as far away from the lot as possible. He'd gone to the front of the club, made a scene at valet parking trying to appear like an innocent man who'd had too much to drink, but Don Thornwall saw him leave and didn't think he was drunk.

When Wesley ran to the terrace, hurried across it, he may not have realized that Jed saw him and took the path to the lot. As for Jed, Wesley only knew that Jed's fingerprints were on the steering wheel of the Porsche. Wesley had to be terrified that Jed was indeed the murderer. "Do you think the lady at the hotel will call her guests about the phone booth?"

"Highly efficient. Smart." He grinned. "We bonded over an elegant Persian named Lydia."

Annie's lips quirked. Who could resist Max? Blond, handsome, sexy, and a man who appreciated cats. Maybe the call would come and they would know everything.

"Okay." His gaze were searching. "Own up."

How did he know? Was she not only an open book, but as readable as the electronic marquee at Times Square?

Annie popped up from her swivel chair, motioned for Max to join her at the worktable. She pointed at the letters on her map of the club and its grounds. "Eileen and Vera and Wesley were on the terrace. Edward had left to walk home on the golf path." She pointed to the *EI* on the golf path, then used her thick-tipped marker to place a *D* next to the winding walk between the terrace and the overflow lot. "Dave came through the woods to the path and that's when he saw Wesley returning to the terrace. Dave almost stepped onto the path but stopped when Jed came toward him, heading for the lot. By the time Dave got to the lot, the Porsche was leaving." On the path, she drew a *W* with an arrow toward the terrace and a *J* with an arrow toward the lot. "Jed likely saw his father's shock when he came to the terrace and went to the lot. He found Shell's body and feared his father had lost his temper, killed Shell. No wonder he tried to get rid of the body. He thought he was protecting his dad."

Annie imagined Jed's frantic struggle to heft Shell into the car if he found her dead on the ground or, if she was strangled as she sat in the driver's seat, move the body across the console to the passenger seat. Then he got into the car, left the lot, and took the back road to the golf path. The Porsche followed the golf path, its headlights off, to the bridge over the lagoon at nine. Jed maneuvered the car into the lagoon, taking down a railing and a post, then raced across the course to the front parking lot, valet parking, and the colonel's distinctive key fob.

All the while, fireworks exploded above in the night sky, plumes of red and gold, starbursts of blue and orange.

"Either Wesley killed Shell or the murderer was waiting for Shell when she reached the Porsche. Shell's death didn't take long. She left the terrace about ten fifteen. She was likely dead within minutes. If Wesley found her dead, the murderer probably watched him from the shadow of the pines. Wesley ran back to the terrace. The murderer would have followed, cautiously, and heard Jed's running steps in time to hide again. Within a minute or so, here came Dave. Unless Dave arrived first and killed Shell. In that case, he was near the Porsche and remained unseen by both Wesley and Jed."

Max pulled out his cell. "Time to call Billy."

Annie placed a hand on his arm. "I don't believe Wesley committed the murder. He didn't need to stand near the terrace French doors to talk to Shell. He'd already spoken to her at the dance. From what Clarissa told you, Richard's conversation with the murderer reveals Shell and the murderer agreed on a plan in that conversation near the French doors."

Max looked thoughtful. "Billy knows about the call Richard received. He'll agree Richard's conversation weighs against Wesley as the murderer. But you need to tell him what you've found out."

"Let's talk to Maggie and Edward first." Annie felt she owed that much to Wesley. She had set out to find what she could about that night. Either Maggie or Edward could have been on the edge of the terrace and slipped behind the grandstand to reach the path before Wesley followed Shell.

"All right. I'll drop by Edward's office. You talk to Maggie. Let's meet at the station"—he looked at his watch—"in forty-five minutes."

Max was halfway to the storeroom door when his cell rang. He glanced at caller ID, gave Annie a thumbs-up as he answered. "Miss Barton, thanks for calling." He clicked speakerphone and held it up for Annie to hear.

"I said I would talk to my guests." Beatrice Barton's tone made it clear: What she promised, she did. "Joan Talbot was on the porch at nine P.M. The Talbots in three have been coming for years from Columbia. Joan is a poet. Roland teaches philosophy at the university. Joan's originally from Kansas and she loves thunderstorms. She was in one of the rockers, watching the lightning and taking pictures. She said she was the only person on the porch."

Max's expression was eager. "Did she see the caller at the phone booth?" Even if Joan Talbot was looking up at the jagged flashes of lightning, her field of vision included the phone booth.

Annie clenched her hands. The answer was so close . . . Wesley, Vera, Jed, Dave, Maggie, Eileen, Edward, a familiar face hid a murderous secret.

"The thunder and lightning were intense." Miss Barton's tone was measured, a woman reporting what she had been told. "Joan said the storm reminded her of growing up in Kansas. High wind. Slanting rain. She was surprised to see a pedestrian. She said as much as she loved storms, it was foolish to be out on that sidewalk. For that reason, she was interested and she watched. The person—"

"Person?" Max was sharp. "Man or woman?"

"Joan said it was a man or possibly a woman in a man's raincoat and cap. The hat was an ivy cap. In a flash of lightning, the cap appeared to be a brown tweed. She estimated the individual's height at between five feet six inches and five feet ten inches. She watched the person approach the phone booth and step inside. She wondered if it was some kind of emergency that brought someone out to use a pay phone on such a night. She also wondered why someone in a well-cut raincoat—really it was quite similar to her husband's London Fog—didn't have a cell phone, but thought perhaps they had lost or misplaced it."

"She saw the person step into the phone booth?"

"Yes. She thought the entire episode was rather curious because the caller remained in the booth for such a long time. Joan said she was getting chilled—you know how the air can cool when we have a summer storm—and she decided to go inside. The caller was still in the booth at that point and it was about a quarter after nine."

Annie doubted the murderer's phone call lasted long, a few minutes at most. The murderer remained in the booth, staying sheltered until time to meet Richard on the pier. That suggested the appointment was made for not long after the call. Richard probably arrived within ten minutes. He, too, would be drenched but he probably thought a little water was worth money in his pocket.

Max glanced across the storeroom at Annie, held up his right hand with fingers crossed. "Did she get a picture?"

Annie felt a flicker of hope. They might yet identify the caller. Forensic science could divine an incredible amount of information from a photograph.

"Joan Talbot is quite precise. She described every detail of what she saw. Had she photographed the person, she would have mentioned the fact. I will ask her and notify you if there is a picture."

When the call ended, Max was rueful. "More. Not enough. There was no reason for her to take photos of the booth. She was interested in lightning. But Joan Talbot confirms someone was there at nine o'clock. Billy will have to take this seriously whether they find fingerprints or not."

15

Annie spoke in a rush before Maggie Peterson could hang up. "Jed Hurst is in jail."

A startled breath. "That has to be wrong. Sandy—"

Annie knew that their daughter, a junior at Clemson, was working as a summer biology intern at the South Carolina Aquarium in Charleston.

"—babysat Jed and Hayley for years. He's a sweet boy. He didn't like Shell but he would never hurt anyone. Not Jed. There has to be a mistake."

"Max and I agree. We're trying to find out more about what happened during the fireworks. I talked to Dave." There was no revealing gasp, but tension radiated over the connection. "He's trying to help, too." Did Maggie think her husband was guilty? Or was she the murderer who slipped to the overflow lot and waited for Shell? "Dave told me he started off across the golf course, then turned around and headed for the overflow lot."

There wasn't a hint of a breath from Maggie.

Annie picked her words carefully. "Dave arrived at the lot in time to see the Porsche pulling out onto the back road."

"He saw the Porsche leave?" Maggie's voice lifted.

"Yes." Did Maggie know that Shell was already dead and someone else had driven the Porsche? Or was the fact that Dave saw the car leave reassuring to Maggie, proof that neither she nor Dave could be linked to Shell after the Porsche left?

"We haven't talked about that night." Now Maggie was careful in what she said. "He said he had been a fool about Shell. A damned idiot." Her voice was level, no emotion revealed. "He said he was sorry. He said, 'Thank God, she blew me off. She was trash.'" Quoted words in an uninflected tone. Finally, quietly, "Things are going to be all right." There was not so much happiness as a dazed sense of relief. Then, in a rush, "What can I do to help about Jed?"

"I'm asking everyone to tell me where they were after the fireworks started."

There was a considering pause. "Why does that matter?"

"You may have seen something or someone that tells us more about what happened to Shell. It helped to ask Dave. Now we know what time the Porsche left the lot. Maybe you can help us, too."

"I don't think so." She sounded weary. "When Dave stormed out of the dance, I knew she'd blown him off. I went out the front door of the club. I thought maybe he'd walked around to get the car. He was so mad I doubted he even thought about me at all and I didn't know how I would get home. He wasn't there and I saw the keys on the valet board. I waited awhile and then I got scared that he was with her after all and they were going to go away. I knew all about it. Friends had told me about them and then I found out that he'd sold a lot of stock. I found some plane tickets hidden in his sock drawer. He never was any good at hiding things. I started to cry and I told the boy I'd take the keys and he didn't know what to do but I grabbed them and ran into the front lot. I drove home and sat in the empty house, staring at nothing, imagining he was gone forever. He came home about an hour later. I had to let him in. We looked at each other and then I turned and ran to the bedroom and locked the door. He talked to me through the door. I couldn't face him then. I said, tomorrow, we'd talk tomorrow." When she spoke, her voice was shaky. "We didn't talk about that night."

The rubber plant in the outer room of Edward Irwin Investments appeared even more listless. If the plant didn't get water soon, the leaves would curl up in defeat and begin to drop. The office was as shabby, small, quiet, dusty, and sad as the day he first came. Max walked to the open door of Edward's office.

Edward's worried face turned toward him. He said nothing. Maybe he was waiting for doom. Max had a sense that Edward was as wilted as his office plant, simply sitting, waiting, perhaps for an ending, without hope of a beginning.

Again Max stood on the far side of the desk. "You know they found Shell's body."

Edward seemed to be circling the statement, as if wary of a trap. "I saw the story in the *Gazette*."

"You were on the terrace the night she died."

"I went home." He seemed to push out the words.

"What time did you leave the terrace?"

Edward pulled his shoulders back. His cheeks puffed out. "I don't have to talk to you."

Max sat on the edge of the desk, folded his arms. "The police are holding Jed Hurst."

Surprise jerked Edward's sparse eyebrows high. "Jed?" He sagged against his chair in relief. "If he's the one, then why don't you leave me alone?"

"He's innocent." Max spoke quietly. "An innocent kid shouldn't go to jail. Do you agree?"

Edward's eyes dropped to his desktop. "The police must have some grounds to hold him."

"They do. But he's innocent. We've found out enough"—Max could see the terrace in his mind, Shell slender and arrogant, sure of her beauty and her power, walking toward the path, Vera watching, Jed near the grandstand, Wesley starting after Shell—"to know the murderer either followed her from the terrace or was waiting at her car. That's where you can help. If you are innocent, you have no reason not to tell me when you left the terrace and where you went."

Edward's face was suddenly still. He looked at Max. Something flickered deep in his watery brown eyes. Fear? Despair? Uncertainty?

Max was intent. If only he could ask the right question. "Did you see Shell leave the terrace?"

It was as if Edward had been handed a lifeline. The words came fast, jerkily. "I left right after the fireworks started. My head hurt. Eileen decided to stay. I walked home."

Max felt a sick whip of disappointment. Not the right question. He tried again. "When was the last time you saw Shell?"

Edward's gaze slipped away. He didn't look at Max. "I don't know. Maybe as the dance ended. I wasn't paying any attention."

The lie hung between them.

"After she threatened you with jail, you didn't pay any attention?"

Edward's stare was dull, defeated. "I never wanted to see her again."

Billy Cameron was patient. He took notes. When both Annie and Max were done, he slowly shook his head. "So everybody's said where they were. Maybe that's true. Maybe not. And maybe"—he looked at Annie—"you're right about Wesley finding her dead and the kid running there later and panicking and getting rid of the body, but somebody killed her. We've got Wesley, Jed, and Dave all at the lot at the right time. But we don't have any proof." His head swung toward Max. "As for the phone booth, we don't have a murder investigation into the death of Richard Ely."

Max started to interrupt, but Billy held up a hand. "Yeah, yeah, yeah. I know what you believe. Richard was blackmailing somebody. You're right that a call went from the booth to his house at nine oh-three P.M. the night of the storm. You did some good legwork to track down the Talbot woman. But her description could fit anybody. So, that's no help." He gave a grim smile. "I don't think the judge will give me a warrant to search for a well-cut London Fog raincoat. And you left a name off your list." He didn't wait for Max to ask. "Maybe Jed Hurst was all geared up in his dad's London Fog and ivy cap."

Max didn't bother to answer. His expression spoke for him.

Billy looked wry. "I get you. Too subtle for a kid and how would he pay off Richard? The kid can't sell his silver spoon yet." Billy rubbed one cheek with knuckles. "There's not a whisper of proof but your scenario makes sense." The phone on his desk buzzed. He glanced down, picked up the receiver, punched a button. He listened, wrote on a notepad. He hung up, then lifted blue eyes to look at Max. "Hyla found prints in the phone booth. Lots of them are old, smudged, don't matter. Several are recent, clear, distinct. She ran everything she picked up against the prints Mavis took. Like you said, everybody was quite willing to help their law enforcement officer. All of them knew they'd never set foot in that MG. So we got their prints and"—he sounded grim, not relieved—"we have a match. One of our helpful citizens sure as hell made a call from that booth, but we'll never prove it was the call to Richard Ely."

Annie felt the beginning of enormous relief. A match . . .

Faces flickered in her mind like jerky footage in an old black-and-white film. Dave with his bullish masculinity, the once beautiful Maggie diminished by illness and infidelity, imperious Eileen proud of her family and social standing, frightened Edward facing disgrace, possibly jail, reckless Vera terrified for her son, and third-generation rich Wesley butting against realities where money couldn't help. "Oh, Billy, now Jed will be safe."

Billy's face was stolid, his words clipped. "Yeah, I can pin those prints to one of the suspects. But there's no way to prove those prints were made when the call to Richard was placed, no way to prove Richard was murdered, no way to tie the killer to Shell. No way."

Annie heard a familiar name with a quiver of shock.

The webcam picture of the yacht's saloon lacked clarity, but there was no mistaking the expressions on three distinctive faces. Emma Clyde's square jaw jutted with determination. Spiky blue hair mirrored her eyes and matched a swirling caftan. It was apparently a blue day. Laurel Roethke's dreamy gaze had a mystical quality. The exquisite cut of a long-sleeve chiffon blouse with alternating bands of pale green and beige emphasized an aura of elegance and Elvira otherworldliness. Henny Brawley's intelligent brown eyes narrowed in concentration. She folded her arms, austere and formidable in a cream turtleneck and black linen trousers.

Henny broke the silence. "How utterly frustrating."

Emma barked. "There has to be a way."

Laurel turned a thoughtful gaze toward Annie.

Max's arm slipped around Annie's shoulders, a hand tightening protectively on her arm.

Dorothy L, startled by his sudden movement, jumped to the floor and looked back at the sofa.

"I wonder." Laurel's husky voice was speculative.

Annie stiffened. When Laurel had that look . . .

Laurel smoothed a tendril of golden hair. "Dear Annie. You've made such a point of speaking to all of them. It wouldn't come as a surprise for you to make contact, possibly intimate puzzlement at some discrepancy and suggest a meeting at some secluded spot and, of course, there would be brave minions of the law secreted—"

"Ma. No." Max was emphatic.

Annie tried to consider the possibility in an academic fashion. Deep inside, she felt a flicker of terror. Now that they knew, she could see the danger, the coldness, the intelligence at work. Only a fool would arrange such a meeting.

Emma's bulldog face scrunched in thought. "Annie nattering about discrepancies won't break through that composure. We need some kind of shock."

Henny pushed up from the cane chair, paced restlessly. She moved with the grace of both an athlete and an actress. She'd been the mainstay of the island's little theater for years. She stopped, faced the camera, flung out a hand. "It's like slamming into a glass wall.

We can see through the barrier, but we can't break through. We know everything, yet safe on the other side of the barrier, the murderer has no fears, unaware that we know."

Laurel murmured dreamily. "That's why"—she glanced toward Annie—"I thought if we arranged a surprise—"

Annie came to her feet, clapped her hands together.

Laurel looked hopeful.

Max rose, too. "Absolutely not. No assignations in a remote area."

Annie was ebullient. "We know. The murderer doesn't know. Don't you see?"

Four faces stared at her, Emma with an impatient frown, Laurel with an eager light in dark blue eyes, Henny with a quirked eyebrow, Max with his jaw set.

Annie spoke rapidly, forcefully, excitedly.

Emma raised an eyebrow in surprise. "Quite clever. Amazing."

Annie charitably decided Emma wasn't amazed at Annie's perspicaciousness, rather at the outlines of an elaborate trap for an unwary killer.

Ideas came at a rapid clip. Henny provided a roster of names with brief descriptions. They pulled and tugged at the plan, made modifications, expanded, deleted.

"Would that we were there. But now we must leave the execution to the force in place." Emma clearly thought the second team was in charge. She glanced from Annie to Max and back. "As Marigold often says when resolution rests upon Inspector Houlihan, 'I have provided clear instruction. The matter is now in the lap of the gods.'" Emma rose majestically and sailed to the wet bar at one end of the saloon. "This calls for a libation."

Max moved to their wet bar.

Soon, they rose and held their glasses in a toast. "Until tomorrow night . . ."

Mavis Cameron appeared as always behind the counter at the station, self-possessed, calm, pleasant, but there was a flash of curiosity in her mild gaze as she waved them through the swinging gate.

Max tapped on Billy's door, opened it. It was yet another beautiful day in paradise, the early-morning sun streaming through the harbor windows, highlighting Billy's blond hair with its frosting of white, emphasizing the tired pouches beneath his eyes, turning the yellow varnish of his desk a bright gold. He, too, was, as usual, crisp in a white shirt and khaki trousers, grooved lines at the side of compressed lips the only sign of fatigue and stress. He waved a hand toward the straight chairs. His beginning wasn't promising. "I've got ten minutes. The mayor's due. I have to arraign the kid today. I don't like it, but I can't back off. We've got him dead to right on the MG and disposing of the body. The circuit solicitor's pressing me to file murder charges. I won't do it, but I don't have enough evidence to get anyone else. Those prints in the phone booth could have been made any day anytime, and you can bet that's what the murderer will claim. Another day, another week. As for the description, it could be anybody. Plus we don't have a homicide investigation for Richard Ely. Right now we're up a creek."

Annie was decisive. "We have a plan."

His eyes checked the wall clock. "Be quick."

It didn't take long, contact Jerry O'Reilly, arrange for calls to country club members, persuade the innocent to cooperate, line up the supporting cast.

He looked from one to the other, back again. Finally, slowly, he nodded. "There's no law against you calling on people to do their civic duty. If people want to show up, fine. If not . . ." He shrugged. "We'll cover you." His smile was dry. "We'll simply be cooperating with a citizen request. We'll set up a videocam on the terrace and hook up the sound to the overflow lot. If you get something, we'll be there. If you don't . . ."

Annie laced her fingers together. Definitely there was no guarantee. If they failed, pressure would mount on Billy to charge Jed with murder. "We have to count on shock. The murderer has no idea there is suspicion of murder in Richard's death, no idea the fingerprints were found in the phone booth, no idea someone watched from the Mermaid Hotel."

Billy didn't look convinced. "None of this works unless you can turn out a raft of people. Why would anyone come?"

Annie had an answer. "We'll make the invitation too hard to resist. A thrill a minute for those who enjoy being on the edge of a murder case. That will get most of them. Some will come because they like the Hursts or think Jed's going to be a Masters champion someday." Once again faces flickered in her mind. "As for those involved, all of them are decent people but one. They'll come because they want to do the right thing." She hoped.

Billy had been a cop for a long time. "If they don't?"

Max had an answer. "We expand the supporting cast."

Billy looked toward the window.

Annie knew he wasn't seeing the harbor bright on a sunny July morning, white sails brilliant, steel gray porpoises arching in their aquatic ballet, green water tipped by whitecaps, gulls wheeling as they swooped down for prey. The intercom on his desk buzzed.

Billy's big hand reached out, flicked.

"Mayor Cosgrove is here." Mavis's voice was as colorless as winter fog.

"Right. I'll come out to meet him." Billy stood, looked at Annie and Max. He gestured with a thumb. "Go to the break room. You might as well start there. When you're finished, check to see if the coast is clear and His Honor's waddled away before you leave."

The mayor was no friend to Billy, but Annie and Max also ranked high on His Honor's aversion list.

Billy moved toward the door as they stood. He gave them a final brief look. "Seven o'clock. We'll be in the overflow lot."

Max opened the door to the break room, held the door for Annie. Two stricken faces turned toward them and Annie understood Billy's oblique comment. Yes, Vera and Wesley Hurst were the right place to start.

Vera's well-groomed perfection was a distant memory. Her thin face with the prominent jaw was pale as ash, her eyes red-rimmed, her dark hair tangled, in need of a brush. She lifted a shaking hand to her throat. "Leave us alone. We're in big trouble. Stop hounding us."

Wesley pushed up from a pale orange plastic chair. He no longer looked like a preppy habitué of the yacht club, his smooth face drawn and haggard, his eyes haunted. "Damn you people."

"I thought"—Vera's voice cracked—"maybe they were coming to say we could take Jed home." Her face screwed up and she cried as if the tears would never stop.

Annie took a step toward her, held out a hand. "We want Jed to be free. He's innocent. We know who the murderer is and we've come to ask you to help us. Please"—her voice wobbled—"listen to us." She talked fast and hard.

Vera lifted her face, never minding the wetness of her cheeks. "You can save Jed?"

Max's voice was gentle. "We can save Jed. You have to trust us."

Wesley's lips trembled. "I've been nuts. Jed's fingerprints . . . I knew he couldn't hurt anyone but I didn't know anything I could say would help him. Yeah. I found her dead. I'll swear to it. I'll do anything you want me to do."

Annie leaned against a railing near the wheelhouse of the *Miss Jolene*. The ferry plowed westward, the morning sun still high in the sky. She welcomed the breeze off the water and the sense of freshness and freedom so different from the heavy anguish in the break room of the Broward's Rock Police Station. Please God, she and Max could bring peace to two terrified parents and freedom to a kid who had tried to protect his dad. She glanced at her watch. The run to the mainland took forty-five minutes. In another fifteen minutes, she would reach Chastain, the lovely old town on a high bluff overlooking the river. Antebellum homes, some among the oldest in South Carolina, drew tourists every day. On the outskirts of the small and elegant town sat a redbrick college. Waiting to meet her were some of the best and brightest from the Chastain College drama department faculty and students. Thanks to cell phones, Henny had already spoken to Roderick Fraley, the drama department chair, an old friend and one of her fellow actors in summer theater in Savannah.

Annie would meet them in the main hallway of the drama building. She could hear Henny's well-modulated voice in her memory. "Roderick is tall, a gaunt face, rather an Abe Lincoln physique. Amelia Wellington looks like everyone's Aunt Mary. She's about five-four, snowy white hair, a camellia complexion, soft brown eyes, a dumpling figure. Morgan Bitter has a Brian Cox face, once seen, never forgotten. Smooth brown hair, black slash eyebrows, sharp features, medium height. Robin Visey is flat-out gorgeous, shoulder-length dark hair, slender, tall. They won't let you down."

Jerry O'Reilly's anxious gaze moved from Max to Vera and Wesley Hurst. Jerry's freckled face didn't have a glimmer of its usual charm. "Tonight?" He puffed his cheeks in a grimace and looked as though he would like to be anywhere but the office of the service manager for the Broward's Rock Golf and Country Club. "On the terrace?" Clearly he was flailing about in his mind, searching for some way to gracefully refuse.

Wesley hunched forward in his chair, his haggard face relentless, unyielding. "I'll rent the whole damn club. Listen, Jerry, this has to happen." The tone was harsh. Wesley was a man fighting for his son.

Jerry rubbed the side of his neck. "Mr. Hurst, I understand you've got a problem. But club members don't like to get involved—"

Max interrupted. "Jed's a junior champion. People like him. Look, Jerry, you don't have to know much about any of this. Wesley's renting the terrace, inviting people who were here for the fireworks to help him find out more about what happened to his wife that night. We'll handle the rest of it. All you have to do is get the grandstand set up and make sure all the waitstaff who were on duty that night are here. I'll take full responsibility."

Ingrid Webb held the door for a reluctant customer. "We'll reopen later this afternoon. Some technical difficulties necessitate our closing."

The rawhide wiry blonde wasn't happy. "I haven't finished my shopping."

Ingrid gave a bright smile, spoke loud enough for the customers now filing toward the door. "A special thank-you for everyone's understanding." She glanced at a stack of new Kate Carlisle books. "A free copy for each of you."

The coppery tanned blonde took the book with a frown, but when she saw the cover, her eyes lighted. "Oh, a mystery about a rare book . . ."

When the door closed after the last straggler, Ingrid hurried down the aisle. Joyce Thornwall and Pamela Potts each sat at tables separated by the length of the coffee area with cell phones and a country club directory. Joyce was calm, unhurried, her smooth white hair unruffled. She ticked off the fifth name on her list, pressed numbers. Pamela, glasses pushed high on her nose, spoke in her customary precise tone. "Mrs. Vinson, so glad to find you at home. As an outstanding citizen of our island, I know you will be pleased to help the Hurst family as they seek to discover more about the evening Shell Hurst disappeared . . ."

I n an Australian slouch hat, aviator glasses, a Hawaiian shirt left over from an aloha party, chinos rolled to the knees, and black high-top sneakers, Max doubted his mother would recognize him. He pedaled his bike through a familiar neighborhood. He started four doors away from his quarry's home. He parked the bike on its stand in the shade of a live oak and mounted the steps of an antebellum house with upper and lower verandahs and ionic columns. A green jardiniere with tall stalks of flowering acanthus sat to the left of a white door inset with art glass. Max rang the bell.

An elderly lady answered. Tall and spare, her strong features were set in a forbidding frown, perhaps in response to vacationers' garb not usually glimpsed on a neighborhood street.

Max swept off his hat and gave a courtly half bow. "Ma'am, if I may have only a moment of your time. I'm a representative of the neighborhood watch association and we are doing a survey on neighborhood awareness. There was a car stolen on the night of July tenth. You may remember that was the night of the big rainstorm. Did you see any cars on the street at approximately nine P.M. July tenth . . . ?"

All the way back to the island, Annie worried whether there was any chance their plan might succeed. It seemed forever before early evening.

When she and Max arrived at the country club, Max headed straight for the terrace to check on preparations there.

She waited in the main entryway for her guests to arrive, then led them to a private dining room. The buffet on a sideboard held an appealing assortment of sandwiches, cheeses, salads, fruit, and desserts. Instead of wine, there were soft drinks, lemonade, and tea. This was not an evening for relaxation.

Annie waited until her guests had filled their plates, then joined them at a round table. She spooned Camembert onto a rye cracker. The club's tuna fish salad was famous for a dash of paprika. She ate a few bites, put down her fork. She glanced toward the door. It was securely closed and no one was in the room except for herself, four actors, and a twenty-something with a scruffy early beard, sailor's singlet, and khaki shorts.

Amelia Wellington was perfectly attired for a casual country club

257

evening in a V-neck black eyelet tank top and vibrant floral-patterned maxi skirt with an embroidered obi belt.

Morgan Bitter saw her looking at him and immediately changed from a sardonic observer to the bland mien of a man who knows he isn't to be noticed for himself, receding into the waitstaff uniform.

Robin Visey was elegant in a dress not quite as dramatic as that worn by Shell Hurst on her last night but spectacular in itself, a bow-shoulder red crepe gown that molded to her lithe, lean, model's figure. Her dark hair swirled in lustrous curls, her classic features exquisite and perfect.

Roderick Fraley, according to plan, wore a short-sleeve white shirt, black trousers, and black dress shoes. Heavy cranial bones emphasized deep-set eyes that were a curious mixture of green and gray. High cheekbones and a squarish chin looked somehow unfinished, as if a sculptor hadn't quite completed his task. An imposing man, tall and a little stooped, he transformed ugliness to power. "I've instructed everyone on what they are to do." He gestured toward the unidentified twenty-something. "Bobby has his equipment." A tilt of his head indicated a tripod and assorted wires tumbled in one corner of the room. "Now"—he reached to the floor, lifted an attaché case, pulled out a pad—"let's get the blocking set. We can run through placement after we finish eating."

Annie cast an anxious glance at the sky. Black thunderclouds banked against the western horizon, blotting out the sun, leaching color from the terrace. The pines looked dark and primeval beyond the bleachers. Strings of small colored lights on the magnolias and live oaks were pinpoints of cheer in the gloom. However, the golden glow from the torchieres seemed like isolated plumes of light, merely deepening the surrounding shadows. No light shone from the French doors. On the night of the Fourth, the lights in the club had been turned off to enhance the brightness of the fireworks. If they were turned on now, the glow through the panes would make the terrace more cheerful. But it was important to keep the surroundings as near that night as possible.

Perhaps thirty-five people were arranged on the bleachers, not the shoulder-to-shoulder audience on the night of the Fourth. About forty others dotted the terrace, standing stiff and silent. Upon arrival each had been asked to stand as nearly as they recalled to their location midway through the fireworks display. Despite dressy casual clothes and tanned faces, there was no aura of a holiday.

Max gave Annie a quick nod and walked unhurriedly across the terrace to stand near the bleachers.

Despite the shadows, Annie recognized many members. The Lady Luck Dance Club was well represented. Vera and Wesley Hurst stood in the center of the terrace very much by themselves. It was as though a marker had inscribed a circle around them. No one came nearer than four or five feet, not even the dance club members. Wendy Carlson's eyes were huge in her sweet heart-shaped face. She slid occasional glances toward Vera and Wesley. Wendy's smooth-faced lawyer husband appeared bland, as always. Rose Wheeler's flowing drapery was reminiscent of a midnight gathering of dancing fairies but her gaze was sharp and curious. Her tall husband stood with folded arms, shoulders hunched, a man clearly wishing he were elsewhere. The Porters radiated excitement, Lou's gooseberry eyes darting from face to face, Buddy's pudgy cheeks blood-pressure red.

Annie saw other familiar faces, women with whom she played tennis, lean and tanned golfing couples, a canasta group, a Mahjong league, several book clubs, two golf pros, several tennis instructors.

Colonel Hudson, white hair and white mustache neatly trimmed, bony face set in hard lines, stood with his arms behind his back, ramrod straight. Next to him, Jerry O'Reilly's rounded face creased in worry. When he saw Annie's glance, he gave an almost imperceptible nod, a confirmation that the waitstaff was in place around the terrace, just as they had been the night of the Fourth.

Except, of course, for Richard Ely.

There might be latecomers to the terrace, those who were always fashionably late, but those who mattered were present. They'd been asked to dress as they had that night.

Vera Hurst's sprightly and cheerful short-sleeve navy ruffled blouse and belted floral skirt made her haggard, drawn face more obvious. Coral lipstick appeared garish in contrast to her pallor. Tonight Wesley's bow tie wasn't askew and his cummerbund fit smoothly, but he'd lost the affable look of a man sure of deference and attention. His sandy hair was a perfect length, product of an expensive cut, but his smooth-shaven face had an unaccustomed gravity and his eyes a hollow look.

Jed Hurst hunkered against the end of the bleachers, almost invisible in the shadows. His face was a pale blob above a cherry red polo. He stood with his hands jammed deep into the pockets of khaki shorts. Annie wished she'd been at the police station to see his reunion with his parents after his release. Tonight Hayley was with him near the bleachers though the night of the Fourth she'd been at the pool with friends.

Eileen Irwin's ice blond hair was drawn into coronet braids, making her face even more severe than usual, cheekbones jutting, chin sharp. Pale pink gloss did nothing to soften the thin line of lips pressed tightly together. Cool blue eyes moved steadily around the terrace.

She appeared regal, the sequins on her black blouse reflecting light from a nearby torchiere. Edward Irwin nervously brushed back a strand of graying hair. Behind the lens of his glasses, his brown eyes looked worried. He was a bit shorter than Eileen. Stooped shoulders made him look even less impressive. He didn't look comfortable in his too-tight tuxedo.

Maggie Peterson stood near one of the tall urns placed at intervals between the French doors. Annie remembered when Maggie Peterson's pale lilac chiffon dress was a perfect foil for her glossy dark hair and violet eyes. Now she was frail, face and arms thin, the dress hanging too loose. Dave Peterson stood by himself at the east edge of the terrace. Midway through the fireworks he had been striding through the pines, nearing the oyster-shell path to the overflow lot.

Annie located Morgan Bitter. In a short-sleeve white shirt, black trousers, and black shoes, he was indistinguishable from any other member of the waitstaff, brown hair smoothly combed, black slash eyebrows and thin features in a composed, respectful attitude, just as Richard Ely would have stood unobtrusively, eyes alert. At the moment Bitter remained in the shadows near the French door.

Amelia Wellington, Robin Visey, and Roderick Fraley weren't yet onstage. The distant bells of St. Mary's by the Sea signaled the hour, seven sweet peals.

Vera Hurst and Wesley Hurst looked toward her. Their expressions were so similar, fear and a final demanding stare. *Can I trust you? If I tell the truth, what's going to happen?*

Annie mouthed the words. "For Jed."

Near the bleachers, Max gave her a thumbs-up. If all worked out as they hoped, she and Max would remain unnoticed until the final confrontation was set in motion.

Now everything depended upon Wesley and Vera.

Wesley took a deep breath. "Ladies and gentlemen." Wesley's voice was hoarse.

Annie gripped her hands in a tight grasp. Many gatherings at the club in support of a school or a charity opened with such a greeting.

Tonight a desperate family risked accusations, jail, perhaps prison, to save an innocent boy.

16

"Thank you for coming." Hollow-eyed and grim, Wesley hunched his shoulders. The shadows were deepening. His somber tone was a match for the darkness of the sky, the heavy weight of humid air.

The audience on the terrace and in the bleachers was utterly still.

"We've asked you here to help us find the truth to"—a pause—"to the disappearance of Shell Hurst. I want everyone to think about the terrace midway through the fireworks. Please listen as we try to trace what Shell did and said that night. Then we'll ask anyone"—he looked around the terrace, gazed up at the bleachers—"who can help us to speak up."

Wendy Carlson fingered a carnelian necklace at her throat. She looked schoolgirlish in a cream chiffon dress with a high neck and princess waist. As a dance club member, she was always cheerful and eager. Tonight her eyes were huge and her voice thin as she recalled the terrace. "I saw Shell standing near the French door. Her back was to me. She was talking to someone but the shadow by the vase was deep. I don't know who was there."

A French door opened. Robin Visey swept out onto the terrace, young, beautiful, confident.

"Tonight I am Shell Hurst." Robin's throaty voice had a performer's reach, audible to all on the terrace and in the bleachers. "I spoke with someone who stood there." A slender hand pointed at the splotch of darkness by the vase.

Morgan Bitter in his role as a waiter moved quietly to the other side of the vase, visible to Robin playing the part of Shell, but not visible to anyone standing in the shadow of the vase.

Footsteps sounded on the flagstones at the edge of the terrace.

Guests on the terrace and in the bleachers shifted. Quick-drawn breaths sounded, faint as the rustle of an unseen woman's dress on a dark night.

A hooded figure in a white robe moved steadily across the terrace, evoking the fear of a thousand nightmares. There was no face in the hood, only white cloth with slanted eyeholes.

Annie was forewarned yet her throat constricted.

The hood and long robe totally enveloped the new arrival. Where there should have been a face, the almond-shaped holes afforded vision. Covered arms were folded, hands hidden in loose sleeves. The smooth gliding steps gave no hint of sex, no clue to identity.

The only sound on the quiet terrace was the soft spat of the footsteps. The forbidding apparition moved toward the beautiful woman in the elegant red dress, slipped past her, and stepped into the shadow by the vase.

The actress in red, playing the role of Shell, turned toward the splotch of shadow. Without words, she pantomimed conversation.

On the far side of the vase, Morgan Bitter edged forward, head cocked in a listening pose, a waiter eavesdropping.

The woman in red and the robed figure bent toward each other, as if exchanging information.

With a careless nod, the actress turned away, walked across the terrace.

The robed figure slipped silently along the French doors, reached the edge of the terrace, turned and walked swiftly toward the far end of the bleachers, then disappeared from sight.

Annie slid a glance over one particular face.

Utter immobility. Not a flicker of movement.

The actress in the red dress strolled at a casual pace to the end of the terrace. She paused, spoke to a stiff and silent Vera. The actress continued across the terrace, paused for a moment by Lou Porter who quivered with excitement The actress moved on, reached the bleachers. Jed Hurst pressed back against the metal frame. She didn't look toward him. Jed watched her walk toward the path.

A satisfied smile with a hint of insolence gave her lovely face an air of arrogant complacency. She reached the beginning of the oyster-shell path that twined into the darkness of the pines.

On the terrace, Wesley jammed his hands into his trouser pockets. His face was hard and ridged as he watched the actress step onto the shells, which crackled beneath spiked red heels. In a moment, she reached the turn in the path and was lost to sight.

Vera hurried across the terrace to Wesley. She gripped his arm, jerked her head toward the path. He frowned, appeared resistant. Vera leaned forward. He listened, abruptly nodded. Vera dropped her hand and he turned away.

Wesley skirted his way through the silent figures on the terrace.

Many of them took a half step back. Their eyes dropped to avoid looking at him. Wesley reached the path. He stared straight ahead.

Jed drew farther back into the shadow of the bleachers. His sister held tight to one hand.

A bright white cone of light abruptly shone from the top of the bleachers, illuminating Max in a vivid spot. He stood at ease in a polo and gray slacks, the casual dress for an evening at the country club, but his face was somber.

Annie looked at the top row in the bleachers where the unshaven Bobby had rigged his lights.

Wesley disappeared around a pittosporum shrub.

Max gestured toward the path to the overflow lot. "On the night of July fourth, those of you on the terrace and in the bleachers saw Shell Hurst moments before she was murdered."

The silence was intense.

"Shell walked to her car." Max's voice was level and all the more impressive for the lack of drama. "She stopped by the driver's door. The murderer slipped out from a hiding place, came up behind her, threw a tightly rolled silk shawl over her head, and strangled her. Death came quickly. However, the murderer must have had an instant of terror. Someone was coming. The murderer darted into the shadows by a pine. Wesley arrived and found his wife's body."

The spotlight shifted.

Wesley Hurst had returned to the terrace. Now he stood in the bright circle of light a few feet from the path into the woods. The harsh light emphasized purple shadows beneath his eyes and deep lines grooved on either side of his mouth. "I found her. She was lying on the ground next to her car. I got down beside her, turned her over. There was a light up in the tree, and her face . . . She was dead." His voice was husky, shaking. "I should have done something, called somebody, but I was scared." He stared toward Max, though likely he could see nothing against the glare of the white spot. "God, I was scared. I left her there. I ran like hell back to the terrace. Fireworks were blazing up above and everybody making noise and all I could think of was getting out of there. It was hard to get across the terrace. So many people. I got to the other side and told Vera to go home and not to talk to anybody. I told her somebody'd killed Shell and we had to act like nothing was wrong. I ran around to the front of the club and acted like I'd had too much to drink and raised hell about the car. I didn't want anyone to think about me being with Shell. I wanted everybody to think I'd been in the bar. Jerry took me home in a golf cart. I sat up all night, waiting for the police to come." He swallowed, rubbed the back of a fist against his face. "I was wrong to leave her there." For an instant, there was horror and sadness in his eyes. "I was so damned scared."

The spotlight went black.

The bright cone blazed to encircle Jed Hurst. Hayley squinted against the glare.

Jed took a deep breath. "I didn't know what had happened. I saw Dad run back from the lot. He didn't see me next to the bleachers. I knew something bad had happened. I didn't know what I could do but I thought I'd better go see." He stopped, bowed his head. He looked pitiably young. Finally, he looked up and the unsparing light showed a trembling jaw. The words came in jerks. "I got there and I saw her car. I couldn't figure why Dad had run away. I didn't see her anywhere. I came around the pine. She was lying on her back. Her face . . . It was awful. I knew she was dead. I thought . . . I didn't know what to think."

"God, Jed, I'm sorry." Wesley's shaking voice came from the nearby shadows. "I didn't hurt her. I found her that way."

Jed's face crumpled. "I went kind of crazy. I'd told a lot of guys that I was going to do something to make her back off from my sister. Shell was . . . Anyway, that doesn't matter now. But I thought we'd all be in big trouble. Then I thought . . . well, nobody was in the lot . . . the fireworks were exploding and most people wouldn't start home until the show was over and I thought if I could get her out of there, nobody would know what had happened." He took a deep breath. "I pulled her to the other side of the car and got her into the passenger seat." The thinness of his quivering voice brought the horror near. "Once I got the car started, I drove out and turned on the road that runs behind the golf course. When I got close to the fourth hole I thought maybe I could get rid of the car, get rid . . . of her. I turned off the lights and drove on the golf cart path to the bridge near nine. I got the Porsche halfway across, then got out and leaned in and put it in neutral. I slammed the door and went behind and pushed. The Porsche crashed through the railing and into the lagoon. But once it was gone, it was like somebody put a big red arrow there. Railing gone. Something went through and into the lagoon. Then I thought of using another car, butting it into the railing but not going down. I ran across the course and came around to the front parking lot. At the valet board, I saw Colonel Hudson's keys. I knew the car. I hated to do it. God, it was a sweet car."

There was an angry rumble from Colonel Hudson, still standing at parade rest.

Jed looked out, squeezing his eyes against the sharp light. "I'm sorry, Colonel Hudson. My dad will find you another classic MG, perfect just like the one you had. But that night, I knew where your car was parked. I took the keys and got the MG and went back around the course and onto the path and banged into the post. I turned and ran. I went home."

The spotlight on Jed went dark.

Sharp white light encircled Dave Peterson.

Big, burly, but now without bluster. "I'd started home, walking across the golf course. I changed my mind, decided to find Shell, tell her"—a pause—"what I thought of her. Yeah." His face was hard. "I was going to tell her off. I knew she'd parked in the overflow lot. She came into the dance late from the terrace. I got to the path but I heard someone coming fast from the lot. I stepped off the path into the pines. Wesley ran past toward the terrace. I thought that was odd. I got back on the path, then shells crackled again, someone coming from the terrace. I didn't want to see anybody. I figured I'd made enough of a spectacle of myself at the dance. I got back off the path and Jed loped around the bend. I thought he was just in a hurry to get to his car. Anyway, I gave him a few minutes, then I took the path to the lot. When I got there, the Porsche was heading out onto the back road. I was too late to talk to Shell, then I decided I didn't give a damn anyway. I took the back road on foot to the front of the club, but when I got to the valet board, Maggie had taken the car so I took the back road again and walked home."

Darkness.

The circle of light illuminated Max. "Jed was scared because he knew that no one had come after his dad to the parking lot. He thought his dad had killed Shell. But we know what happened."

The spotlight shifted to the edge of the terrace on the far side of the bleachers.

The sinister hooded figure edged along the side of the terrace. The passage of the light made it clear that at night the murderer could have moved unseen in thick shadows there, unnoticed as fireworks exploded above the terrace, lifting the gaze of viewers on the terrace and in the bleachers to the spangles in the velvet sky.

The hooded apparition slipped among the crowd to the center of the terrace. Annie walked across the flagstones and stepped into the circle of light, quite close to the hooded figure. "As soon as Jed drove the car out onto the back road, the murderer returned to the terrace. Tonight we intend to reveal the identity of Shell Hurst's murderer, the person who spoke to Shell near the French door, the person who slipped across the terrace and came around the end of the bleachers to hurry to the overflow lot. Now I'd like for these people to join me." She called out the names.

They came, one by one.

Vera Hurst's face was pale and stricken. Her green eyes implored Annie: *We've done what you asked. We've told damning facts. We've put ourselves in great danger of arrest. Help us.*

Wesley was a far cry from the preppy sailor accustomed always to deference and comfort, but he had the air of a man awakening from a nightmare. He gazed at his son with tears in his eyes.

Dave Peterson stood protectively near Maggie. His beefy face projected defiance. Maggie placed a cautionary hand on his arm, but she looked at peace, no longer drained by despair.

Eileen Irwin's sharp features reflected distaste. She stood quite tall and straight, gaze unwavering, disassociating herself from a tawdry encounter. Edward's round face was anxious and uncertain. His shoulders slumped and the ill-fitting dinner jacket pulled over his paunch.

"The murderer"—Annie looked at each in turn—"feels quite safe. The murderer doesn't know two critical facts." She looked at each in turn, let her words hang in the sultry air. "A waiter overheard the murderer's conversation with Shell when they agreed to meet at the Porsche." Annie pointed across the terrace at the vase.

Morgan Bitter stepped from the shadow into a second bright circle of light, looking like a member of the waitstaff. The light clicked off, leaving Annie and the other dance club members in a single circle of brightness.

"The Tuesday following Shell's disappearance, I spoke to Richard Ely, the waiter who overheard that conversation. He told me he'd see what he could find out, people who talked to Shell. But Richard has his own plan. He called a member of the dance club."

There was no change on one particular face though surely there was the beginning of uneasiness.

"Tuesday night that member called Richard. The call was placed at nine oh-three P.M. from the public phone booth on Main Street opposite the Mermaid Hotel. The booth is one block from Fish Haul Pier. Richard's end of the conversation was overhead by his former wife. Richard Ely told his caller, 'I always try to accommodate club members, help them avoid any . . . trouble. It's often been my pleasure to serve members above and beyond my duties and I've been generously rewarded. I was near the French door when you and Shell Hurst spoke. I heard you plan to . . .'"

The murderer's lips tightened.

Annie felt a flicker of hope. Now there was worry. She continued steadily, "Richard agreed to meet his caller at the end of Fish Haul Pier despite a deluge of rain from a huge thunderstorm. Richard didn't mind getting wet because he expected a nice payoff. He didn't know Shell was dead but he figured the member didn't want to be connected in any way with Shell's mysterious disappearance. Instead, Richard died from a blow to the back of his head. The murderer eased his body over the railing into the Sound. A shrimp trawler pulled him out of the water. Now, it's time for our witnesses."

A second circle of brightness illuminated Max. "This afternoon I went door-to-door in a neighborhood within walking distance of the country club. My first witness is Gail Farraday."

A stout, ruddy-faced woman strode into the light. Her black hair was cropped short. She looked athletic in a cream polo and navy Bermuda shorts and thick-soled running shoes.

The murderer's lips parted in shock.

The stout woman's bright dark eyes gazed at Annie, Vera, Wesley, and Jed Hurst, Maggie and Dave Peterson, Eileen and Edward Irwin. "Have to say"—her brusque voice had a faintly British accent—"didn't know much about any of this. But truth is truth. The night of that storm, I was out in my garden. I'm a gardening fool. Sometimes in a heavy rain the waterspout near my daylilies spews out like a hose. Daylilies like lots of water but not that much. Anyway, sheets of rain were coming down. I knew I'd better check. It was raining heavily, but I turned on the garden lights and I could see well enough. It was about a quarter to nine. I was out there in a poncho, working with a trowel to clear out the spout, when one of the garage doors next to our house opened. I looked up. Nasty night to drive out. Lightning. Thunder. There was a huge rumble, then a brilliant flash as the car backed out of the drive. The car belongs to him." She pointed a stubby finger.

Edward Irwin's face was pasty. He looked desperately around the terrace. "Not me. Never. I didn't go out that night. I swear to God."

Max lifted his hand. "The second witness."

Amelia Wellington bustled into the spotlight. Soft white curls framed a dumpling face. Annie arranged for the actress to play the part of the vacationing poet who'd observed the visitor to the phone booth from the upper porch of the Mermaid Hotel. The poet could testify at a trial, but she'd not been able to come back to the island on short notice. "Oh dear me, I had no idea of the importance of what I saw. It was the night of July tenth. Such a huge storm. I was watching the lightning from the second-story verandah of the Mermaid Hotel. The verandah overlooks Main Street. All the shops were closed but the street lamp next to the phone booth provides quite a strong light. If it hadn't been storming, I might not have noticed the pedestrian. But someone walking in that kind of storm was strange." She looked straight at a rigid, listening figure. "Quite striking, the ivy cap and the well-cut London Fog raincoat. Curious. A man's raincoat, but as soon as I saw the face—"

"It wasn't me." Edward's voice rose. He moved away from Eileen.

Eileen's hard face turned toward him, a gleam of anger in her cold blue eyes. "Your car. Your raincoat. The raincoat was still wet the next morning. Of course, she tried to blackmail you—"

Max was sharp. "How did you know about the blackmail, Eileen?"

"Edward told me." The blue eyes shifted to Max. "I never thought he would kill her."

Annie wasn't surprised that Eileen was ready to abandon Edward, but there were indrawn breaths of surprise and looks of dismay on the faces of many on the terrace.

Edward's lips trembled. He stared at his wife. "I didn't tell you about Shell." There was a curl of horror in his shaking voice. "I never would have told you." He took a ragged breath. "I saw you talking to her on the terrace after the dance and I knew you knew. Did she call you, too? Or did you eavesdrop that morning when she called me? But you were the one talking to her that night. You were in the shadow by the vase and a huge firework exploded right up above you. I saw the look on your face. You knew. I thought maybe you were going to pay her, keep her from going to the police. But I never told you what she'd said."

Max took a step toward Eileen. "Did Shell call and tell you? Did you overhear Edward talking to her? Did you call to ask her what was going on and she twitted you that the fine name of Eileen Irwin was about to be fodder for the tabloids? Whatever. You knew about the blackmail. You don't give a damn about Edward, but you won't have your name dragged through scandal. Did you set up the meeting in the overflow lot to try and talk Shell out of her scheme? Did she laugh at you?"

Eileen lifted her chin, her gaze imperious beneath the white blond coronet braids. Her features sharpened, high cheekbones jutting, bony chin rigid. Thin lips curved in what was meant as a dismissive smile but turned her expression into a chilling caricature of a wealthy woman dealing with bumptious social inferiors. "I've listened to enough of this nonsense. I don't know anything about blackmail. I have no idea where Edward went in his car that night. As for Shell"— a dismissive wave of long thin fingers—"I never left the terrace that night until I went inside to get my shawl—"

"That's a lie." The crisp declaration came from high in the bleachers. Sue Ralston, the club's senior women's singles champion, edged her way to the steps on the east side. "I'd just started down the treads. I was looking down. You walked past the bleachers, heading for the pines. In your right hand, you carried a length of silk. I saw a flash of red."

Eileen's features flattened as she stared upward.

Annie felt as if they'd hit a grand slam. Bringing everyone together, calling on club members to help, had unearthed a fact that proved Eileen to be a liar and linked her to murder. Here was a real witness, not an actress, and this would be what Billy needed to file a murder charge.

Sue Ralston looked down, face composed, arms folded. "I'd often admired that shawl. There was just enough of the dragon visible for me to identify it."

Eileen didn't move. She didn't look toward the path to the overflow lot despite the sound of running footsteps.

Billy Cameron strode across the terrace, hand near his holstered gun. He reached Eileen, faced her. "Eileen Irwin, you are under arrest for the murder of Shell Hurst and Richard Ely."

17

Colonel Hudson's polo shirt and white trousers were as crisp as any uniform. He looked distinguished, white hair and mustache trimmed with military precision, carriage commanding. He stopped in front of the cash desk, gave Annie an admiring nod. "I came by to say you and your husband"—he looked around inquiringly—"handled the affair at the club very well indeed."

Max was midway up the central aisle. "The Intrepid Trio is ready—Oh, sorry. Good morning, Colonel."

"Good to see you. Like to commend you both. Too often we don't take time to recognize meritorious service. I've just been to the mayor's office, insisted there be a citation presented to Chief Cameron. He handled a dicey situation perfectly. I understand that woman's gibbering with rage, demanding she be released, that she was defending herself from attack. Pretty hard to make that claim when a woman's strangled from behind and a man hit on the back of the skull and pushed into the water. And"—his dark eyes gleamed with satisfaction— "I've had a word with that young scamp Jed Hurst. Have to say he looked like a man ready to head for the hills the minute he saw me. But no one under my command ever claimed I didn't recognize guts and promote the men who could size up a situation and take action. Damn shame about my car. But that young man can be an officer our forces need. Think of it. Finds a dead woman. Thinks his staff is involved. Quick as rip figures out a solution. Body in the car, back road to the golf cart path, bam through the bridge on the ninth hole. No car. Runs across the course. Steals a car. Back to the bridge. Wham. Now the missing railing accounted for. I've had a talk with that young man. Needs an appointment to a service academy. Good for the golf team, too. I'm seeing to it." He gave a decided nod, then looked around. "Nice place here. Think I'll take a look around." With that he turned and marched down the central aisle.

Max jerked a thumb. "The Intrepid Trio awaits us via webcam."

As they started down the corridor, Ingrid slipped behind the cash desk. "It's cool where they are." She couldn't quite hide her envy. Outside the temperature had already hit ninety-three and it was only ten o'clock in the morning. "Tell them to bring me a chunk of ice."

Annie grinned. "I don't think it's that cool."

"If they keep going. Lots of glaciers in Greenland," Ingrid said wistfully. "I'll bet they're wearing sweaters."

In fact, when Annie stepped into the storeroom, she was immediately greeted by cheers from three sweatered ladies lounging in the saloon of *Marigold's Pleasure.*

Emma looked like a chunky polar bear in a heavy white cardigan that contrasted with a deep purple caftan. "Billy Cameron sent us the video from the videocam they set up on the terrace. As it goes to show, there's always evidence if you keep looking."

Laurel beamed at Emma. "But you have such an advantage."

Emma's face began to draw down into a resentful square.

"Dear Emma," Laurel cooed, "you outthink everyone."

Henny's beautifully modulated voice was soothing. "That's usually the case, but it does look as though this month's paintings are still a puzzle for you, Emma."

Emma lifted her head, yellow spiky hair bright in a shaft of morning sunlight as the crested cockatoo watched her from a nearby perch. "Oh"—her tone was careless with an undercurrent of triumph—"I'd been intending to tell you. Other things on my mind. Child's play actually. The first painting—"

A rap on the open door and Colonel Hudson stepped inside. "Sorry to interrupt. Clever idea those watercolors. Mysteries are favorites of mine between flights. Great rest for the mind. The first painting is *Death in a White Tie* by Ngaio Marsh, the second is *The Fifth Man* by Manning Coles, the third is *Do Not Murder before Christmas* by Jack Iams, the fourth is *To Catch a Thief* by David Dodge, and the fifth is *The Case of the Spurious Spinster* by Erle Stanley Gardner."

"Well done." Henny clapped.

The colonel looked at the computer screen, stood a little straighter. "Forgive me for my interruption. But"—his tone was gallant as his eyes settled on Laurel, undeniably beautiful in a pale pink cashmere sweater and white wool trousers—"I see that I may have the opportunity to meet three lovely ladies." He moved nearer the screen, shoulders back, stomach flat, eyes trained on Laurel, a man with a mission.

Annie doubted he remembered he had won a new mystery and free coffee for a month.